Aberdeenshire Library and Information Service
www.aberdeenshire.gov.uk/alis

Boyer, G.G.

The return of
Morgette / G.G.
Boyer

D1348747

1635742

THE RETURN OF MORGETTE

Legendary gunfighter and lawman Dolf Morgette is heading back home to Idaho for his son's wedding, but soon he learns he may be attending a funeral instead. Junior Morgette, the marshall of Pinebluff, has been drygulched and is near death.

Dolf needless to say is worried sick about his son and he is eager to get back to him as soon as possible, but there are various obstacles in his way, not least a gang of rustlers, gold-stealing thieves and a range full of outlaws.

THE RETURN OF
MORGETTE

G. G. Boyer

GUNSMOKE

This hardback edition 2004
by BBC Audiobooks Ltd
by arrangement with
Golden West Literary Agency

ISBN 1 4056 8004 0

British Library Cataloguing in Publication Data available.

Printed and bound in Great Britain by
Antony Rowe Ltd., Chippenham, Wiltshire

THE RETURN OF MORGETTE

CHAPTER 1

"RIFLE shot," Doc Hennessey identified the sound mentally. His next thought as he saw Junior Morgette spin around and topple over was, "Some s.o.b.'s shot young Morgette."

It wasn't exactly unexpected. He'd made enemies of a number of hardcases as Pinebluff's town marshal. Doc's eyes swept the nearby woods, to see where the drygulcher might be concealed, as he swiftly snatched a long-barreled Colt from his medical bag beside him. A lingering wisp of smoke revealed where the shot had been fired. Doc thought he could see someone running up a hill through the dense spruce-shaded undergrowth and eased off two carefully aimed shots at the motion. At that range he didn't expect to hit anyone for sure, but he wanted to make certain whoever it was kept going and didn't try to pump another bullet into Junior.

Then, smoking pistol still in one hand and bag in the other Doc sprinted toward the prostrate figure. "Helluva way for a Morgette to get shot," he was thinking. "Playing left field for the local nine." Despite the wry reflection he was in great anxiety. His next thought was, "If the kid's killed I deserve the blame. I knew they'd be after him. His pa'll never forgive me."

Doc and Dolf Morgette senior had been sidekicks a decade before in a bloody range war. Dolf was now in Alaska, or maybe on his way home expecting to attend Junior's wedding. Be a helluva note, Doc thought grimly, if it turns out to be comin' home for a funeral instead.

Doc got to Junior in a dead heat with the boy's uncle Matt. Doc's first thought when he saw the spreading bloody spot where the bullet had entered his back near his heart was, "Maybe there ain't gonna be a wedding."

He glanced up and looked into Matt's eyes. "Still breathin'," he said. "I'll have plenty of help here. You go after whoever was up there." He indicated the hill with his thumb.

Buck Henry ran up in time to hear that remark. "I'll go along," he said and actually led the way at a fast trot, Matt following. Buck was Dolf Morgette's brother-in-law and a full-blooded Indian. He was carrying a rifle that he'd quickly snatched from a boot on someone's tethered mount.

The rest of the ball players and most of the crowd from the small bleachers had started to assemble around Doc and Junior. Catherine Green, who expected to marry Junior, was one of the first. She came flying, holding her skirts up. Breathlessly, she knelt beside Junior, looking awfully close to tears.

"Will he live?" she asked Doc.

Doc gave her one of his typically blunt diagnoses. "I don't know," he said. Then to Dr. Priddy, his new partner, who had also run up, he said, "Get a wagon. Some of you other galoots bring that barn door over here." He pointed to the door hanging by one hinge on a dilapidated shed next to the ball field.

They got Junior in the wagon, Catherine cradling his head in her lap as they drove, getting blood all over her skirt. Doc rode beside her trying to keep Junior's air passages open. She tried to shut out the sound of his pitiful labored breathing, staring in fascinated horror at the bubbles that rose with each gasp, issuing from both his mouth and nose. "Oh my God!" she said. But she kept the even worse thought unsaid—he's dying! And there's not a single thing anyone can do—not even Doc.

He was still alive when they got him to the small, neat hospital that served Pinebluff. Several men awkwardly maneuvered him into Doc's operating room and onto the table.

"O.K., everybody out," Doc ordered. "Me an' Doc Priddy an' the nurse will handle it now." He patted Catherine's shoulder as he herded her outside. "I'll let you know as soon as we know. Wait in my office where nobody'll bother you."

She tried to sit in a chair and look at some of Doc's reading material to keep her sanity, but the words on the pages were incomprehensible. She was close to hysteria, jumping up every few minutes and pacing the floor, digging her nails into her palms.

"I'm always the practical one," she tried to argue some calmness into herself. "I've got to get a grip on myself."

But she kept listening to the sound of muffled voices from the room where the doctors were working, attempting to make out some word that would give her a clue to Junior's condition. Desperately as she tried she couldn't understand what they were saying, though occasionally she could discern the anxious tone. The sun was lowering behind the western mountain range and still they hadn't come out.

"Please God," she prayed, "let him live. I love him so."

Sheriff Morgan Casey had been at the ball game, so it was no problem to get ahold of him and persuade him to accompany Matt and Buck in trailing the rifleman. Matt showed him the empty rifle shell, a .40-82, when he and Buck came back from their preliminary look up on the hill.

"Musta been pretty scared," the sheriff allowed, "or he'd a taken time to pick that up. I would've. You say the tracks lead up over the ridge? Probably staked a hoss up there. Let's get mounted and on that trail before the sun goes down."

They easily found where the shooter had mounted his horse and tore away at a gallop. The tracks were simple to follow while the rider was putting some quick distance between him and the scene of the crime. Then he apparently got a grip on his panic and made an attempt to cover his trail. He was no match for an experienced native tracker like Buck, who had practically been born to the skill. The fugitive had taken to a stream for a while, then sought rocky ground to exit, but they were close enough behind him that even the water dripping from his mount's legs was still plainly visible in droplets on the limestone scarp. If it hadn't been, Buck's sharp eyes would have readily spied displaced twigs and leaves, as well as the disturbance of small patches of sand in depressions in the rock. After a few miles the rider ahead had become bolder, probably thinking he had covered his trail sufficiently. The tracks had led over the timbered ridge between Pinebluff and the Mustang River, then down to the river and into the well-traveled road that paralleled it. The rider may have thought the many other tracks there would confuse anyone following. But he hadn't counted on an Indian trailer being ready at hand. Buck was able to follow unerringly and keep at a steady lope once on the road, even though the many other hoofprints would have totally confused an inexperienced eye. Sheriff Casey had been as anxious to stay on the trail as they were till the tracks headed into the wagon trail leading to the Kelbo ranch. Then he pulled in his mount. When Buck and Matt came back to see why he'd stopped, he said, "You sure that trail leads up there?"

"Sure, I'm sure," Buck stated. He pointed to the ground. "Trail's plain as day." Casey squinted at it, seeming uncertain.

"Well, I guess you know your business," but he followed reluctantly, appearing to grow more nervous by the minute. He glanced at the westering sun several times as they rode, Matt noticed. His actions were sufficiently unusual that Matt's suspicions were aroused.

A good many people besides Matt had noticed that Sheriff Casey had got pretty "thick" with the Kelbos whenever they came to town, playing poker and drinking with them in the saloons. This knowledge prompted Matt to wonder if the sheriff was eyeing the sun's progress toward the horizon in hopes they'd lose the trail when night overtook them. If so, he was disappointed. They followed the tracks right into the Kelbo ranch just as the sun dipped behind the hills. Everyone knew that the Kelbos had reason to hold a grudge against Junior. Just the night before he'd had to arrest Yancey Kelbo again for being drunk and disorderly in a saloon. This time Yancey had put up a fight and had been soundly thrashed by Junior, who had acquired his father's knack for bareknuckle fighting. All the Morgettes had the brute tenacity and speed that made for good fist fighters. Young Billy Joe Kelbo had tried to mix into the affair and had been taken in by Junior's deputy, Simp Parsons. The brothers had both spent the night in the cooler. Matt thought, "They could have stayed in town, and either one of 'em coulda done that shootin'. But I'd bet on Yancey. The kid's too green. Yancey's mean."

Old Man Kelbo, a lean six-foot-six Texan with a forbidding face and manner that scared a lot of people, came out of the ranch house as they rode up. "Just as though he was expecting us," Matt thought. Most ranchers would have greeted them with a "Howdy, light and rest yore jeans," probably followed by an invitation to supper in view of the time of day. But Kelbo didn't say anything. He simply glared at them. Sheriff Casey appeared hesitant to state their business, but finally told the old man why they were there.

Kelbo spat into the dust. "Warn't none o' my boys," he stated. "They all been here all day. Look around fer that hoss you bin trackin' if yer a mind to."

Casey appeared relieved. Matt caught the implication in Kelbo's words and manner that had caused Casey's relief. His manner had suggested that the Kelbos had a sweaty horse that anybody might want to see safely hidden by now. Matt knew he was lying about his boys. He'd seen them both in town just about an hour before the ball game had started, but he didn't see any point in saying so. Casey looked at Matt for an O.K. to give it up and was disappointed. Matt said, "Why not look around anyhow as long as there's some light. See if that cayuse's tracks go on through."

Casey shook his head in exasperation. "You fellers can look around all you like. It's gettin' dark. I'm headed back to town. There ain't nothin' to see here or Kelbo wouldn't be so all fired willin' to let us look, would he?" He winked at the Old Man as he said it. Kelbo laughed harshly.

"Yer damn' well told," the Old Man stated. He laughed again.

Matt looked at Casey in disgust, then silently pulled his mount around and headed back toward Pinebluff. He'd have bet if they'd had enough light to scour the country they'd have found a hot, sweaty horse hidden that would lay down tracks like those they'd followed, and not over a mile or two from the ranch either.

"Don't fergit what them tracks looked like," he cautioned Buck, "not that you're apt to."

Buck nodded. Like most Indians he could remember a set of horse tracks he'd seen ten years before, if there'd been some reason to notice them especially. It was something like a Chinese remembering his complex alphabet whenever he needed to call on it. Few whites would understand this. Matt did. He had a little of it himself. Although it might have taken him a lot longer, he probably could have followed that set of tracks to the Kelbos' himself.

CHAPTER 2

OLD Man Kelbo kept his sons at a respectable distance, living alone in the ranch house, with the boys consigned to the bunk house along with the cowboys. The next morning he sent Elmo, his Negro man who had been with him since Texas, to fetch Yancey up to the house. Yancey's stomach began to feel queasy when he got the summons. He had an idea what it was all about and didn't relish facing his father. The news of Junior Morgette's having been shot had been carried out from town by some of the cowboys, but Yancey himself had known all about it before then. He was also aware that people would naturally think he had a prime motive, though no one mentioned it to him. Nonetheless, he could tell what they were thinking by some of the looks he'd gotten from the boys, including his own brothers, down at the bunk house. The shooting also explained why Sheriff Casey had been up to the ranch house earlier. Yancey was puzzled though because Casey hadn't been down to question him.

As it happened, Old Man Kelbo's first awareness of the attempted murder of Junior Morgette came from the sheriff. His outward coolness had been an act, a bluff. The Old Man had been through a lot of trouble and managed to keep a whole hide. He was trouble wise. Therefore, his bold front—as though he had nothing to conceal—had come naturally, and he had been gratified to see it work on the Sheriff's party. He had thought of sending down for Yancey right after the sheriff left, having seen his son come in earlier and turn his horse into the corral. But Old Man Kelbo was usually a deliberate man, unless his temper bested him. This cautiousness now stayed his hand. He wanted to think the matter over. Why would Yancey do a damn' fool thing like turn his sweaty horse out in plain sight if he'd done the shooting and could rightly expect to be trailed? He knew his son wasn't that dumb. He resolved to think it over and sweat the truth out of Yancey in the morning, meanwhile letting him squirm if he had some reason to do so. He did make a circuit of the ranch headquarters himself before full dark to see if he could pick up tracks of the animal the sheriff's party had been following. He couldn't be sure in the dimming light, but he followed a set of tracks that skirted the building area and continued on down to the creek, losing the trail in the water. He saddled up and was out early to see if he could find where the horse had come out of the stream and where it had gone then, but was unsuccessful. He wasn't entirely certain that he had the right set of tracks either, not having the same unerring eye for identifying tracks that Buck Henry did. Few whites did. Most ranchers could trail and read sign, but only one in a thousand could read hoofprints like an Indian, with the certainty with which a later generation would be able to identify fingerprints. Still puzzling over what he knew, and even more so over what he didn't know but suspected, he'd ridden back to the house, tethered his horse, and sent Elmo down for Yancey.

He glared at Yancey as soon as he entered the house. Knowing what was probably coming, the younger man squirmed like a little boy. He was damn' glad he was too old to be worked over anymore with a tug strap. Nonetheless, he was just as much in dread of the Old Man as he'd been as a kid. Old Man Kelbo's frosty stare was even more awesome because his piercing gray eyes, one slightly squinted, peered down from his towering height of six-foot-six— half a foot taller than any of his boys.

"How old're you, Yancey?" the Old Man grated out in a low, deadly voice. He worked up a snarl on his leathery, hawk-like face as he slid the words out.

"Aw, Pappy," Yancey complained. "I'm thirty. You know that." He was practically hanging his head. Despite having killed a few men himself, Yancey cowered like a whipped dog before this gaunt-faced threatening giant with the unruly iron gray hair and blazing eyes.

"How much do you weigh?" the Old Man asked, in the same tone.

"A hunnert ninety pound, I'd guess," Yancey blurted out meekly.

The Old Man eyed him in silent disgust for several dragging seconds. Then he growled, "That sure makes you the biggest, dumbest, damn' fool I know that's old enough to know better then." He paused but didn't expect a reply, nor did he get one. Yancey tried to meet his father's icy glare and failed. The Old Man opened up again. "Here we are a-tryin' ta git a foothold on a new range, oughta be walkin' soft an' playin' our cards close to our chest. An' what do you do? Tangle with the law, like a damn' fool! Not only that but after young Morgette dragged yer face around in the sawdust in that saloon you decide to git even by dry-gulchin' the kid no sooner'n I pay yer bail. Don't you know Morgette's old man is the handiest sonofabitch with a gun walkin' the face o' the earth? He'll be down on us like a duck on a June bug. And now I'd bet yer fixin' to lie to me about it. Anybody not tetched knows it was you shot the kid." This was pure bluff to see what Yancey might spill out.

"Pappy, I swear I didn't do it!" Yancey blurted, looking like a cow about to go under in quicksand.

"Oh sure! That damn' Matt Morgette and the Injun kid dragged the sheriff out here not an hour behind you, onto yer tracks every step o' the way. If the sheriff wasn't eatin' at the same trough with us you'd be down in the jug right now. That Injun knows. An' Matt Morgette knows. An' when Dolf Morgette hits here he'll know. You know what that adds up to? Big trouble. We're gonna hafta put that whole bunch outa the way somehow before they git us. That's the kinda trouble you got us into."

"I still say I didn't do it."

"Then who the hell did? You ain't got no reason to lie to me. I'd rather you hadn't, but if yuh did, it's done."

"Somebody who hotfooted it out here musta done it if them tracks led here," Yancey insisted. "Them Injuns don't make mistakes about trackin'. But it wasn't me."

"You come high-tailin' in about an hour ahead o' the sheriff."

"Sure. I was there at the ball game and saw Morgette get it an' dragged my freight. But if I'd knowed whoever did it was gonna head out here I'd sure as hell have stayed there or headed somewhere else. I ain't that dumb."

"Well, I gotta admit that makes sense. Was you at that game with anyone that'd know yuh?"

"No I wasn't. I sure as hell wish I had been." Then a new idea occurred to him. "Who've we got in our crowd that'd want to see me get the blame?"

That was a shrewd speculation that hit home with the Old Man and set him figuring. An enemy in their crowd could sure undo them this early in the game. The Old Man, ready to dismiss Yancey, replied, "Nobody that I know of. An' I ain't sayin' I believe yuh yet. An' I ain't sayin' I don't." Actually he was satisfied Yancey hadn't pulled the trigger on young Morgette. But he might know who did. May have paid one of their hardcase hired hands to do it.

Another thought riled the Old Man just then.

"Why the hell didn't you come and tell me young Morgette was shot if you knew. Why did you let me find it out from Casey first? I had to do some damn' fancy talkin'."

"I didn't know that whoever did it was gonna lead 'em out here. If I had I couldn't have told you—like I said, I wouldn't have been here. I was as surprised to see 'em as you were."

"Damn' lucky fer yuh I got rid of 'em with a pat story or you'd likely be in the cooler anyhow, whether Casey's taking sweetheart money from us or not."

Yancey saw an opening to change the subject and said, "Smith just come in a little while ago. There'll be another big herd o' them Canadian hosses through fast."

The Old Man nodded idly, reloading his pipe, wrapped in thought. Yancey stood waiting for him to say something. As though just discovering him there his father looked up questioningly.

"I said," Yancey started to repeat his message and was interrupted by the Old Man's, "I know what the hell yuh said. Git on with it; don't stand there like a cow steppin' on her own teat!"

Yancey left abruptly, heaving a huge gusty sigh of relief once outside, then hurried down toward the bunk house and cooking cabins partially hidden in the cottonwoods near the creek. Once out of sight of the main house he pulled a half-pint bottle of whiskey from under his coat and drained half of it in one swig. Then he rolled a cigarette and got that going to his satisfaction, inhaling a huge drag and blowing it out with gusto. "Jee–zuz!" he sighed aloud. "I sure wish to hell I knew who tried to beef young Morgette." He thought, "If he dies—or maybe even if he don't—his old man'll hunt me down like a jackrabbit." He considered high-tailing back to Texas, better yet to Mexico or South America. Then he recalled how sweet the pickings would be if their plans all worked out here. The money was already starting to roll in. He suddenly felt lucky, confident he'd skin out of the mess he was in. He told himself, "I always have." He pulled out the whiskey, downed the rest and tossed the bottle into the brush. All the Kelbos had been in and out of lots of trouble—especially Yancey. Whiskey had been at the root of most of his troubles, he reflected. "At least I never cracked my marbles gittin' throwed from a bronc, like Billy Joe," he muttered, thinking of his unpredictable youngest brother. "It's a miracle he didn't start shootin' when we had our run-in with Morgette the other night."

He shook his head ruefully and continued on toward the bunk house. Through the trees, he glimpsed his father mount his horse then head him at a lope toward town. He thought, "I wonder what he's up to now? He's sure been spending a lot of time in town just lately." But the thought never entered his head to ask the old man. He knew better.

Tom Miller, manager of the Gould Company bank in Pinebluff, was another who, like Yancey, was curious about Old Man Kelbo's frequent visits to town. Unlike Yancey, he knew at least one place that the elder Kelbo stopped on those visits. He had frequently observed him, as he did this morning, pass beneath the brightly painted sign of Gould's new competitors across the street, Kellums and Krieger, and then duck his head to go through the door of their bank. Watching Kelbo had briefly interrupted Tom's perusal of a letter from his boss, Alby Gould. He returned his attention to it now, especially the part about a honeymoon, which came as a total surprise.

> . . . *you probably recall Victoria Wheat—a local girl. We have just been married and will be coming to Pinebluff on our honeymoon. Expect us on the 8 A.M. at the Junction on the twentieth. We will want transportation directly to the ranch. Please tell no one that we're*

coming as we'd like a few days alone. Of course I expect you to alert the help at the ranch, but tell them to keep it under their hats.

Tom remembered Victoria Wheat, and not entirely because she was a lovely young lady that few men ever forgot. Tom Miller knew something about Victoria's past, as he knew many things the locals considered secrets. Tom was a watcher and listener and as a result learned a lot. Moreover, he was a thinker. Many people came to him for advice, others for a shoulder to cry on. He listened to their troubles since it was good business. As for advice, sometimes he gave it and it was usually sound. Because people confided in him he had been made aware that Alby's new wife had once been desperately in love with Dolf Morgette. Dolf was on everyone's mind just then since his son had been shot the day before, and it was generally known that Dolf was on his way home, expecting to attend Junior's wedding. The whole community was now tensely awaiting Dolf's arrival, wondering what that violent man might do to Yancey Kelbo, whom everyone suspected had pulled the trigger on Junior. But that wasn't the thought uppermost in Tom Miller's mind. Instead he considered the intriguing possibility that Dolf and Victoria might run into each other again. He wondered if Victoria still cared for him—it had only been three years. And how might Dolf still feel about her, although he too was now remarried? They might by chance come in on the same train. How would they handle a chance meeting? He wondered how much she may have told Alby of her past. "Nothing, I'd bet," he said to himself. Nonetheless Alby was no fool. He probably knew, or at least suspected.

At this point Miller noted Kelbo's departure from the bank across the street. Shortly afterwards, Alex Krieger came down the sidewalk and entered the bank. "Back from his *vacation*, I guess," Tom muttered under his breath, then thought, "I wonder what he was really doing? He isn't the type to take vacations; he'll die happy at his desk when he's ninety or so, if I'm any judge. He's been up to something out of town."

Angus Kellums covertly eyed everyone who entered his bank. He had a private office with frosted glass windows, but preferred the railed-in area outside so he could "keep an eye on business," as he thought of it. Actually he was simply nosy. He immediately noted Krieger's entrance and was glad he hadn't arrived before Kelbo had finished his conversation with him. He hoped his partner hadn't even seen Kelbo. Nonetheless he was relieved to have Krieger back in town. He was anxious to hear how he had made out on a deal they were both developing. He perfunctorily shook hands.

"C'mon inside," he suggested. They disappeared into the inner sanctum where, significantly, only Kellums, the senior partner, had a desk. He silently seated himself and lighted a cigar, not offering his partner one. He puffed slowly not wishing to appear too eager.

Krieger read him, and consciously sought to nettle him by firing up his own cigar in a leisurely fashion, puffing on it slowly several times, pretending to get it properly lit. Then, still evading what he knew was on Kellums' mind, he said, "I saw that long drink of water, Kelbo, leave just now. What the hell did he want?"

He watched Kellums' face twitch once or twice, involuntarily. He had noticed that the older man had been growing more nervous and irritable in recent weeks. Something was deeply bothering him that he was trying to conceal with little success. Krieger watched the other's agitation with some satisfaction; there was no love lost between them, though they worked well together due to a common interest in getting rich. Finally Kellums said, "He must have cashed a check. I didn't talk to him." Actually they'd been in earnest conversation in the office during Kelbo's entire visit, Kellums just stepping outside again shortly before his partner arrived. Krieger suspected as much, but let it pass. He remained silent, waiting out Kellums, who was becoming irritated by Krieger's failure to report what he was anxious to hear.

Kellums made a poor attempt to conceal his agitation, his tic fluttering spasmodically, much to his irritation. The tic had developed only in the past month or so. He tried to shield it from Krieger with the hand holding his cigar and was further displeased to note that his hand was shaking like that of a palsied old man. It would have enraged him to know that that was exactly what Krieger considered him. Finally he blurted out, "Well, did you find old Wheat?" He was referring to Victoria's father, who had left

Pinebluff a few years before, one jump ahead of the law, and as far as anyone knew, one jump ahead of a slug from Dolf Morgette's .45. Wheat had once been the ruling political power in the area, and was suspected of having ordered the murders of Dolf's father and two older brothers during the Pinebluff War, as it had been called. Ed Pardeau, as sheriff, had been Wheat's trigger man and had actually done the dirty work, finally being killed by Dolf. Despite his fugitive status, Mark Wheat still owned a sizeable portion of the town and the surrounding Quarter Lien district. This is what interested the two bankers; both of them were land and money hungry and didn't scruple about how they acquired either. In this they were typical of their class and the times.

To Kellums' question regarding Wheat, Krieger replied, "Of course I found him. Right where we thought he'd be—in Mexico, Guaymas in fact. Living like a king with a young Mexican wife."

"How'd an old bastard like him get a young wife?"

Krieger laughed as he said, "He didn't make any bones about that. He told me he bought her. Maybe you should do it when you retire." He snorted at the idea of his dried-up partner with a woman, especially a young one. Then he thought, "Maybe it would do Kellums good." He was beginning to look at times like he might explode, probably from the pressure of realizing that this was his last chance to make it big. He'd been a banker since the '50s in San Francisco and had actually worked for General Sherman, who at that time had been a banker there. But he'd failed to really prosper in the business. Something seemed to be lacking in him, although he had the calculating avarice that all of them did, Krieger thought. He'd tried to put the finger on what it was before. Now, watching the anxious senior partner it suddenly came to him: he's not cool in the clutch.

Regarding Wheat's purchase of a wife, Kellums hadn't even grinned. He merely said, "So much the better. He'll probably need money. We can keep him under our thumb with regular payments. Does he know what the hell his stuff is worth now that the mines have reopened?"

"Of course he does. It cost me ten grand up front."

"Jeezuz! Wait'll the Big Man hears about that. Our tails will be in it."

Kreiger thought of that, in fact had been thinking about it all the way home. He and his partner were simply front men for the silent partner who had put up the money for the bank. He shrugged. "He'll have to live with it. Wheat is shrewd. And tough."

Kellums looked sour as hell at the prosepct. "You tell him then." Then after thinking for a moment, he added, "You should have told that bastard Wheat you'd tell Dolf Morgette where to find him if he didn't play ball."

"I didn't think of it, but where the hell would getting Wheat killed help us?"

"Maybe his daughter would deal."

"Fat chance. It's a damn' good thing we didn't too. I picked up a New York paper in Ogden on the way up. Alby Gould just married Wheat's daughter."

Kellums looked shocked for just a second, his eyes opening wider. Then he quickly masked his surprise, rapidly turning over the implications of that in his mind.

"I hope to hell you tied Wheat up good with that ten grand."

"I did. Got all the papers here in my grip. As soon as we file 'em we'll own as much of the Quarter Lien, for all practical purposes, as the Morgette outfit—and about half the town too."

"Good," Kellums said. "That ought to keep the Old Man happy in view of young Gould gettin' hitched to Wheat's daughter. He mentioned we might have to have Wheat rubbed out. Thought his daughter would be softer. Fat chance now with Gould behind her. How long did you get it for?"

"Five years. By then we'll either make it or break it."

"Don't say break it," Kellums snapped. "I'm too damn' old to start over." He sighed, off guard for the moment. Krieger was amazed at how old and tired he looked. Kellums pulled himself together and took a puff on his cigar and discovered it had gone out. His hand shook violently as he relit it. "Goddam' nerves," he complained, not caring about the admission, since he couldn't conceal it anyhow.

"You need a vacation," Krieger said, almost sympathetically.

"Not likely. I'd spend all my time wondering how things are working out here. We still don't have the stretch of ground we really need. How do you suppose we can get our hands on that?"

Krieger shrugged. "Damfino. It's a cinch we ain't gonna scare the Morgettes off of it. Kelbo's got those nesters out of our way that were in there along the river, but he isn't about to scare out the Morgettes."

"Did you hear what someone did to young Junior Morgette?"

"How the hell could I help it? Hen Beeler gabbed about it all the way up from the Junction on the stage. He says everyone figures Yancey Kelbo was the trigger man."

"I wouldn't be too sure of that," Kellums stated. "Someone may have taken a good opportunity to get even with the kid and have it blamed on Yancey. He's roughed up a lot of others. He'll be as tough as his old man if he lives. And that reminds me, his old man is due in pretty soon expecting to go to a wedding. If he goes to a funeral instead we might be lookin' for a new crowd to handle our delicate little jobs, because he just might take a notion to kill Yancey Kelbo. If he does, he'll have to get his whole crowd, and between 'em I'd put my money on Morgette, from what I've heard."

"No lie," Krieger agreed. "Besides, he'd have plenty of help."

"Well," Kellums sighed, "that still doesn't solve the big problem. How do we get that strip along the river from the Morgettes before the whole world knows the railroad is planning to come in here? If the Old Man wasn't on their board of directors the word would've been out by now. We haven't got much time."

"Well, you might make 'em an offer they can't turn down, if Old Whatsis will stand for it."

Kellums shook his head. "No deal. The idea is to make some money on it sellin' it to his own company."

"Well," Krieger said, "maybe he won't get the Morgette real estate then. Hell, we got everything going for us now, except that. He'll get greedy and sink us all. But one thing is damn' certain. With Dolf Morgette comin' back he sure as sin isn't going to be able to use the Kelbos for that job like we've done on a bunch of scared hoemen."

"Maybe Dolf won't get home," Kellums said, slyly.

"What the hell does that mean?" Krieger asked.

"Just a hunch."

"I don't want a damn' thing to do with tryin' to kill that one," Krieger said. "It's been tried before. I plan to die from fallin' off my wallet at a ripe old age. Morgette doesn't kill off worth a damn. My advice to you is that if you're plannin' to sic Old Man Kelbo and his boys on Dolf that you call it off—or distance yourself from the deal a helluva long ways."

That was the way the meeting ended. Kellums wouldn't say any more about his hunch regarding Dolf Morgette, wouldn't admit if it was anything more than a hunch.

As Krieger left he reflected on his own plan to profit from their knowledge of the impending railroad right of way. He'd been quietly courting Theodora Morgette, Dolf's ex-wife, who with Matt Morgette now owned the piece of property they needed. He had found her extremely susceptible to a smooth line of flattery. Krieger was thinking she wouldn't be too hard to take, even if he had to marry her. She wants too much for the land, so it may come to that. She was a mighty handsome woman but, he had to admit, she was nonetheless a big damn' fool to fall for his oily line. "Oh well," he told himself, "brainy women make troublesome wives, I've been told."

CHAPTER 3

DOLF Morgette was southbound, midway between Seattle and San Francisco on the steamer *Port Discovery*, when his son Junior was shot. Maggie, his wife, had decided to go directly to Idaho from Seattle while he went by ship to Frisco and picked up Amy, his daughter by his first marriage. She had been there attending school.

"You go ahead," Maggie had insisted. "This way I'll have a few extra days with father."

Her father, Chief Henry, was nationally renowned for having whipped the yellow-striped britches off the U. S. cavalry a decade before. He finally had been allowed to return north years after his final surrender and banishment to Indian Territory. He was given a new reservation too. Dolf knew the Chief wanted to see his grandson, Henry, and suspected he'd particularly like to spend some time with him alone.

Maggie hadn't aired her other thoughts. She dreaded meeting Dolf's white San Francisco friends, the socially prominent Alexanders. She knew that Dolf once had been very close to Will Alexander's daughter, Diana. It seemed important to her that Dolf clearly recognize she trusted him alone now with Diana. All factors considered she was relieved when Dolf agreed she should go home directly. She would have preferred that he come too, but understood his reluctance to have Amy travel alone, even though she was now sixteen.

Before he left Seattle Dolf arranged to ship home his horse, Wowakan, and dog, Jim Too, and most of his baggage on the same train Maggie would be on. He had wired Will Alexander his expected arrival time in San Francisco and was not surprised to see his friend waiting at the gang plank. He had half expected to see Will's whole family and Amy as well.

They shook hands warmly. "Alaska must be the fountain of youth," Will observed. "You look ten years younger."

"No worries," Dolf replied. "I had a ton of 'em when I was here last year."

This caused a brief frown to cross Will's face. He knew Dolf was soon to be weighed down with additional heavy worries. The previous year Dolf had thought Maggie and Henry had been drowned in a spring ice jam and flood in Alaska. Now Will had a telegram advising Dolf that his son by his first wife was lingering close to death. He decided to delay the news awhile. His friend at least deserved a peaceful lunch first.

Will himself looked spry and chipper for a man over sixty and Dolf said, "You don't look too bad for an old geezer yourself."

Will grinned. "Man's as old as he feels. Just turned sixteen this A.M. C'mon. I've got my buggy waitin'. Drove myself." He steered Dolf up the dock. "Clemmy's layin' on lunch for us. I'll have Eustace pick up your bags."

On the way up to his mansion Will explained Amy's absence. "She and Diana went down to the ranch as soon as school let out." He didn't add that he'd wired Diana to return at once so Amy could go to her brother's side, if there was time.

Will's wife Clemmy greeted Dolf like a long-lost brother, as he knew she would, then stuffed a huge lunch into him. After lunch, being aware of the bad news, she discreetly left Will and Dolf just as they were firing up two of Will's cigars.

"I'm afraid I've got some bad news," Will started in without beating around the bush.

"Who's been killed now?" Dolf spilled out the first thought that flashed through his mind. In view of his past this was a natural response. So many he'd cared for in the past had gone quickly and violently.

"Nobody dead yet as far as I know," Will quickly reassured him. "Your brother Matt wired me knowin' you were headed here. Your son got shot a couple of days ago. He's still hangin' on. I wired Matt right back for more details. Here's his answer. I already read it." He pulled a telegram from his inside coat pocket and handed it to Dolf. It read:

JUNIOR STILL HANGING ON STOP SHOT IN THE BACK BY UNKNOWN PARTY STOP DOC THINKS HE'S GOT A FIFTY-FIFTY CHANCE STOP I SUSPECT A NEW CROWD OF LOCAL HARDCASES NAMED KELBO STOP JUNIOR ARRESTED A PAIR OF THEM THE NIGHT BEFORE HE WAS SHOT STOP GET HERE AS SOON AS YOU CAN STOP WILL MEET YOU AT JUNCTION STOP WIRE YOUR EXPECTED ARRIVAL TIME STOP

MATT

Dolf re-read it, then stared out the window silently for awhile. He carefully masked his inner turmoil. He loved his son deeply. His gut had tensed into a tight knot as soon as Will had given him the bad news. Will left him to his thoughts. Dolf had had reservations about Junior following in his footsteps as a lawman. But he was going on twenty-one and tough as they came. Even at that he would have voiced objections except that their old friend, Hal Green, was now mayor of Pinebluff. The town was experiencing a new mining boom due to rich new discoveries and undergoing a revival of the wild and woolly late '70s period. Hal had his hands full keeping the lid on all the usual explosive potential of card sharps, red-eye, women, and footloose adventurers. He figured if he couldn't get one Morgette he'd settle for another.

Dolf snapped out of his reverie shortly, a feeling of great urgency pressing him. "I've got to get up home quick, Will. What's the best way to go?"

"Already got your ticket. Leaves at 4 P.M. I'll bring Amy along myself later. Was aimin' to go up there and look over the new prospects anyhow for me and old George Hearst. We'll be just twelve hours or so behind you."

Will pulled out his gold turnip-watch. "Got about an hour to get you to the ferry. Plenty of time. Let's splice the main brace—you could probably use one." He pulled a bottle of cognac from the sideboard, but rather than pouring a fashionable snifter, sloshed out half a water glass apiece.

Dolf hoped Will didn't notice the tremor in his hand as he accepted the glass. Dolf's nerves were all steel when faced with a life and death situation in a gunfight, but where family and friends were concerned he was as vulnerable as a sentimental woman.

On the way to the ferry Will brought up another matter on his mind. "I hate to bother you at a time like this, Dolf, but I've got a proposition I'd like you to think over."

Dolf glanced expectantly at Will, a man to whom he owed a great deal. Regardless of his own circumstances, he'd have tried anything short of the impossible for Will. The latter hesitated.

"Spill it," Dolf urged.

"Well," Will said, "first off I'm a pretty big stock holder in Wells Fargo." He paused and took a deep breath, letting it out gustily. "I really hate to ask a favor at a time like this," he confessed.

"So? Ask it anyhow."

He handed Dolf a fat envelope. "It's all here. Jim Hume, who's Wells Fargo's chief of detectives, has a proposition to offer you. If you take it, wire him according to the instructions inside. If you don't I won't blame you and it'll be all the same."

Once on the train Dolf took out the bulging envelope from Wells Fargo. Inside were copies of a number of reports from company detectives, whom Hume had apparently sent into the Pinebluff District in the past few months, several other documents, plus a cover letter addressed to Dolf, which he read first. Hume wrote:

The company needs a good man to coordinate its whole operation at Pinebluff. On the recommendations of both Will Alexander and Wyatt Earp, I'm offering you the job. I want you to hire some good guards, see that they pay attention to business, and also want you to do some detective work. Read the enclosed reports. They will give you some leads as to who may be behind the recent robberies where we've had to eat the losses. It looks like someone on the inside may be handing out information, since only our three biggest shipments were hit, and no others. I would keep an eye on our present agent as a possible suspect. Anybody can tell when a stage is carrying bullion, of course, by the fact that it has a shotgun messenger, but knowing which were the big *shipments suggests an inside job. Contact Ben Page at Pinebluff, who is our biggest shipper. I am writing him that you will probably be our new man in charge. I have not told our agent yet and will leave that up to you. The enclosed papers include your appointment directly under me and will serve as authorization to take over the whole Pinebluff operation if you take the job, including hiring and firing. I am authorized to pay you $500.00 a month and some substantial added bonuses in the right circumstances. [Dolf knew enough about the company's operations from his past experience as a lawman to read "right circumstances" as "We pay a bonus if you get rid of the right people, and no questions asked here about how."] If you accept the offer, wire to B. F. Smith, Box 100, San Francisco and say: "Have bought the horse and will deliver."*

The enclosed reports will give you a general picture. I think that there is a large confederation of outlaws in cahoots with the local law and perhaps some influential people as well. I don't know who they are but the gang is also into large scale stealing of horses and cattle. A family consisting of a father and several boys by the name of Kelbo have been there for about a year. The rustling started on a large scale after they moved in. They have a record for the same all over the West and have been run out of Texas, New Mexico, and Arizona, dating back to the late '70s. So you can pretty well figure who's doing the dirty work. I don't trust Sheriff Casey either; you may know him from past experience. You can judge better than I can what sort he is if you worked with him before. I have arranged a commission for you as a U.S. deputy marshal if you accept our offer. All you need to do is take the enclosed commission to a judge or anyone authorized to do it and have the oath administered and send it to the U.S. marshal for Idaho.

Dolf then read through a series of individual reports that simply confirmed in a little more detail what Hume's letter had summarized. One especially attracted his notice and caused him to wonder if Hume had carelessly left it with others or had hurriedly overlooked its contents. This report stated that with respect to the several nesters that had been harassed out of the country, local suspicion in some quarters pointed to Matt Morgette, the largest cattleman in the district. It added that he was the tough brother of the notorious gunman and killer, Dolf Morgette, who had left the country some years before after a series of killings. Details on the latter were not supplied. Thanks a heap Wells Fargo, he thought. If all your detectives are as sloppy as this one there's no tellin' what could happen to an innocent feller. He wondered how many the company had sent "over to the majority" on that sort of slipshod investigating and reporting—and gladly paid bonuses for the mistake in the bargain.

Nonetheless, in view of what appeared to be afoot on his home range, he could see the advantage of the Wells Fargo position as well as of being a U.S. deputy marshal. At the very least it would allow him to carry a concealed weapon legally. Otherwise he envisioned himself being harassed by the likes of Morgan Casey, who he knew all too well from their mutual service under Ed Pardeau in the old days. The knowledge had not left a good taste in his mouth either. He could envision Casey meeting him at the stage when he hit town and frisking him on general principle, just like Tobe Mulveen, who had succeeded Pardeau as sheriff. Tobe had almost made a life work of harassing Dolf whenever he got the chance. Casey would probably do that too if he could, thinking that when Dolf was in town there was always trouble, just as Mulveen had.

"Well," Dolf said to himself. "I can guaran-damn-tee 'em there's gonna be trouble when I hit town this time."

As soon as he got to Pocatello he took advantage of a train delay to get sworn in as a deputy marshal and get his oath in the mail. He also sent Hume his cryptic message via B. F. Smith accepting Wells Fargo's offer.

At Butte he took a short stroll to stretch his legs and check at the depot for the telegram he was expecting. He was deeply concerned about Junior's condition and hoped to get a wire at Ogden or Pocatello from Matt, but he was disappointed. In Pocatello he'd sent Matt an urgent plea to wire him at Butte and let him know how Junior was coming along. He remembered the old saw about no news being good news, but was more inclined to think they might be trying to spare him the tragic blow till they could tell him personally. At the depot he found the hoped-for wire waiting for him.

*THE KID IS CONSCIOUS STOP DOC SAYS QUIT WORRY-
ING STOP JUNIOR SAYS TELL THE OLD MAN MOR-
GETTES ARE HARD TO KILL STOP YOU OUGHT TO
KNOW STOP SEE YOU SOON STOP*

MATT

At this news Dolf felt as though a huge stone had been rolled off
of him. He hadn't realized how tense and concerned he'd been.
He'd only been able to sleep in short, restless snatches since leaving
San Francisco. Now he suddenly felt like he'd like to sleep a long
while. He was relaxed and smiling to himself when the slug
whistled by his head, slapped into the brick depot wall and
ricocheted away in the night with a spiteful whine. He didn't see a
muzzle flash and assumed the gunman was behind him across the
tracks. He leaped toward the shelter of the nearest doorway, which
was also shrouded in darkness, jerking his .45 as he went. As he'd
expected, a second shot followed the first. Just one guy, he thought.
If there'd been more they'd have shot together. He poked his head
out to scan the darkened tracks. A row of flatcars was dimly
outlined in the light from the depot and from a switch engine
moving toward him from somewhere down the tracks. He thought
someone moved on the other side of the cars but couldn't be sure,
training his pistol on the spot. Another shot issued from that area,
going far wide of him. He returned it with three rapid shots,
spacing them in a fan to sweep the possible spot where the gunman
might be. He cautiously remained under cover. You never knew
when someone might get lucky. He heard shouts in the near
distance; the shots had obviously aroused a great deal of curiosity
among reckless souls who risked having their lights put out by
coming to investigate before they were sure it was safe. Dolf's train,
which was on the main line on the other side of the depot, started
to pull out. He debated running for it or staying to explain to the
local law what the shooting was about. He'd have liked to know who
was shooting at him, in case he'd tagged him. "The hell with it," he
grunted. "I'll read it in the papers." He risked breaking from the
door, but instead of crossing the lighted platform he darted around
the dark side of the building and caught his train on the run as it

gathered speed. "I can't risk sitting it out in the local jug with Junior in the shape he's in." He knew that his credentials would probably get him out on his own recognizance, but that would take time. Boarding the train on the run, he bumped into a passenger in the vestibule undoubtedly curious about the shooting.

"What the hell was all the shooting about?" the other asked him.

"Mad dog," Dolf told him. "The marshal shot it over there." He pointed beyond the depot as the train drew away in the dark.

"Good thing," the fellow said. "It might have bit some kid."

Dolf forbore commenting that he hadn't heard that adults were immune to rabies. He went through the train and regained his seat. He was asleep a minute after sprawling comfortably in the seat, which he had all to himself. A carpet bag makes a better pillow than a saddle, he thought drowsily as he dropped off, his hat pulled over his eyes.

CHAPTER 4

DOLF hit the Junction on the 8 A.M. train. He spotted Matt already mounted, leading his horse Wowakan. His rifle was even strapped in a boot on Wowakan's saddle. Matt's a typical Morgette, Dolf thought, doesn't forget a thing. At the same time it reminded him how tense local affairs must have got in a hurry. Matt rode over to meet him as he jumped down from the train. He didn't take time to dismount or shake hands. "Junior's doin' fine," he reassured Dolf right off, then, "If you got any baggage, we'll pick it up later, unless it's something like diamonds. Sneaky lookin' crew tailed me down most of the way. Thought I didn't see 'em, but I was watchin' my back trail. Probably the Kelbos. My guess is they're waitin' back down the road for us somewhere, figurin' the ball may open as soon as you get in. Probably aim to get in the first lick."

Dolf mounted Wowakan wordlessly, then spoke for the first time, "It's yore party, little brother. You lead the way."

Matt hung spurs to his horse and tore for the woods, riding at right angles to the road to Pinebluff, Dolf following, their thundering departure inviting wondering stares from the passengers out stretching their legs. Matt drew his horse in, once they were safely concealed in the timber. He offered his hand. "I'm sure as hell glad you're back. The Kelbos know we got the deadwood on 'em for the shooting. So does that damn' worthless sheriff, Morgan Casey." He told Dolf how he and Maggie's brother Buck had led the sheriff straight to Kelbo's.

"Why the hell didn't he arrest Kelbo?" Dolf asked.

"Claimed we didn't have any proof, in so many words. If Buck and I had stayed up there without the sheriff I imagine we'd still be up there."

"Couldn't Casey read the tracks himself?"

"Hell yes! He could! I could! The schoolmarm could've! I wanted him to look around the place, at least for Yancey Kelbo's horse—Yancey was the one Junior roughed up and threw in the jug the night before he was shot. I told him we should circle for the tracks goin' on through and he said it was gettin' dark and he didn't have time to fool around anymore—I could do as I damn pleased. That's when I gave him up for a hopeless case."

Dolf recalled Hume's surmise that the sheriff was hand in glove with the Kelbos, but said nothing.

Matt said, "We'll have to settle with the Kelbos personal, I reckon."

Dolf nodded silently. It was a familiar old story to him. That had been the way, in the end, that he'd had to settle with the murderers of his father and two older brothers. He thought, this time, *maybe*, it'll be different, with the Wells Fargo backing me. *Maybe!*

"We'd better keep movin' at a good clip," Matt suggested, urging his horse into motion again. "If that was the Kelbos they probably had someone come to the Junction to watch for us. Knowin' we ain't comin' by the road they'll try to head us off."

Dolf had been thinking the same thing. It might be possible, if the Kelbos had learned the country well enough by then, to cut them off at the long open park known as Eagle Meadow. That is, if it really was the Kelbos. The Morgette brothers kept their horses at a steady, mile-eating lope whenever the terrain permitted. Dolf was relieved to see they'd won the race to Eagle Meadow, if someone was indeed on their trail. The meadow was occupied by a herd of grazing elk that galloped away into the far timber at first sight of them. If a party following them had arrived first and was waiting in ambush, it was unlikely the elk would have returned to their grazing so soon.

Dolf and Matt pulled up midway in the meadow to let their mounts blow and look around; also to listen.

"If anyone's comin'," Dolf said, "we beat 'em here anyhow. No other place they could get ahead of us, short of town."

"Someone's comin' all right," Matt said, pointing. Dolf had seen the riders emerge from the trees a couple of miles away before Matt pointed. Matt then took a pair of field glasses from his saddle bags and coolly scanned the approaching group. "Eight or ten," he estimated. "One's Old Man Kelbo. He's a tall drink of water. Can't mistake him. Can recognize some Kelbo hosses too. Must have all his boys along." He put the glasses away, eyeing Dolf for a lead.

"Let's head for the timber and drop our greetin' card on 'em, then high-tail for town," Dolf suggested.

They raced to the far end of the meadow, halting again. Dolf dismounted and drew his .45-90 from the scabbard. When the riders were within a half mile he dropped a couple of long shots among them. He was sure they heard the mellow boom of the big rifle, even if they couldn't hear the heavy slugs whistle by. They pulled in their mounts, apparently for a short council.

"Shells for that cannon in yore saddle bags, left side," Matt told Dolf.

Dolf reloaded, calmly watching the pursuing party, which fanned out abreast, well spread out, and started their horses at a rapid walk for the partially concealed Morgettes.

"Just like the cavalry," Matt observed. "Looks like they mean business. Do we fight or skedaddle?"

"Both," Dolf said. "They started it. We'll have to give 'em a lickin' sooner or later."

He watched the horsemen, now clearly ten in number, break into a gallop, shooting rifles at long range. He heard only one bullet whiz above them in the trees. Carefully he took aim using a tree for a rest and squeezed off a shot, bringing down the lead horse. The others, as he suspected, pulled up, unnerved by that kind of shooting. He squeezed off a second shot and dropped one of the milling riders from his saddle. That conclusively ended the charge. Several of the riders were spurring out of range at top speed. He dropped a couple of random shots after them and drew a volley from three who were rolling the dead horse off the lead rider.

"Let's go," he yelled to Matt. "My guess is they won't be following us very close from here on in."

They took a more leisurely pace, trotting side by side, but kept a close watch on their back trail, stopping briefly whenever they could get a long view of it, to look and listen.

Dolf asked at one stop, "Where's Maggie and the kid?"

"Gone out to her paw's camp since Junior's on the mend. Took the dog too, since he doesn't know any of us. He sure looked all over for you."

Dolf had felt like he was truly home when he first arrived at the Junction. Despite the need to be alert for an ambush, he had savored the familiar land and the tall snow-capped mountains, which seemed closer than they actually were. He and Matt had made their way into the foot hills, threading among tall stands of lodgepole pine and white spruce, with their delicate bluish-green needles that never failed to please his eye. They had ascended to Eagle Meadow through stands of juniper and towering yellow pine, finally reaching the higher levels where larch and aspen were also found. Serviceberries and huckleberries grew in thick abundance here and there. Once in the high meadow itself they rode among purple heather and columbine, with vast fields of syringa visible on the higher slopes. This lush and varied growth characterized their route right to the edge of town. Two mining booms had robbed some of the slopes adjoining the town of their timber, used for cribbing in the mines. However, tall conifers dotted the town proper, just as he remembered them, with wild flowers growing in the yards and empty lots.

When Dolf had last seen Pinebluff it was on its way to becoming a ghost town: few people or conveyances were to be seen in the streets. Now it seemed to have returned to the boom days of the late '70s, the wide dirt streets teaming with pedestrians, buggies, and wagons. Large ore wagons moved slowly down the road to the smelters over on Pine Creek at the edge of town. Their steady hammering carried clearly across town. Dolf imagined they went day and night just as in the first big boom. There were no empty boarded-up buildings now. From the edge of town, where the miners' shacks clustered, to the middle of town at Main and Pine, every building seemed to be reoccupied. The downtown district even boasted some new board walks. Newly painted signs hung across the sidewalks on mercantile houses that were again doing a thriving business. Dolf felt for a brief instant like he'd taken ten years off his life and was again a deputy sheriff in the old boom town. Then he recalled the grim business that faced him now. Even with Junior on the mend he had his work cut out for him. In many ways it would be just like it had been a decade before when he was a lawman there—with one exception: he'd be calling the shots this time.

Their first destination at Pinebluff was naturally the hospital. Neither of them was prepared for the scene that greeted them upon entering since Matt had last heard that Junior was doing fine.

The first person Dolf saw as he entered was not Doc, from whom he'd anticipated a hearty welcome, but his former wife, Theodora, Junior's mother. She rose swiftly as he entered and crossed to him just as though bitter years hadn't come between them. The stricken look on her face warned him that something was terribly wrong. Whatever else her short-comings may have been, he was sure she loved Junior, their first born child and only son, in the ardent way that only a mother can. She flew into his arms now for comfort, just as she always had long ago.

"He's dying!" she moaned on his shoulder. "He's got a fever of 106 and pneumonia has set in. Doc's in there with him now." Dolf's heart sank into his boots.

"Take me to him. I want to see him while he's still alive," Dolf ordered. Theodora dumbly led him down the hall, Doc looking up briefly as they entered the room. He and Doc Priddy were both packing cracked ice around Junior, Doc putting a sack of ice on Junior's forehead. Doc's face was haggard from days of worry and strain. His eyes met and locked with Dolf's, then he shook his head uncertainly.

"Crisis," he stated. "Next half hour may tell the story. Better pray."

On that Dolf had beat him to the draw by several seconds. His son's bluish-white, emaciated face, eyes deeply sunken and closed, body propped up on pillows so that he could at least draw in short, rasping ragged gasps of breath through his wide open mouth, tested Dolf's nerve to the core. He didn't see how anyone that looked that bad could live. Nonetheless, he didn't abandon hope. It wasn't his nature.

"He was doin' O.K. till this morning, talkin' to his ma. Then he started to get delirious," Doc explained. "We'd better send for Catherine and Mum." Mum was Dolf's strong-willed grandmother. The thought of her moral force gave Dolf heart.

"I'll go," Matt volunteered from the door to which he'd followed Dolf and Theodora.

Doc suddenly looked exasperated. "O.K., everybody out now," he ordered. "He needs all the air he can get."

Catherine Green arrived breathlessly, looking frightened and close to collapse. She blindly ran back to Junior, recognizing no one as she passed. Doc eyed her severely as she entered, having driven the others out, then seeing her stricken look he relented and smiled weakly.

"I want to kiss him while he's still alive," she pleaded.

"Go ahead," Doc said. "Maybe you'll wake him up like in the fairy tale. I need to get him awake so he can swallow. Got one last cure up my sleeve."

She approached the limp figure in the bed apprehensively, taking Junior's hand in her own. He had pulled it out from under Doc's ice packs himself and had been fidgeting with his covers. Catherine leaned over and very gently kissed his burning cheek. As she did he opened his eyes.

"I think he's comin' around," Doc whispered.

Junior looked at Catherine. "Honey," he gasped with some difficulty. "I knew you'd bring some cold lemonade."

Doc snatched the ice pack off Junior's head. "Here," he ordered Catherine. "Help me get him up higher so he can drink this lemonade." Doc had snatched up a cup of brown liquid he had ready.

Between them they helped Junior get Doc's concoction down. He made faces and had a tough time breathing between swallows, but dutifully took it all, the effort sapping the last of his energy. Then they eased him back on the pillows, his eyes already closed again. They both watched him anxiously. "May be my imagination but I think he's breathing easier already," Doc said, replacing the ice pack on Junior's brow.

"Should I go now?" Catherine asked, not wanting to go, pleading with her eyes to stay.

"I don't think so," Doc opined. "You may be what he needs. Keep holdin' his hand. Here, I'll get you a chair an' you stay right with him for awhile. Call me if you need help. I'll be out with Dolf."

"Is Dolf there?" she asked, dismayed. "I didn't even see him."

Doc smiled. "He'll understand. Don't worry about it."

Dolf's grandmother, known simply as Mum, met Doc in the hall. He held his finger to his lips. "Go peek," he said, "but don't go in. Doctor's orders." For once the formidable Mum followed the doctor's orders. Everyone recognized her as a power unto herself, under normal circumstances. She exerted a moral force on everyone she came in contact with. She'd seen a lot of trouble in her slightly over four score years and survived it with flying colors. As a young bride of not quite sixteen she'd filled an Indian with buckshot for trying to run off the filly that her husband had given her as a wedding present. During the Civil War, after General Ewing had issued his famous (or infamous) order number nine, she'd staunchly stood off a band of marauding Reb guerrillas who'd come to burn them out because Dolf's father and brothers had gone to join the Union Army. She'd been backed in this by Dolf himself, which he recalled vividly as she sailed in, hugging him briefly, then headed back to look in on Junior. She was only a couple of inches shorter than Dolf and still had a lot of good flesh and muscle on her. As Matt had once observed to Dolf, he'd bet her against the two of them in a hay-pitching contest. It would still be a good bet, Dolf guessed.

"What do you think?" Mum whispered, rejoining Doc after her peek.

"He's still got a fightin' chance," Doc stated.

Mum's jaw tightened. "Morgettes always figured a fightin' chance gave us the odds."

She and Doc went back out together. Mum made up for her brief greeting to Dolf by giving him a bear hug. "You're gettin' fat," she allowed, not really meaning it, just joshing him. He was lean and hard as a board from running behind his dog team all winter just to keep in shape. In Alaska the trap line he'd been running was some fifty miles long.

A pall hung over the group waiting outside but they tried to make cheerful conversation. Theodora clung to Dolf's big hand for comfort. At a time like this all past scores were forgotten. Doc tiptoed in to check on the patient. He found Catherine fast asleep, her head leaning on the bed, oblivious to the ice packs. Junior's hand was on her head. His eyes were open and lucid. Doc moved into the room and knew that Junior recognized him. "You're gonna make it, kid," Doc assured him.

"I know it," Junior replied. "I have to." He looked tenderly at Catherine, then closed his eyes and drifted off into a sound sleep.

Later Catherine joined the group in the waiting room. It was a happier looking crowd. She asked Doc, "What was that you gave Junior?"

"Remember Strong Bull's remedy that pulled Dolf through up at Chief Henry's camp when you were nursing him back in '85?"

She looked puzzled for a moment, then remembered. She recalled Doc saying at the time, "Yuh never know, Catherine. If it works, don't knock it. Did yuh find out what was in the cup of water Strong Bull gave Dolf?"

She also remembered her reply, which had been "Ugh!" Now she asked Doc, "You didn't?"

"I did!" he said. "Ground red ants. Like I said, if it works, don't knock it. So far it's worked twice for Morgettes that I know of."

CHAPTER 5

THE women had left the hospital. Theodora was staying in town with Catherine Green. Quiet, tactful Catherine was one of the few women she liked. Mum had invited everyone over for supper and gone home to get it started. "You, too, Doc," she said, "if you think Junior'll be outa danger."

"We'll see," Doc said. "Doc Priddy'll be back here by then I reckon."

Once alone with Dolf and Matt, Doc reached into the bottom of a medicine cabinet. "Got some special remedy for us walking wounded." He pulled out a bottle of 100 proof Kentucky bourbon and poured three stiff hookers into water glasses. He winked at Matt and glanced at Dolf, saying, "I know one's yore limit, old pard, but you never said what caliber: .22 or .45. This one's a .45." He hoisted the glass. "To the kid. He's gonna make it this time for sure."

They all drank to that. Doc passed around the cigars, then collapsed into his swivel desk chair, leaning back and propping his feet up on his desk. "First time I've relaxed since the kid was shot," he said. "I think I'll take Mum up on supper. Ain't had a square meal since then either. Then I'm gonna sleep till next Wednesday."

"Tomorrow's Wednesday," Matt said.

"I know. That's what I said." He lifted the bottle and offered it around. Dolf still had half his drink left. Matt took a small refill.

Dolf and Matt then told Doc about their run-in with the Kelbos.

Doc leaned back again and blew cigar smoke at the ceiling. "You know," he said, "we're gonna have to kill those sonsabitchin' Kelbos for the good of the community."

"If it comes to that," Dolf agreed.

"May already have done for one of 'em, but if they complain they'll give themselves away. They weren't tryin' to serve subpoenas on us, exactly," Dolf said, then added, "Well, I guess I'll mosey up to Mum's. Comin' little brother?"

"Might's well. We got lots to talk about I haven't told you yet."

"See you at Mum's," Doc said. "Gonna check in on Junior again. Nurse is back with him, so I reckon he's O.K. If there's any change for the worse I'll let you know right away." He walked them to the door.

Dolf and Matt were out on the walk, Doc still standing in the door, when a cavalcade of riders escorting a wagon turned the nearest corner.

"Oh, oh," Matt cautioned. "Big trouble. That's the Kelbos. I can imagine what's in the wagon. Looks like Doc's got another customer."

Overhearing, Doc said, "That answers one question. Your clay pigeon isn't dead yet."

Old Man Kelbo was driving the wagon. Dolf suspected it had been the Old Man's horse he'd shot. Seeing the Morgette brothers, the Kelbos passed some low-voiced remarks between them. It wasn't hard to guess what they were saying, probably something like, "That must be Dolf Morgette with his brother—the damned old grey wolf himself." They kept coming steadily and pulled up in front of the hospital. A number of townsmen were gathering, attracted by the cavalcade.

The Old Man stopped the wagon at the front walk. He didn't get down, instead glaring at the Morgettes. He wore a pistol and his rifle was propped up on the seat beside him.

"You'd be Dolf Morgette?" he finally said, pointing a long gnarled finger.

Dolf said nothing. The horsemen, four in number, spread out.

"I said," the Old Man bawled, "you'd be Dolf Morgette. I got some Morgette handiwork here in the wagon. My boy. Maybe dead already. You, Doc. C'mere an' help us get him inside."

Doc eyed him coldly. "I got a stretcher in here. Send one of yer boys for it and carry him in yourself. You ain't helpless."

No Kelbo moved, waiting for a signal from the Old Man. He

waved them back. "No, by damn," he said. "Let them Morgettes carry him in. One o' them done it."

Sensing what might be coming several townsmen, whose curiosity fought with their discretion and lost, began to move toward cover. Neither Morgette moved or replied. Doc drifted back out of the door. The Old Man jumped down, turning to get his rifle. Dolf spoke for the first time, recognizing what was shaping up.

"Move that rifle and I'll kill you, Kelbo." Dolf moved swiftly forward, jerking a long-barreled Colt with the blinding speed for which he was famous. He swept the pistol over the rest of them, arresting their motions toward their weapons. Matt had also jerked his pistol. At Dolf's command the Old Man had frozen with his hand on the rifle. Slowly he removed it and turned toward Dolf, his face turning beet red.

"You Morgettes killed my boy, you sonsabitches!" he shouted. Everyone in hearing knew what calling a Morgette a sonofabitch meant. They weren't disappointed.

"You got a pistol on," Dolf said, replacing his almost as swiftly as he'd drawn it. "Go after it."

The Old Man hesitated. "Go after it," Dolf hissed, close to his face, "if yer not too damn' yellow."

Kelbo knew he'd talked himself into a shooting situation. He'd rather die than "skin it back," so he made a motion to draw and was buffaloed on the side of his head by Dolf's long Colt barrel. Losing his hat, he collapsed disjointedly into the road. As soon as he hit the Old Man, Dolf made a lightning swing of his pistol to again cover the four Kelbo boys. "Now," he ordered, "take 'em out real easy and drop 'em."

A new voice emphasized the order from the hospital door. "Do like he says," Doc ordered. "This thing's full of double-aught buck." He swung his locally famous double-barreled Greener back and forth to cover them all. "I'd as soon work on all of yuh instead o' just that one in the wagon."

One by one the Kelbo boys slowly withdrew their pistols and carefully let them drop to the dirt. "That's better," Doc said. "Now any one of you damn' fools can come get a stretcher for the one's hurt. An' a pail o' water to toss on your old man."

That defused the situation. All the fight had been taken out of them for the moment. Dolf and Matt stayed around in case these hardcases were unreasonable enough to give Doc trouble despite their grim need for his services. Simp Parsons, who had been Junior's deputy, was now acting as town marshal; notified of the trouble he arrived at a trot. He took in the situation at a glance. His first action was to collect the dropped weapons. He sent one of the nearby gawkers over to Packard and Underwater's Livery for a grain sack to hold the collected weapons. Only after taking that precaution, collecting the Old Man's pistol and rifle as well, did he greet Dolf. "Glad to see yuh home," he said, but not shaking hands since both his and Dolf's right hands still held pistols. They both laughed and reholstered their weapons. "What happened?" Simp asked, and received a brief recital. "Want me to run the bastards in?" he said.

Dolf shrugged. "What for? They'll be right back out in the A.M. at the latest." It was a generosity he'd soon regret.

The next city official on the scene was Mayor Hal Green, just in from his ranch. His daughter Catherine had told him Dolf was at the hospital and he arrived just as several dippers of cold water were being sloshed in Old Man Kelbo's face. Kelbo didn't know which end he sat on at first, getting partially to his feet once, then toppling back over like a drunk. Finally he oriented himself and regained his senses, glaring like a mad bull. His terrible temper again unwisely drove his tongue. "You!" he pointed at Dolf. "You, or your brother shot my son this morning. I'll get you two if it's the last thing I do."

"I notice the hole was in the front when they carried your boy in," Dolf said quietly, carefully refraining from admitting he'd done the job. "I got a son inside and the hole's in the back." He stepped close to the Old Man, who was now surrounded by his four other sons. "The whole country knows who the hell shot him. If I burned down you and all your damn' sons like mad dogs nobody would hold it against me."

Simp Parsons moved up between them. Facing the Kelbos he ordered, "Either get inside or get outa here before I jug you all."

They reluctantly shuffled into the hospital with surly faces. Watching them Dolf said to Matt, "Best one of us stay with Junior all the time from now on. We'll move him to the house as soon as he can stand it."

"I'll go on guard for now," Simp volunteered.

Only then did Hal Green step up and shake Dolf's hand. "Am I ever glad to see you, Dolf," he greeted him. This place is getting as bad as '79. How about taking a job as chief of police? I just got the council to approve a six-man force."

Dolf laughed. "Hold on, I just got here. We'll have to talk. How about comin' out to Mum's for supper? We can confab there."

"You got a customer for supper and a confab. First I gotta go get somebody to spell Simp in there. Already got a couple of special police lined up. I'll see you later."

"I suppose we'd better stay out of Doc's way," Dolf told Matt. Doc Priddy had also hustled in while Dolf was talking to Hal Green. "They're probably operating already."

"I 'spect," Matt agreed. "Doc oughta take off one of the kid's legs. I never heard of a one-legged cow thief." Then added more practically, "Suppose Junior'll be O.K. in there with all that scum?"

Dolf thought a moment. "He oughta be O.K. for now," he said. "We'll get him out as soon as Doc says it's O.K. to move him. I wouldn't put anything past that crew from the looks of 'em. I wonder where the rest of the gang went that jumped us this morning?"

By this time they were mounted and on their way over to Mum's. "They don't come in town much," Matt said. "Warrants out for most of 'em from lord only knows where. I suspect they're part of a big rustling gang that operates all over the West. The word is they run stolen horses an' cattle both. Some claim the horse operation drives herds as far as from Canada to Mexico and back, and from out here over into the Dakotas. We just lost some horses this week. About fifty. I got young Buck Henry and Clem Yoder out now on the trail of a big herd headed south. Our stock's probably in it. Been losin' cattle too. Spring roundup for everybody was way short, especially for after a fair winter. All started since the Kelbos and their hardcases hit the country. Since then stages are gettin' stuck up too."

"I know," Dolf said. "That's why Wells Fargo hired me."

Matt looked puzzled. "I meant to ask you. How come you of all people took that kind of job? I thought you had your fill of it. Besides we expected you'd be goin' right back to Alaska."

"Did it for a friend," Dolf explained. "Temporary."

"It might be more temporary than you think if the Kelbos ever get the drop on you. Friends're your weakness."

"And family," Dolf added. "I reckon I'll stay around awhile to see that you youngsters get the hang of it."

"Of what?" Matt asked slyly.

"Polecat huntin'. It's an old Morgette specialty. Pa asked me to pass it along but I been neglecting my responsibility."

Matt laughed. "You could hunt them with your eyes shut around here lately. You couldn't throw a rock in town day or night without hittin' one."

Dolf sighed inwardly. "Welcome home," he greeted himself.

CHAPTER 6

THOSE at Mum's house for supper hadn't really expected Doc to make it, and certainly not the way he did. He came in late without knocking, out of breath, startling everyone at the big kitchen table.

"You gotta get the hell outa here, Dolf—you and Matt both. That idiot Morgan Casey has a posse on the way over to surround the place."

"What he hell for?" Dolf asked calmly without rising.

"Old Man Kelbo claims you shot his kid. Filed an attempted murder charge."

"That's no lie," Dolf said, "I shot his kid. Sorry it wasn't the old man, but the bunch was millin' around at least 500 yards away."

"Never mind. Just get the hell outa here. You ain't got time to argue."

"I'm not runnin'," Dolf stated flatly. "Tired of always runnin'."

"Good," Mum said. "I'll get my shotgun out." As good as her word she went to the pantry and returned with a big double barrel.

Catherine Green and Theodora both looked apprehensive. Matt, who was cut off the same Morgette bolt of cloth as Dolf, contributed the laugh. "I think I'll finish my huckleberry pie an' coffee before the shootin' starts." And dug right in.

Hal Green was more explosive. "That damn' fool Casey oughta be hung. He's in cahoots with Kelbo and the crowd backing him. If you end up in his jail he's apt to let 'em drag you out and hang you, or shoot you. Might be better to light out till we can arrange some protection."

"Nope," Dolf stated. "Let 'em come. I'll prefer counter charges of assault and attempted murder of a federal officer."

"Make that chief of police too," Hal added. "I'll swear I hired you by mail last week."

Dolf grinned. "Makes it sound better for sure. I'll take the job. I'm beginning to think this place needs a damn' good shakin' up. I owe Pinebluff plenty. Every time I come to town somebody trys to throw me in jail." About the immediate threat he said, "You women folks go upstairs. Take a lamp. You too Mum. If anyone tries to come up besides us plug 'em. Matt and Doc, prop a chair under the front door knob unless Mum's found a key since I was here last. And make sure all the shades are down."

He silently eased open the door of the now darkened kitchen and listened. He could hear movement, boots on the uneven ground, where someone was unsuccessful at an attempt at stealth. Someone else uttered a low-voiced caution to be quiet. A voice very close by said in almost a whisper, "The damn' light went out. Suppose they know we're comin'?"

"Naw. They went in the other room. I could see the lamp movin' thataway."

"Let's hope so. I don't like this a bit."

There was no reply. Dolf noiselessly eased the door shut. Hal Green, directly behind him, asked in a whisper, "Anyone out there yet?"

"Full of 'em," Dolf replied.

"Maybe I can slip out and go uptown for some of our boys. I've got a little organization called the Civic Protection League."

Dolf grinned in the darkness. He recognized the name for "vigilantes" regardless of what "word sharps" like Hal Green called them.

"You'd get shot sure as hell, Hal. There's a bunch of nervous dudes crawlin' around the bushes, afraid the big bad Morgette boys'll yell boo at 'em."

Matt and Doc tiptoed softly back into the kitchen. Dolf said in a low voice, "The yard is crawlin' with 'em."

"What now?" Matt asked.

"Let 'em turn loose their wolf. If they try to rush us a couple of shots'll scare 'em off if I'm any judge. We could probably run most of 'em into Canada with corncobs and lightnin' bugs."

"Unless the Kelbos are with 'em," Doc cautioned. "And they are.

That's how I got tipped off they were comin'. They had the sheriff with 'em down at the hospital. Overheard 'em schemin' when they thought me and Priddy were still operating on the kid."

"What're the Kelbo kid's chances, by the way?" Dolf asked.

"Better'n Junior's were."

They were cut off by a hail from the yard. Dolf recognized the sheriff's voice.

"Hey, Morgettes," he yelled. "Anybody home?"

"Let him sweat awhile," Dolf ordered. "Maybe he'll get up nerve enough to come to the door just like the 'quality.' He knows damn' well we're home."

There was a long silence, followed by intentionally loud footsteps on the back porch. After a pause, whoever the brave soul was rapped on the door. "It's the sheriff," he yelled again. "I wanta talk to you, Dolf."

Dolf got a picture of Morgan Casey out there probably peeing down his leg, and certainly not with a gun in his hand. "I'm gonna grab him and get him in here," Dolf whispered. He swiftly opened the door, collected a handful of Casey's shirt front and jerked him inside, kicking the door shut. He shoved a six-shooter in the sheriff's ribs. "Don't move, Casey," he snapped.

"I won't," Casey quavered. "I won't." He fervently prayed that none of his nervous posse would start shooting.

They got Casey's gun and frisked him for a hideout. "Now," Dolf announced, "we're in a negotiatin' position. Casey, yell to those sonsabitches with you and tell 'em to get back away from the house." He kept a grip of the collar of Casey's shirt in back and pushed him to the door. "Open it a crack and tell 'em."

"Suppose they start shootin' when the door opens?"

Dolf prodded him with his pistol again. "Do as I say."

Casey opened the door and quickly yelled. "It's the sheriff, boys! Get back away from the house!"

There was no response. "Do as I say!" Morgan yelled. "Or I'm done for! Git back, fer Crissakes!"

"The damn' fool," a voice said. It sounded like Old Man Kelbo. Then Dolf recognized the voice of the sheriff's brother, Ed. "O.K. Morg," he yelled. "I'll git 'em back away. C'mon boys. They got us in a crack." Then he yelled again. "Hey Dolf. We only want to talk to you and Matt down at the jail. Nobody's gonna hurt yuh!"

Dolf thought, "Not now they won't hurt us, that's for sure." He yelled back. "We'll come down to the jail by ourselves. Clear out with that mob. Especially the Kelbos."

There was no immediate reply. Dolf could imagine a heavy strategy meeting going on over that proposition. He again jabbed the sheriff with his six-shooter. "Tell 'em to do what I say."

"Hey Ed," the sheriff yelled to his brother. "Clear out. They'll come down on their own."

Morgan Casey believed Dolf would keep his word, although he still hoped the Morgettes would be killed or sent to the pen for a long stretch, for the sake of his own bread and butter. He, nonetheless, had a wholehearted respect for all of them; they were distinguished for both guts and honesty.

After several minutes the customary silence of a small town night settled down outside. "I'll go look around," Hal Green volunteered.

"I'll go with you," Doc said.

They quietly slipped out into the darkness. After several minutes they returned.

"Nary a soul," Doc announced.

"Good," Dolf said.

"I still don't think it's a good idea to go down to the jail in the dark," Hal cautioned.

"Neither do I," Doc chipped in.

"How about you, Matt?" Dolf inquired.

"You're the boss, Dolf. I don't care when we go."

"Good," Dolf said. "I don't think it's a good idea to go down there in the dark either. There's probably a Kelbo rifle stickin' outa every dark alley between here an' there, waitin' for us to go by like a bunch of nice little ducks all in a row at the shootin' gallery."

"Hey, wait a minute," the sheriff protested weakly. "What the hell is this? You promised to go down to the jail."

"Shut up," Dolf said. "I didn't say when. We're probably savin' yer life. If the Kelbos tried to dry gulch us I'd shoot out yer liver first of all. If I'm any judge the Old Man is pretty close to a mad dog. He's the kind would cut off his arm because he pounded his thumb with a hammer. Do it before he cooled down and thought what he was doin'. We'll go down to your jail when I'm damn' good and ready." Turning to Hal he said, "Let's go where we can talk for a little while. I want you to get the ladies out of here first of all, in case that crowd comes back later because we don't show up. Got a couple of other items I'd like you to handle too." He drew Hal into the other part of the house. When they returned the women were with them. "I'll take care of it, Dolf," Hal was saying. "You can count on that."

CHAPTER 7

AFTER leaving Mum's house, the sheriff's brother, Ed, had discharged his posse. He was now in charge as undersheriff in the absence of Morgan. When the Morgettes didn't show up shortly at the jail, he grew more agitated with each passing minute. Adding to his queasiness were the looks he'd been getting from Old Man Kelbo. Furthermore, he had his suspicions where the four Kelbo boys were. Those suspicions coincided with Dolf's, who had figured they'd be waiting in ambush for him and Matt to come down the darkened streets like innocent damn' fools to surrender. Ed expected the sound of gunfire at any moment and feared his brother was apt to be the first to die. He knew Dolf Morgette was certain to come with a cocked six-shooter held to Morgan's spine. Ed nervously rolled a cigarette, spilling a great deal of tobacco in the attempt. With that lit he eyed Old Man Kelbo. "Where's yer boys?" he wanted to know.

"The question is, where the hell 'r' the Morgettes?"

"I dunno."

"I told you and your brother it was a damn' fool stunt for him to walk up on that porch. We shoulda made a sieve outa the place."

"There were women in there."

"We coulda let 'em out fust."

"Maybe yer right," Casey allowed.

"O' course I'm right ya idjit. Your brother and the Morgettes ain't showed up have they? By now they're hid out an' took yer brother with 'em fer insurance. Yuh won't see any of 'em afore mornin', if then. Well I'm gonna be right here waitin'. Those two belong in jail. They maybe kilt my baby boy, Billy Joe. He's a layin' down there lookin' powerful low."

Ed stifled a snort since baby Billy weighed 180 pounds. He also forbore to mention Junior Morgette, down there looking very little better, and that the whole country figured a Kelbo bullet had put him there. But Ed was wholeheartedly scared by this vicious, half-crazy old man with the evil eyes, and kept mum. Finally after a couple of uncomfortable hours dragged by, he headed back to the cot in the rear office. Old Man Kelbo, who had been dozing in a chair, woke up.

"Where the hell you goin'?"

"Might as well get some shut-eye," Ed said. "If yuh want to get some yourself you're welcome to the bed in any cell in the place that's empty."

The old man only grunted. Ed spent a restless nightmare-filled night, getting up gladly at first light. He started a fire in the office stove and set a pot of coffee on. He hoped Old Man Kelbo had left but was disappointed—he came downstairs followed by his boys, Yancey, Lute, Jud, and Rafe. Ed hadn't heard them come in the night before.

Without preamble Old Man Kelbo said, "If them Morgettes don't show up in the next half hour we're gonna go out an' scour the country. You can come along 'r not as yuh please."

"I'd better stay here in case somethin' breaks," Ed said, glad at the thought of getting rid of them. When he was around them, especially the Old Man, he felt like he was sitting on a keg of powder with a sputtering fuse.

Even Old Man Kelbo would have been surprised to know just how far out in the country the Morgettes had taken the unwilling sheriff. While Ed Casey was starting his pot of coffee at the office, Matt Morgette was doing the same over a small fire well into the timber above the Junction.

"Best not go down before train time," Dolf cautioned. "Maybe somebody telegraphed over here about keepin' an eye out for us."

"This is kidnappin', yuh know," Casey complained for about the tenth time. "When we do get back to town I'm gonna run yuh both in for that too."

Dolf looked over at him contemptuously. "Well, Matt," he said, "if that's the case we'd better be sure the sheriff here never gets back to town."

"Right," Matt agreed. "Got all them deep prospect holes and old abandoned mineshafts all over the country. We could claim we turned him loose up in the hills and he must have walked into one. Better yet just claim we kicked him outa Mum's an' never saw him again."

"Course they still might try to get us fer capturin' him. But I never saw a warrant when he showed up at Mum's." Dolf eyed Casey with mock severity. "Did you have a warrant?"

Casey kept his mouth shut.

"Well, did you?" Dolf pressed him, then answered his own question. "Hell no, you didn't. No judge or J.P. in his right mind would issue a warrant on a Kelbo's word alone, without more evidence than they got. You let 'em stampede you. You don't really think one of us shot his son, do you?"

The sheriff looked thoroughly uncomfortable. Naturally he wanted to think the Morgettes had shot Billy Joe, but mainly because it pleased him to think so. However he was by no means certain they really had. The Kelbos certainly hadn't told him a straight story. According to them the two Morgettes had ambushed them without provocation. That didn't make sense even to the sheriff who knew the Morgettes better than that. Casey had been jealous of Dolf ever since they'd been deputies together under Sheriff Ed Pardeau years before. Casey had gloated when Pardeau finally ran off with Dolf's wife, Theodora, and eventually married her after Dolf had gone to the pen.

"You don't have to answer that either, Morg," Dolf said regarding his last question. "But you'll know for sure what happened if the good Lord lets us live till noon. We're gonna show you some sights today."

They heard the train's whistle in the distance. Dolf checked his watch. "That's funny, it's close to on time," he said. It was traditionally late and, as a result, known as the Northern Bullet. "Best I get on down to meet Will."

He'd known Will Alexander would be on this train, since Will had contacted him with a wire at Butte, telling him he'd be later than expected because Diana and Amy missed their train up to

Frisco. What he hadn't mentioned was that, in addition to Dolf's daughter Amy, he'd have his own family along. That had been Diana's doing. She'd insisted on coming. In view of how Dolf's wife, Maggie, might take that, Diana's mother had tactfully decided to come too. Through Hal Green, Dolf expected a buggy and escort to be waiting for Will's party. But he'd brought an extra saddled horse for Will. He needed an influential outside witness like Will for what he had in mind later in the day. He was about to get more influential witnesses than he'd bargained for.

Dolf left Sheriff Casey with Matt and rode down, leading Will's saddled mount. The Morgettes were known for raising fine saddle horses throughout the Northwest, having a herd of over one thousand, one of the largest in the country. Dolf had picked a horse for Will on Matt's recommendation; a large bay gelding with plenty of speed and bottom. It was one of Matt's personal string. Because of the touchy local situation Dolf remained astride Wowakan ready to run if necessary, and also kept a tight lead on the other horse.

Dolf looked around the station and spotted what had to be the rig Hal Green had sent since it was the only one in sight. He was little short of astonished to see who the driver was though.

"Hal sent me, Dolf," the driver assured him quickly, as soon as Dolf approached, recognizing that he might seem like an odd choice.

"Hello, Tobe," Dolf said. This was Tobe Mulveen, formerly sheriff, who had once almost made a career of keeping Dolf in his jail. Dolf drew beside the two seater and shook Tobe's huge paw.

"Surprised to see me?" Tobe said.

Dolf grinned. "You know it. But I figure Hal Green knows what he's doin'."

Tobe himself grinned then. "Matter o' fact I'm workin' for you now. Hal told me you're chief of police, or will be if you ever get back to town. I'm one of the new cops he hired."

Dolf thought about that and reached a quick conclusion. "Well, I'll be jiggered," he said. "I couldn't ask for a better one." He meant it. Tobe was a good man in a fight, big, bull-like, and totally fearless.

Just then Will jumped down from the train and turned to help the others out. Dolf was surprised to see Diana jump off the train, followed by her mother, with Amy last.

"How about holdin' these hosses, Tobe," he said. He sprang off Wowakan and went quickly forward to greet them all.

Will pumped his hand. "Brought the whole tribe, as you can see. And that ain't all. Wait'll you see who else'll be comin' out in a minute." He was beaming happily.

Dolf folded Amy into his arms, gave her a big hug, kissed her cheek and netted a smack on the lips in return. "Pa," she exclaimed, then choked up. She hugged him hard, tears in her eyes. The sight of her tugged at his heart, reviving an old memory. At sixteen she was almost a woman. And a dead ringer for her mother, Theodora, when Dolf had first laid eyes on her long ago and fallen hopelessly in love. Clemmy and Diana both kissed him full on the mouth, Diana holding him long and tight, not caring what anyone thought of it. Her warmth poignantly reminded Dolf of how close they'd been. But he got the surprise of the day when Will said, "And look who else is here—and you'd better notice her wedding ring or get into trouble right off."

Dolf turned to see Victoria Wheat coming daintily down onto the step stool, then onto the ground. She looked as regal as she always had, small, straight-backed, slightly voluptuous with those entrancing gray eyes wreathed by honey-colored hair. He sensed Diana carefully observing their meeting. She knew enough about them both to suspect how it had been once between them. Then Alby Gould appeared at the top of the steps and bounced down athletically. Before Victoria had a chance to kiss even Dolf's cheek, Gould thrust out his hand. "I say, Morgette, bully to see you again." He pumped Dolf's hand enthusiastically.

Dolf was drowned for a moment in a chorus of conflicting chatter from everyone. He did manage to congratulate Alby and Victoria on their marriage. Finally he was able to draw Will aside. "I've got some important things you've got to know right now." He quickly started to fill Will in on what had been happening.

When Will got the drift of his news he interrupted. "Wait a minute. I think you ought to get Alby Gould over here to hear all this too."

"I should have thought of that," Dolf agreed. "If we only had an extra horse he could come with us while the ladies go with Tobe Mulveen over there. Couldn't have a better witness than Alby."

"We got lots of extra horses," Will said. "Got a whole car full. They'll be siding in a minute. Now let's get Alby."

"You sound like old friends."

"We are. I've know him since Ogden. We all got on there. Him from the East and us from the West."

Will beckoned Gould over and the three of them were in earnest conversation for a few minutes.

"I'm your man," Gould said eagerly as Dolf finished briefing them.

"What's all this man talk?" Diana asked, unwilling to be left out any longer.

Will, who always treated her like the son he'd never had, didn't hesitate to tell her the gist of what had been said, while Alby quickly told Victoria what was happening.

"You ladies can go back with Tobe Mulveen," Dolf explained. "If there isn't room for all your truck, check it with the express agent. We'll get it later."

Diana planted herself in front of Dolf. "I'm no lady," she said. "I've got Henry W. Halleck over there in that car. I'm going with you."

"No. It might be dangerous." Dolf looked to Will for support.

He should have remembered that Diana had a habit of getting her way. "Take me or I'll follow you anyhow," she insisted.

Will grinned. "It seems to me, Dolf, that you said we'd have the sheriff along. Surely we'll be safe with him around."

The humor of that tickled Dolf. He also knew that Will could never say no to his spirited daughter. Besides he remembered how Diana had ridden Henry W. Halleck wildly through the darkened streets of San Francisco, carrying Will's double-barreled shotgun to his rescue. He thought she could well be better than most men in a pinch. It had been her instinctive, quick shooting that had actually saved his life that night.

"Saddle up," was all Dolf said. Diana gave him a mock salute.

Victoria Wheat watched the cavalcade leave with her new husband on one of Will's horses. She argued with herself. "I'm married now. Why should I feel this way over Dolf going off with Diana? I don't mind Alby going off with her and he's my husband."

But she found no answer. At least not one with which she was happy.

A short ride brought Dolf's crew to where Matt was detaining Sheriff Morgan Casey. The latter recognized Alby Gould. "Mr. Gould," he said, "thank God you're here. These Morgettes have kidnapped me."

"I know." Alby gave him small consolation. "I don't blame them, under the circumstances."

"But . . ."

"Dry up," Dolf said.

While this was transpiring Diana's eyes met Matt's. She thought, here's Dolf ten years ago. "I'm Diana Alexander," she introduced herself coolly.

"I'm Dolf's brother, Matt," he said, feeling somehow tongue-tied like a small awkward boy at the sudden appearance of this green-eyed goddess with the long auburn hair. He wondered how the devil she'd got here with this rough crowd.

Dolf led the party over the same trail he and Matt had followed the day before. He was gratified at the sight of something he'd hoped for, a ring of buzzards circling over the end of Eagle Meadow. The dead Kelbo horse would still be there. But first he said, "I want you to follow their tracks from where they came out of the timber and started after us." To Morgan Casey he sarcastically suggested, "You outa pay particular attention, Morg. Matt tells me you have a lot of trouble trackin'—at least you did the other day when the tracks of whoever shot Junior led right to the Kelbo ranch."

Casey looked sullen. "So what? They mighta kept right on goin' just like I told Matt."

"Why didn't you circle to see?"

"Gettin' too dark."

Matt snorted. "You coulda asked yer pals, the Kelbos, to put us up till morning."

Casey ignored the gibe.

"Who're those fellows comin' this way?" Will asked, pointing to two horsemen coming their way at a lope.

"That oughta be Hal Green and Ben Page from town if everything worked out like we planned," Dolf said. For Will's benefit he added, "Hal's mayor. Ben manages the big mine." He positively identified the two as they came closer and then introduced everyone as they joined the group. Hal Green looked hard at Diana, as though to say, "I mighta known it with a Morgette around, they even find women on mountain tops," but he withheld comment, only grinning at Dolf and winking.

Dolf retraced the tracks of the entire action of the day before, explaining what had occurred. It was plain as day anyhow from the tracks in the soft ground. All of them, even Diana, had had enough ranching experience at one time or another to decipher tracks this plain. The Kelbo brand was on the dead horse. A couple of wolves had been eating on the carcass, preventing the buzzards from landing, but they'd run for the deep timber and probably were waiting for a clear coast to return.

Dolf asked the sheriff, "Say, Morg, you don't have trouble reading brands like you do reading tracks, do yuh?"

The sheriff was silent. "Know which Kelbo belongs to that hoss?" Dolf prodded.

Matt said, "I sure as hell do. So does he. It was the Old Man's."

"That right, Morg?" Dolf prodded some more.

"Yeah," Casey reluctantly agreed. "But it don't prove nothin'." The sheriff was lying in his teeth as everyone present knew. His face mirrored it too.

"How about that cavalry charge across the field after me and Matt? They musta chased us two miles before I shot the old man's horse, hoping they'd give it up. What've you got to say about that?"

"When we get back to town I've still gotta book yuh both for a hearing." Casey evaded the obvious. "Old Man Kelbo signed a complaint."

"With an X?" Matt asked.

The sheriff gave him an evil look.

Dolf stood where he and Matt had been when he'd halted the Kelbo charge with his .45-90. The others watched while he counted a number of fresh Kelbo cartridge cases he'd collected along the trail of what he called the cavalry charge.

"I count thirty-two bright, shiny Winchester cases from out there," he said. "What do you make of that Morg?" he asked the sheriff. "We could possibly find another thirty-two if we looked hard. That crew wasn't kidding around. They were after our hides."

"Maybe they shot them shells after you shot the kid."

Alby could stand no more of it. "Sheriff, you're a stupid oaf," he snorted indignantly. "The sign out there is plain as day about exactly what happened. Even I could see that and I'm supposed to be a tenderfoot. A lot of people are going to be interested to hear that you're trying to cover up for a bunch of damn' cow thieves and murderers."

Casey could think of nothing to say and wisely didn't try. Besides, big men of Gould's caliber awed and rattled him. He knew that Gould's parents back East had as much money as the Astors and Vanderbilts. Money impressed Casey a lot.

Alby added, "Firing a barrage like they did shows they intended to kill the Morgettes if they could. Of course a hit at any range would be pure luck from a horse, but they were obviously trying. That's attempted murder, sheriff. What do you say to that?"

"Then let the Morgettes file charges," Casey said sullenly.

"What for?" Dolf asked. "I hear your jail leaks like a sieve where yore friend're concerned."

CHAPTER 8

HAL Green, Will Alexander, and Alby Gould all had legal and political savvy derived from long experience. They recognized that the main problem of the Morgette boys was no longer the charge of shooting young Kelbo. That appeared to be a clear-cut case of self defense and would hold up in court if it came to it, in view of the physical evidence they'd just examined, which any cattle-country jury would understand.

The three of them dropped back for a short confab on how to get the Morgettes out of the more recent charge of kidnapping the sheriff, which just might stick if the boys got an exceptionally knuckle-headed jury.

"I don't think either one of them knows how serious that could be," Green said shaking his head.

"Or give a damn, either," Will pointed out. "They don't think of it as kidnapping, you know. Seen too much trouble. They just see it as stayin' alive. Can you blame 'em?"

"Of course the sheriff was dead wrong," Alby contributed. "But that isn't going to keep him from raising the roof once he's back safe and sound among friends. He's lost a lot of face, and for a politician that means everything, especially one of his two-bit caliber. I've seen enough of 'em to know on my way to the Senate, not that we don't have some there too."

Hal concluded with the notion that had formed in his fertile mind. "If we can save the sheriff's face we may be able to make a deal with him to forget the whole thing. If I know him he isn't half as interested in getting even just now as he is not looking foolish. This is election year. He wants to be elected like most everyone else who's in office."

"You're right as rain, Hal. What do you think, Will?" Alby asked.

"I hope he's right, anyhow. Why not talk to that knothead sheriff, Hal? We can always threaten to put him down a mine shaft as a last resort like the Morgettes did from what Dolf told me back there." They all laughed. But at least Hal knew the Morgettes were capable of it if it came down to a "ground hog" case. Hal had gone through the Pinebluff War with Dolf. The Quarter Lien had uncounted graves he'd filled when pushed to it, most never found yet.

They arranged for Hal to ride alone beside Sheriff Morgan Casey.

"You shoulda come out to look over Eagle Meadow of your own free will before you came after the Morgettes," Hal told Casey. "You're gonna look like a damn' fool for comin' over to drag the Morgettes out in the night without a warrant, just on the say so of a bunch of hard cases like everybody knows the Kelbos are. Especially without investigating first."

Casey bristled. "So what?" The Morgettes can think about it up in the pen. They shouldn't of let Dolf out in the first place. Every time he comes home there's trouble." He carefully avoided mentioning that the Kelbos had told him a cock-and-bull story. He was able to read the tracks up in Eagle Meadow as well as anyone. They testified to exactly what had happened.

Green let Casey's nettled reply go by, having needled the sheriff just enough. Hal knew that Dolf never started the trouble that always greeted him whenever he came home. Others with old grudges did that.

Hal jeered, "The Morgettes being in the pen'll be small consolation to you if you don't get reelected. "You'll be the first sheriff we've had laughed out of office."

"Waddya mean?"

"Well, for one thing the Morgettes got a lot of friends, and a lot of sympathizers, to say nothing of money behind 'em. Worse yet, the West loves a joke. Put all that together. It adds up to votes, but not for you. The horse is on you for goin' over to pinch the Morgettes and getting captured yourself like a damn' tenderfoot. Around here, as you damn' well know, you might not even get a grand jury to indict 'em. In fact I'd bet you can't. They'll laugh ya outa court and maybe give Dolf a medal to boot."

Casey knew Hal was right. He rode along in gloomy silence. The point was so well taken he wasn't even angry, just worried. He loved being sheriff. Finally he said, "So what's your bright idea about what I oughta do?"

Hal suppressed a grin. "I think you ought to make a deal."

"Like what?" the sheriff asked, definitely rising to the bait. "I ain't makin' any promises, mind you," he added hastily, but it was obvious he was eager to do just that. "Figures you'd be interested in a deal to get yore friends off, to say nothing of yourself," he blustered. "You were there too when they nabbed me."

"So what?" Hal countered. "You get off if we do."

"So spit it out."

"When we hit town I think you ought to let it out that you went out to Eagle Meadow to investigate like you should have done in the first place. You can say you took the Morgettes along under arrest. I'll print that in the paper so everyone in creation will know it. You'll look good. Otherwise I print what really happened and emphasize that you didn't even have a warrant when you came to get the Morgettes."

Casey rode awhile in silence. Finally he offered Hal his hand on it. "You got a deal." Hal was surprised at the eagerness with which the sheriff shook hands, revealing his true depth of agitation over the possibility of looking stupid—and, as a result, maybe losing the next election.

"What're you two scheming about?" Dolf asked, dropping back to join them from where he, Matt, and Diana had been riding together, talking and laughing occasionally. Dolf had deliberately found a reason to leave Matt and Diana alone; he had a hunch that some sort of chemistry had taken hold there and it pleased him.

"I just sold the sheriff a good idea for all of us," Hal said diplomatically. He explained the deal. All Dolf did was nod. Hal took that for an affirmative, knowing that Dolf was no fool. "I'll tell Matt so he doesn't spill the beans," Dolf said as he rode forward to rejoin his brother and Diana. Hal was delighted to see how carefree the two Morgettes could be even in this tight situation. "Why not," he thought, "they've been in what amounts to a war for ten years on and off—they got used to it. Probably seems normal to them." He felt like a weight had been lifted from his shoulders. He slowed his mount to rejoin Gould and Will. "We cut a deal," he said. "I thought old Morg would kiss my hand. If I'd known how sensitive he is about looking foolish I wouldn't have worried half as much. That leaves us just one obstacle to get by and I got that greased, I think."

"What's that?" Will asked.

"We've got to keep Dolf and Matt entirely out of jail. I have Judge Porter standing by to have a bail hearing as soon as we get in. He did it once before for Dolf, right at the jail. I got a hunch it might not be safe to leave those two boys overnight in the lockup. Not with the Kelbos around in the frame of mind they're in, and as cozy as they are with the sheriff's crooked crowd. No tellin' what might happen. The Kelbos're from Texas where they practice an old Mexican custom called *la Ley Fuego*."

"What the hell's that?" Will asked.

"Literally it means 'the law shoot.' They let prisoners escape *a little ways*."

"I've read of that," Alby said.

"Of course," Will said, "I just recalled that's the Mex name for it. They used it in California too. But back in '49 we just figured it was smart poker without using any fancy names. Got rid of a lot of scum that way. Unfortunately some good men got it too, just like the Morgettes might. Only those guys out there didn't have any friends in camp. The Morgettes do."

Hal knew he had a hole card in case all else failed. The Civic Protection League. But he didn't want too much publicity regarding their existence until it was absolutely necessary. If worst came to worst he planned to put a special guard around the jail whether the sheriff liked it or not. He thought it might do Casey some good to think he smells a little hemp in his future. Might be more careful of the birds he flocks with.

Undersheriff Ed Casey wasn't as dumb as Old Man Kelbo would have liked to make him out. Nor was he lacking in backbone as some suspected. He was more inclined to be sneaky about appearances. He'd always observed that it gave him a secret advantage if people underestimated him. He liked it that way. He was thinking of that now as Old Man Kelbo harangued him in the sheriff's inner office, the door shut for privacy. (Ben Page, who was in a big hurry to get back to town, had just ridden in ahead of the others and brought Ed the word that the sheriff was bringing in the Morgettes.)

"You git them Morgettes in the *Juzgado* here," Kelbo growled, "an' keep 'em after dark an' we won't need to worry about no trial where some soft-headed jury can get bamboozled by slick lawyers. And if it does come to a trial and they get off, I'm gonna settle with them personal if it's the last thing I do."

Recalling the record of those with similar aspirations regarding Dolf Morgette, Ed Casey thought, "It just might be the last thing you do, old man. The odds favor it." Ed savored the idea even though he was fully aware how useful the Kelbos had been to his crowd.

"We ain't apt to get the Morgette boys in here overnight," Casey told him. "I remember the last time Morgette came to town old Judge Porter trotted down and had a bail hearing right in the old sheriff's office that burned down. If the bank had been open so Mark Wheat coulda laid his hands on the bail money, Dolf would have walked out the door right there. Morgette's got a lot of big bug friends yet."

Kelbo scratched his grizzled head slyly. "Well, then why don't we see something happens to Judge Porter just to be sure he doesn't come through this time too?"

"Too risky," Ed protested, quickly amazed at Kelbo's callous audacity.

Kelbo assured him, "I don't mean anything permanent. But Porter's always down at the Bonanza Saloon in the afternoon. Got a weakness for the bottle I'd guess. Probably goes home from there and keeps knockin' 'em back. That's probably where he got that tomato nose. Why don't you go down and buy him some extra drinks, then make sure he has a bottle to take home. If he gets suspicious, tell him you're 'lectioneering early fer yer brother."

"What're you aimin' to do if we get the Morgettes in here for the night?" Ed inquired suspiciously.

"Never mind. Just see that they get in a cell we can get a ladder up to," was all the Old Man said. He winked. "And keep the lamp on bright in the hall outside their cell. We'll do the rest." Then another idea struck him. "Just to copper our bet I got another idea. You got a room upstairs where we can hide somebody out?"

Ed eyed him incredulously. "You think I'm crazy enough to let someone git the Morgettes from inside the jail? Everyone'd know we were in cahoots with whoever did it. Might even think I did it myself."

"Not if you were down at the saloon when a bunch of shootin' busted out, up here. Be natural enough for you to come runnin' up here with a bunch of the boys from down at the saloon and find that Simple-Simon jailer, Billy Blackenridge, cold-cocked and the Morgettes dead."

Risky as it seemed there was logic in the idea to Ed's mind. He pondered a moment, swayed by the threatening appearance of Old Man Kelbo and his goading remark, "No guts, no glory. You want them Morgettes out of the way or not?"

Actually Ed was neutral. He knew his brother had always detested Dolf, but there was no great love between him and older brother Morg, who treated him like a janitor most of the time. He sort of admired Dolf. But he knew what side his bread was buttered on. Although he'd never been let in on who the real higher-ups were, he knew they had put out the word to get Morgette. By now he was even aware of the unsuccessful attempt to get Dolf at Butte. He'd wondered how the hell they knew what train Dolf had been on. It had impressed him with their power. He had every reason to believe that if he balked now, Old Man Kelbo might tip off those same powers that be and get his own tail in a bear trap.

"I seen a padlocked room up there at the end of the cell block," Kelbo pressed him. "What's in that?"

"Some extra guns and ammunition for posses and the like. We always keep that locked up tight."

"Not tonight," Kelbo told him. "If it looks like we got Judge Porter out of the way so's the Morgettes'll be boardin' here, I'll send one of my boys over before dark and you take him up there. Can hang the padlock back so's it looks locked."

After Kelbo left, Ed Casey sat at his brother's desk shaking his head. How the hell did we get in this deep, he wondered? He heaved a sigh, reflecting that he was probably too old to go away and start over some other place. Well, he thought, if everything works out I won't have to worry about work anymore after we've milked this one dry. The trouble was, he remembered what had happened to a sheriff and his gang with similar ideas over in Montana. Sheriff Plummer and most of his associates had stretched vigilante rope. It wasn't a happy thought.

On his way out he told Billy Blackenridge, the flunky who acted as turnkey and janitor, "I'll be down at the Bonanza."

On the thirty-mile buggy ride to Pinebluff, Clemmy Alexander had a good opportunity to renew her acquaintance with Victoria. Almost the first thing Victoria did—after the excitement of the men leaving—was to apologize for not sending the Alexanders a wedding invitation. "We got married on the spur of the moment," she explained. "Even Alby's folks didn't hear about it until we stopped on our honeymoon—and did that ever cause a stir."

"I'll bet," Clemmy said. "I see you both survived it."

"He's the apple of their eye, fortunately."

Victoria saw that Amy was growing up to be a picture of her mother, but didn't mention it because she'd been jealous of Theodora since she'd first laid eyes on her: Victoria, age twelve, was attending her first dance when Theodora swept in triumphantly on Dolf's arm. Victoria had had a crush on Dolf even then. Noting Amy's shy good manners, Victoria remarked to herself how different Amy was from her mother and how like Dolf. She'd been unsettled from the excitement of seeing Dolf again and wasn't deceiving herself that she and Alby were a love match. She'd once told Dolf that only a few lucky women got to marry the men they really loved, and that he would always be that one for her. Now she knew how painfully right she had been. She was only twenty five, yet she wondered in panic if her life was over already, which she sometimes felt it was.

Amy shyly watched Victoria whenever she had a chance. This was the sort of woman she wanted to be. She did not picture herself living the rest of her life in a frontier backwater as some rancher's or miner's drudge, not even for a wealthy one. She wanted an education and the natural social grace of ladies of good breeding. The past season, which she'd spent with the Alexanders in San Francisco, left no doubt of that in her mind. She vowed she'd never be a snob or forget her roots, but she sensed that the world offered her more than a simple marriage, a swarm of children, and an endless chain of unvarying years ending in an untended grave, grown over with weeds in some ghost town cemetery. She wanted a cause to pursue. If she'd been a man and lived in the old days she knew that she'd have been a knight on a quest. In her youthful dreams she often thought, "I want a monument when I'm gone, where people will bring their children and say this was so and so and she did such and such." She didn't care what as long as it was a worthy cause that led to being remembered.

Clemmy, riding on the front seat with Mulveen, asked him what grew in that part of the country and how many cows an acre could graze. To his surprise, he found himself liking her from the first, his natural unease around women evaporating without his recognizing it. He was sorry when they pulled into Pinebluff.

On the way up on the train, Will and Victoria had struck a deal for the use of the Wheat mansion during the Alexanders stay in Pinebluff, which could turn out to be for the entire summer, depending on how mining prospects panned out. Now, as it turned out, Victoria and Alby would have to stay there with them for a few days. Tobe drove the ladies directly to the Wheat mansion first.

Dolf had told Tobe to drop Amy at Catherine Green's where her mother was staying temporarily. Tobe told Amy, "I'll run you over to your Ma next."

On their way over there Amy blurted out without thinking, "Why isn't Ma staying with Mum, I wonder." Then she remembered that they didn't get along any too well. Tobe shrugged, "I couldn't say young lady. Probably because your ma wanted to get better acquainted with her future daughter-in-law." For a crude product of the range, Tobe had his diplomatic moments. "Anyhow when we get over there I'll wait on you to see if they're home. They're supposed to be expectin' you. If they are and you want, I'll run you over to the hospital to see your brother."

"I hope he hasn't had another bad spell," Amy said. "I want to see him as soon as I can." They had been exceptionally close after Dolf had been sent to the pen, clinging together like two babes in the woods since Ed Pardeau hadn't been much of a step-father, being too self-centered. If Amy had had much real fathering, it had come from her older brother during those years. Now she was looking forward to truly getting acquainted with her real father this summer.

Somewhat later that afternoon Dolf and his party reached Pinebluff. Sheriff Casey had agreed to let them stop at the hospital before booking them. "I'm gonna have to go with you two though, for appearances."

"Suits me," Dolf agreed.

Meanwhile Hal was going to pick up Judge Porter for an immediate bail hearing in the J. P. chambers at the jail.

Dolf was in Junior's room at the hospital when Hal returned looking disconcerted. Sheriff Casey was outside and out of hearing. Hal announced, "Got some bad news, I'm afraid. Old Porter is drunk as a coot. He's down at his house now, passed out cold. I'm gonna get Doc to go down and see if we can give him something to sober him up. I don't want you two down there in that jail overnight like a couple of sitting ducks if we can help it."

"What do you think we should do now?" Dolf asked.

Hal hesitated. "I guess go on down with Casey and act like nothing's wrong. It won't do not to keep our end of the deal now. Otherwise I'd suggest you go out the back door."

It was an old story to Dolf, but Matt had never been in jail before. Dolf grinned at him as the sheriff was filling in the blotter. "Cheer up, Matt. It's an old Morgette custom," he said.

Morg had a little confab with his brother Ed, who whispered urgently to him before Morg led the prisoners upstairs. "Best cell in the house. Pity you won't be using it long, the way things look."

With that he left them alone. "Think they'll get old Porter sobered up before mornin'?" Matt asked.

"Damfino," Dolf said. "But if I don't come out of here alive, like Hal is frettin' about, it won't be because I scared myself to death worrying about it ahead of time."

He hit the cot and was snoring inside of two or three minutes. Matt shrugged and rolled onto the other cot. Both were happily unaware that Ed Casey had kept his word to Kelbo and smuggled an assassin into the gun closet in case the less risky murder attempt from outside after dark miscarried.

CHAPTER 9

ALBY Gould circled by the Wheat mansion to show Diana Alexander where it was. Then he went immediately to the bank to make sure Tom Miller would stay open in case bail money was needed. Diana found the entire contingent of the Morgette faction's women, except Dolf's wife Maggie, at the Wheat place.

Clemmy, like most everyone else, with the possible exception of Theodora, was enchanted with the down-to-earth quality of Dolf's big strapping grandma. She was calling her Mum already, as Mum had demanded.

Diana, from Dolf's descriptions, hadn't expected Mum to be a sweet little old lady, but this muscular six-footer, who looked a well-preserved sixty, almost floored her. Mum shook her hand with a grip like a dairy farmer (she milked her two cows morning and night). Mum looked Diana over with a twinkle in her eyes. "I hear yer aces with a shotgun," she said for openers.

Diana giggled. "Who told you that?"

"M'grandson. He don't write often but when he does he writes all the news. Said yuh saved his life."

Diana blushed. Mum laughed. "I'll lend yuh my extra shotgun while yer here. Keep yer hand in. Yuh may wanta shoot yourself a Kelbo before yuh leave."

Mum was holding the stage as she usually did. She already had everyone "sandbagged" into coming to her place for supper. She'd argued, "Catherine ain't got the room, an' Victoria didn't even know she was gonna be here, so she hasn't got anything in the house yet." That settled that. She got them all behind her team, in her big farm wagon with boards laid across the sides for seats. "Ain't fancy," she allowed, "but it beats shanks mare 'n' draggin' skirts through the dust."

They left a note on the door for Alby so he'd know where to find them. If Mum had known that her two grandsons were probably going to spend the night in jail, most likely she'd have organized the ladies to pull off a jail delivery. They didn't find out what had happened until Alby came out just as they were all about to sit down to supper.

Mum began to rumble as soon as she got the news that Dolf and Matt were locked up and Judge Porter was in no shape to get them out right away.

"No need to worry," Alby assured her. "Us menfolks have everything under control. Will and Hal are down with Doc sobering up the judge."

That "menfolks" business was his mistake. Mum snorted. "If you *menfolks* knew how to control much youda had me sit up today with that sot Porter and keep him sober. I'da taken a stick of stove wood to 'im if he reached for a bottle. Nobody ever tells me what's goin' on until it's too late."

As a U. S. senator, Alby was not used to being dressed down quite so thoroughly outside the Senate Chamber. He managed it with good grace, however. "You sound just like my mother," he observed, grinning broadly.

"Well, she must have good sense then," Mum stated.

Clemmy tactfully sought to change the subject by saying to Alby, "Victoria told me your wedding was as much a surprise to your family as it was to all of us."

Alby guffawed. "Mater was fit to be tied. But Vicky here finally said 'yes' and I wasn't about to give her a chance to change her mind. Mater came around. And Pater was a brick about it. Gave us a million as a wedding present."

"A million what?" Mum spilled out.

Alby looked at her genuinely puzzled. "Why, a million dollars, of course."

It took awhile for that to settle in with Mum. Finally she asked blandly, "Do you think he'll miss it?"

Alby, not knowing whether he was being ribbed or not, was nonetheless equal to Mum. "I doubt it," he said equally blandly, his eyes twinkling behind his glasses.

"That's good," Mum said, then calmly added, "Have some more of these boiled new spuds." She passed him the big serving dish.

"Thanks," he said. "You're a capital cook, Mum."

That "capital" almost threw her. She looked at Alby suspiciously for a moment and detected no guile. "Dudes sure talk funny," she thought. But she liked something about him. "He's honest," she finally concluded, "that's it." She wasn't used to the idea of the very rich possibly being honest.

"Come around anytime," she told him. "I love to cook."

This light banter didn't succeed in its real purpose—taking their minds off Dolf's and Matt's predicament long enough to enjoy the meal. There was a lot more light chatter, but when they were having some of Mum's famous huckleberry pie with homemade ice cream and coffee, she asked Alby the question that was on all their minds.

"What are you menfolks doin' ta see that my two grandsons survive the night down in that target gallery of a jail? Wouldn't put it past that idjit sheriff to let somethin' happen to 'em down there."

"Well, like I said, the boys are trying to get Porter sober enough to function. If that fails Hal's going to put a special guard on at the jail."

"Suppose the sheriff has some objection—and he will. What then?"

"That's why I picked up a Wells Fargo shotgun down at the bank. The sheriff will have to lump it." He left with his shotgun while the ladies were all trying to do the dishes and getting in each others' way.

"Let's let the rest of these gals take over," Mum suggested to Diana. She'd been sizing up the young woman ever since they'd met. "We'll just get outa their way—I cooked it, it's fair enough if they wanta clean up." She drew Diana into the parlor. "How's yore shotgun finger?" Mum asked her in a low voice. "While the menfolks are supposedly takin' care of everything like a bunch of knuckleheads I got an idea." Diana was all ears. Mum went on conspiratorially, "After I take everybody home you figure an excuse to come back over here with me for awhile."

Diana came up with an instant excuse, "I can bring my horse over. Victoria's hay is moldy. They weren't ready for visitors yet."

The sheriff expected Old Man Kelbo to stop by after he heard they'd locked up Dolf and Matt. "Probably be at least one Kelbo at the hospital with Billy Joe," he told his brother. "That one'll know where the Old Man is. Best you go look him up from what you said."

"The old sonofabitch had better be around," Ed said. "This'll be their best chance. I didn't spend that four bucks to get Porter soused to see it go for nuthin'."

"Put in a bill," Morgan said disgustedly. "Just get the hell out and find him quick. Lord! A whole four bucks!"

It wasn't the Kelbos that showed up at the sheriff's outer office first however. Much to Casey's discomfort it was Mayor Hal Green, Alby, Will Alexander, and Tobe Mulveen. Casey was unaware that another half dozen heavily armed townsmen were seated on the broad front steps of the jail. Green and Will carried Winchesters and Alby had his Wells Fargo gun. Mulveen was packing two six-shooters. They were all wearing the silver scroll of a city policeman, ordered by Hal in anticipation of a larger force.

"What the hell is this?" Casey stormed. The significance of the new badges hadn't hit him yet. "It's agin the law to carry shootin' arns in town 'less yer comin' or goin'. You know that Hal."

Green grinned and affably explained, "This is the new city police force except for Simp Parsons and the chief of police."

Casey looked stunned. "Who's the chief of police?" he managed to ask to cover his discomfiture.

"You got him in a cell upstairs—Dolf Morgette," Hal explained dryly, with a straight face. "We come to have a little meeting with him if you don't mind."

Casey looked like he might be going to have apoplexy. "Mind," he said loudly. "Of course I mind. What sort of fool do you take me for?"

"A big one!" Alby slipped in without hesitation grinning like the fabled Cheshire cat and showing a lot of his big ivory teeth. He was enjoying himself hugely.

Casey glared at him, then around at all the rest. "I ain't a big enough fool to let any of you upstairs and maybe slip them Morgettes a couple of six-shooters."

"Why not bring Dolf down here? We could use your office. We don't have any secrets. You can sit in on the meeting," Hal offered.

"No way," Casey stated firmly.

"O.K. Morg," Hal agreed. "We'll stick around though since this is public property." With that, some maneuver in which the Morgettes would be killed went out the window, Hal figured, not knowing Lute Kelbo was secreted upstairs.

Sheriff Casey withdrew to his office. He pulled a quart of whiskey from his desk drawer and tossed down a substantial belt of it, quickly followed by another. In a way he was relieved. He didn't have the stomach for anything as raw as killing prisoners right in his jail, or even in a phony escape that he suspected most of the electorate would regard with the suspicion it would merit. He figured he'd somehow have to get upstairs and warn Lute Kelbo in the gun closet. He could slip him out the back door that led to the fire escape. He felt a lot better about the whole affair. Neither Kelbo nor the big boss could blame him for this turn of events.

As they arrived, the Kelbos were startled to discover Hal's vigilantes lounging in the dark on the front steps. Neither party spoke, merely eyeing one another with mutual hostility. When the Old Man stepped into the lighted building and saw Hal and the others he drew up like a bristling dog running across a strange pack.

"Siddown on the bench," Kelbo ordered his three boys. They seated themselves opposite Hal's police force. The Old Man swore under his breath. He stalked into the sheriff's private office and slammed the door. In a moment Ed Casey came in, took in the situation with growing alarm, and went into his brother's office. He heard Kelbo demanding of the sheriff, "What the hell's goin' on? You sellin' out on us 'r are you tetched?"

"Neither," Casey replied. "They barged in and just sat down."

"Well run 'em to hell back out. We got a job to do here tonight."

Casey looked desperately pained. "Can't do that."

"Why the hell not?"

"It's the mayor as you damn' well know. He claims that's his new police force."

Old Man Kelbo slipped into one of the irrational moods that always scared Casey half to death. "Give the word and me 'n' the boys'll throw their asses out in the street."

Casey cautioned quickly, "Don't start anything we don't have to. If they're in here they don't know what's goin' on outside. You can still slip a ladder up under the Morgettes' window an' slip 'em a greeting card."

Kelbo snorted. "You must be asleep. There's a half dozen more gun-hung hombres a-squattin' on yer front steps. They'd be down on us like a duck on a June bug."

Casey's jaw dropped. "The hell yuh say? They musta slipped up damn' quiet."

"Well they're out there," Casey's brother Ed confirmed.

Casey felt his sense of relief returning. Much as his brother had wondered earlier, he asked himself, "How the hell did we get in this deep?"

"I got an idea," Kelbo stated. "Yer out here at the edge of town. We can stage a hellacious bunch of shootin' over in the sage brush across the road. That'll draw Green's whole crew over to that side. We might even get 'em to shoot over thataway. Cover the sound of any shootin' they might hear over here."

"Waddaya aim to do?" the sheriff asked.

"Nemmine," Kelbo told him. "Jist leave it to us."

All three went to the door together. They were greeted by an unhappy surprise. Hal Green rose and pointed to a pile of six-shooters and cartridge belts on the floor. "Sheriff, I disarmed these men for you." He indicated the Kelbo boys who sat on the bench looking foolish.

"What the hell do you think yer doin?" Old Man Kelbo exploded.

"Hand yours over too," Hal said quietly. "The sheriff just got through reminding me it's illegal to carry guns except comin' and goin'."

"Well," Kelbo said. "We're all just goin', so hand 'em back."

Hal thought about that. "I ought to run you all in and let you tell it to the judge in the morning."

Old Man Kelbo was now keeping his temper remarkably well, as he could when there was some percentage in it for him. Observing this, Morgan Casey shrewdly wondered if his temper fits were an act.

"Well?" Kelbo said to Hal. "We gotta git out to the ranch. Been wastin' a powerful lot o' time in town lately. You know the ranch ain't gonna run by itself fer long."

Hal knew Kelbo probably had a half dozen other men "to run the ranch," but was just as happy at the thought of having the Kelbos out of town.

"O.K.," he agreed. "Take 'em back and clear out."

Sheriff Casey and his brother weren't as sure the Kelbos would be leaving town as Hal seemed to be. In fact they were both sure they weren't.

After the Kelbos left, Hal told Mulveen, "I hate to work you day and night but I wonder if you'd go over and relieve Simp at the hospital. I think the rest of us better stay here awhile."

It was about a half hour later that a barrage of shots erupted from the gulch across the road below the jail. As Old Man Kelbo had planned, Hal and his men ran outside to join the others, who had spread out along the side of the building the shots had come from.

"Hold your fire," Hal ordered, "till we find out what's going on."

They could hear a couple of bullets thwack against the jail's brick walls high over their heads.

Mum had delivered all the ladies to their respective houses, Theodora and Amy remaining in town with Catherine, even though the ranch was only a few miles out.

Knowing her daughter, Clemmy wasn't at all surprised Diana still had the energy to take her horse, Henry W. Halleck, over to Mum's, despite having been on the go all day. Diana whispered to Clemmy, "Isn't Mum a peach? If I'm late it'll be because we're gabbing. She promised to show me the family album. It's got a daguerreotype of Dolf in knee pants she says. I've got to see that."

She kissed Clemmy goodbye. "If it gets too late I'll stay overnight."

"I wish you wouldn't," Clemmy said. "With all the trouble in town I'll worry about you."

"All the more reason to stay. Mum shouldn't be left alone over there."

She tied Henry W. Halleck on behind Mum's wagon. "Lead on," she told Mum.

Instead of the family album, Mum was showing Diana how to operate her newfangled, lever action twelve-gauge shotgun. "Put a couple of double-aught buck in the magazine first, then some birdshot. The birdshot'll come up first. It holds five and one in the chamber, but I still favor Old Betsy, my double barrel. Besides Betsy's a ten gauge."

Mum drove as quietly as possible through the darkened streets, keeping to the edge of town. She tied her team in a copse of spruces on an empty lot about a block from the jail and put nose bags of oats on them. "That'll keep 'em quiet awhile, I hope," she allowed. "C'mon. Foller me." They slipped through a delivery gate in the high board fence around the rear yard of the jail. "Damn' fool menfolks!" she muttered under her breath. "Gate shoulda been locked." She led the way to the deep shadows beneath the still standing gallows on which they'd hung Len Stabo the year before. There was still a pile of excess lumber below the gallows.

"We'll set," Mum whispered. "And wait. If I'm a good guesser our boys are in the cell where the light is. Nobody's gonna sneak up and pot shot 'em while I kin draw breath!"

When the shooting erupted on the far side of the building, Mum placed her hand reassuringly on Diana's leg. "Sit still. That's probably to git them fool men all over to that side while somebody makes their move over here," she whispered. "Git ready."

Yancey Kelbo and his brother Rafe hastily jockeyed their ladder up under the window of the jail. They were faintly visible in the starlight to the two women in ambush. The bombardment still continued on the far side.

"Wait'll they're half way up," Mum cautioned. She drew a bead. "I'll git the top one. You pepper the other varmint. O.K. shoot."

Yancey Kelbo, fifteen feet off the ground, toppled from the ladder and knocked himself out from the fall. Rafe hit the ground running, not caring what happened to his brother, who had almost knocked him off the ladder falling. Rafe's pants were full of bird shot. He felt like he'd been stung by half the bees in creation.

"Keep the one that's down covered till we know he ain't dangerous," Mum ordered. Yancey was still as death. "Leave his gun here," Mum ordered. "So they'll know what he was up to. He won't be after anybody for a long while I don't guess."

"We'll leave the ladder too," Mum said. "None of this one's

crowd'll be back. This way everybody kin tell just what he was up to when they find him, which won't be long—I'll see to that."

Mum and Diana concealed their guns in the bottom of the wagon, then drove up to the jail after all the shooting had stopped. The old lady got one of the men's attention. She said, "We was drivin' by when the shootin' busted loose and we took cover back over there. Somebody was shootin' over on this side too, near the jail. Maybe you better check." That's how Hal's posse found Yancey so soon—still unconscious.

Mum then dropped Diana off at the Wheat mansion. "We'll have to have tea agin' sometime soon, dearie," she said sweetly, mocking the society dames she'd heard. Diana giggled.

When Diana came in, Clemmy asked, "What in the world was all the shooting? Do you know? I wonder if your father is all right."

Diana said, "We could barely hear it over at Mum's. Of course father's all right; he always takes care of himself. I'm going to hit the hay," she added, using an old ranch expression she'd picked up from their cowboys.

Clemmy kissed her goodnight and watched her ascend the stairs. She wondered if her daughter knew her hair smelled of powder smoke. She knew better than to ask why. It would only turn out that a skunk or a coyote had been after Mum's chickens and they'd shot it. Clemmy didn't realize how close to the truth that came, figuratively speaking.

Some of Hal's posse carried the unconscious Yancey Kelbo into the jail. By then all the others, including the two Casey brothers, were inside.

"Look what we found under a ladder shoved up to the Morgettes' window," Joe Purple announced gleefully. They dumped Yancey on the floor, then rolled him over. His pants were a bloody mess right where he sat.

"Birdshot, I'd guess," Hal stated. "One of you boys dust him?"

"Not me," Purple said. "Couple of ladies came by in a wagon after the shootin' an' said they saw a disturbance over on the other side. We found old Yancey laying under the ladder on the ground. Pretty clear what he was up to, but somebody caught him at it." He looked around. "Any of you other fellows?"

None of the others admitted to the shooting.

Sheriff Casey was the most puzzled of all. Someone had obviously anticipated the Kelbos. He could imagine the Old Man's rage when he found out what had happened. Worse yet, he wasn't sure that Lute upstairs might not have shot the Morgettes during all the excitement. He had to get up there and find out, but he didn't want any company. He wanted to get Lute out of the jail quickly.

"Well, we better take Kelbo down to the hospital," the sheriff allowed. "Hal, how about having some of your boys get him down there."

"Let's put him in a cell and send for one of the Docs. We don't want his crowd bustin' him out. It's plain as hell he was tryin' to get up that ladder and kill the two Morgette boys." Then an unpleasant thought occurred to him. "Hey. How the hell do we know he didn't get up there before he got potted." He raced for the stairs before the sheriff could protest.

Dolf and Matt were both in their cell, backs to the wall away from the window, fully aware of what might be afoot. Hal rushed down the cell block and spotted them.

"Boy, am I glad to see you two," he said.

"That goes both ways," Dolf said. "What the hell's goin' on?"

Hal told him. "Looks like you got a friend you didn't know about," he concluded. "Whoever potted Yancey was over where I should have had brains enough to keep somebody."

"I wonder who," Matt said.

Remembering Mum's double barrel, Dolf thought he had a good idea, but he kept it to himself.

Over the sheriff's protests Hal by threat of force got his way and tossed Yancey Kelbo in a cell. He told Casey, "You're so damn' strong for legal proceedings. If we get old Judge Porter sober we can have some on this bastard along with the Morgettes. And," he added, "I'm gonna stay around with some of the boys to see that this bird doesn't fly the coop. Somebody go get a Doc."

CHAPTER 10

TRUE to his promise, Hal Green finally dragged Judge Porter down to the jail for a bail hearing even if it was 3 A.M. Sheriff Casey came out of his inner sanctum looking very seedy, sporting a two-day growth of beard. Will and Alby had stayed the course, dozing on the outer office benches. The sheriff hadn't extended them the courtesy of empty cells as his brother had the Kelbos. The judge, after a ten hour rest—most of it totally unconscious—looked much the best of any of them.

"Well," Porter ordered Casey, "bring down the Morgette boys."

When they appeared with the sheriff the judge apologized. "Sorry to let you boys stay in here so long. Had a couple of drinks but my old war wounds have obviously reduced my tolerance."

"We understand perfectly your honor," Dolf said with a completely straight face.

"What bullshit," Hal observed to Will in a very low whisper.

"Where are the complaining witnesses?" Porter asked.

"One's upstairs in a cell. The other's down at the hospital," Casey said.

"Well, get 'em. We ain't got all night, Morg. They shoulda been here before now."

"I can't do that judge."

"Why the hell not?"

"They can't walk."

The judge looked around owlishly. He hadn't been told of the "melancholy incident" that had befallen Yancey and Rafe Kelbo. "What the hell happened to 'em?"

"Somebody filled their butts with birdshot, I'd guess," Casey told him.

"How did that come about?" Porter asked for the record, although Hal had already told him.

Hal explained the earlier happenings of the evening officially this time.

"I see. Well then, let's hear what the Morgettes have to say about what they're accused of. We'll handle the Kelbo case later. As I understand this case the Kelbos have accused Dolf and Matt of attempted murder of one Billy Joe Kelbo. What've you got to say about it, Dolf?"

Dolf told him exactly what had happened, seconded by Matt.

"I can vouch for that whole thing," Hal chipped in. He explained how Dolf had taken him, Alby, Will, and the sheriff over the ground the previous day and that the tracks and other evidence completely corroborated Dolf's account. Will and Alby vouched for every word of it. "Ben Page was along too. He'll tell you the same but he's gettin' some shuteye. Gotta be at the mine tomorrow," Hal said. Morgan Casey was discreetly silent on the subject.

The judge speared him with a sharp inquiring look. "What have you got to say about it, sheriff?"

"Well, the tracks and empty shells were like they said, but it's any man's guess what really happened. I ain't sayin' it happened like Morgette says and I ain't sayin' it didn't." He was sticking to his stubborn defense of his cohorts, but liking it less each time.

"Rot!" Porter snapped. "Anybody with good sense could tell what that 'sign' out in Eagle Meadow testifies to. It's almost as good as a photograph of the action. And, besides that, everyone knows the Kelbos are a crooked bunch that've been chased out of every place in the West they ever lived in. I, for one, wouldn't believe them if four angels came in and testified for 'em. I'm turning Dolf and Matt loose on their own recognizance. If the D. A. wants to take it up with the grand jury that's between him and you. When I see those two Kelbos with birdshot in their asses I'm gonna cite 'em for damn' poor judgment for gettin' in rifle range of a Morgette, first of all. Give the boys back their property. Now, I've heard enough to remand those two Kelbos to custody for conspiracy to commit a murder. Casey you bring that one down here from the hospital and jug him. If Yancey's good enough to stand a cell, I reckon his brother will survive."

The proceedings were interrupted by pounding and hollering upstairs. A faint muffled voice could be made out yelling, "Let me outa here goddamit. I've had enough of this."

"Is Yancey delirious?" Porter asked. "Maybe I was a little hasty and both boys should be in the hospital."

Casey tried to prevent a mass exodus of the whole group upstairs to the cells to investigate, but Porter overruled him. They discovered the source of the hullabaloo in the gun closet, just as the sheriff suspected they would.

"Let whoever it is out," the sheriff reluctantly told his brother.

Lute Kelbo stepped out cautiously, looked over the crowd, and stood with open mouth. Seeing the Morgettes he made a move for his pistol, then thought better of it, but did so an instant late. Dolf grabbed him and slammed him up against the wall, dazing him, then relieved him of his pistol, which he shoved in his own belt.

Porter eyed the sheriff hostilely. "How do you explain this man's presence in your jail, fully armed?"

Casey shook his head in genuine bewilderment, since he couldn't figure out how Lute had been locked in.

"I can't," he confessed.

To Lute, who was regaining his senses, Porter said, "You. How the hell did you get up here?"

"None of your damn' business," Lute said defiantly.

"What were you planning to do here?" the judge asked, "as though anyone with any sense couldn't guess. You were here to put the Morgette boys out of the way, right? Well, we'll damn well get to the bottom of this."

Lute was silent.

"Casey, throw him in a cell. I'm scheduling a hearing for eleven A.M. on this whole business in my chambers. I want all three of these Kelbo boys there if you have to bring Yancey and the one down at the hospital on stretchers. Y' understand?"

Casey nodded. He was in a panic, knowing that he too was bound to be implicated. He noticed Hal Green eyeing him and grinning and that didn't help either.

Earlier Billy Blackenridge, who'd been sleeping off one of his jags in an empty cell, as he regularly did, had been awakened by the arguing downstairs. It had taken a few seconds for him to get his bearings, then he had got up, yawned, and stretched. "Dark out," he'd thought. "Best I make my round up here to check everything out so old Casey don't land on me." He had gone to the end of the hall, checked the rear door, then started back. It was then he'd noticed the unlocked gun closet. He had quickly slipped the padlock in the hasp properly and locked it. "Good thing I saw that," he'd thought. "I'd 'a' got blamed sure as hell. I wonder what damn' fool left it open?"

Back downstairs Dolf and Matt were given back their arms and other personal items. Hal said, "I'll run you boys home in my buggy. Oh," he handed Dolf his silver scroll with Chief of Police inscribed on it, "this makes it official."

"Thanks—I think," Dolf said, and grinned. "I had a notion once I'd like to clamp the lid on this town when it was wide open, but I was always playin' second fiddle."

"Well, it's been tryin' to be wide open again. Woulda been except for Junior and Simp." Then after a moment's thought Hal added, "How do you feel about clampin' the lid on it now?"

"Damned if I know."

Dolf and Matt bid goodnight to Will and Alby with thanks for their support, then jumped into Hal's buggy. Once at Mum's she got up and fed them a couple of big steaks before she let them turn in.

Dolf lay awake thinking, "Before I clean up Pinebluff, or get Wells Fargo's ducks in order, I'd better go see Maggie and the kid or she's apt to scalp me. Well, I've got a good excuse for not doin' it till tomorrow at least," he told himself. "I've had my usual homecoming stay in the calaboose. And made a jailbird of little brother too." He smiled over the small consolation of knowing it was all in the best Morgette family tradition. It was only his second night home. "I must be slipping," he thought, grinning in the dark, "last time I got in jail my first night home."

The next day as Dolf approached Chief Henry's camp, Jim Too, Dolf's big hound, spotted his friend—Dolf's big black stallion Wowakan—a mile or more away. It was the first time that Dolf had observed that dogs could recognize individual animals at long distances, just like range-wise people. The hound came at a flat-out run. Dolf dismounted to greet him. The big animal jumped all over him, almost knocking him down, then ran excitedly in circles around them like a puppy. To Dolf's amazement Wowakan took after the dog, trying to nip him, then they played a game, face to face like two dogs, faking, dodging, and gamboling.

"Hey, you two," he said with mock severity. "You've been holding out on the boss." He wondered how long this game had been going on.

Maggie wasn't far behind the hound, coming on horseback at a run on a big Apaloosa, Henry seated before her. She wore tribal clothing. Almost before the pony skidded to a stop, she leaped nimbly down, with Henry under one arm, then set him on his feet. He wore only a breech cloth.

"Pa," he yelled, running to Dolf who stopped to scoop him up. Maggie slipped under his other arm for a long homecoming kiss. It had been only a little over a week since they'd parted, yet it seemed like a long time.

"How's Junior?" she asked.

"Comin' fine now," he told her. He also told her the recent crisis. "Lots of things happening fast, but that can wait. How's your Pa?"

"Very happy. You should see him and his grandson when he thinks no one is watching."

"I intend to. But right now I'd better pay my respects. Got some presents too. The one that'll go over best is comin' later. I got a cowboy bringing out a dozen fat steers."

"You're right about that. As usual the government has us on short rations. Which reminds me, there's something I want to ask you about. But that can wait to."

Dolf knew a little of the greeting ceremony among the Indians, but he also knew they didn't expect a white to know their customs perfectly, if at all. Simple manners and a good heart were recognized for what they were, and were worth their weight in gold. Dolf had learned a good bit of Maggie's tribal tongue from her since, for one reason, they wanted to be sure that little Henry could speak it as well as English; they alternated languages at home.

After the ceremonial greetings and solemn pipe smoking, the

sub-chiefs and important men left Dolf with Chief Henry. Maggie and young Henry joined them then. Unlike most of the men of his tribe, Maggie's father had had only one wife and had never taken another after Maggie's mother had died of fever during their confinement in the malarial Indian Nations. He had been very lonesome, his tepee kept only by a widowed sister, and was pathetically happy to have Maggie, the great warrior she had married, and their son all in his lodge.

Maggie had already told her father of their travels and adventures since she had left home with Dolf. Now Dolf brought them up to date on his crowded week since he'd left Maggie in Seattle. When Dolf came to the part about his not only accepting one lawman's job, with Wells Fargo, but a second as a U. S. deputy marshal, and still another as Pinebluff's chief of police, Maggie didn't try to conceal her dismay and disapproval.

Dolf looked grave. "It isn't the law primarily. I've come home into the middle of what's become a feud. I can't walk out on my son and brother and go back to Alaska yet. The law jobs'll help me help them."

Still, Maggie feared for his safety. He had survived so much deadly peril in the past by such narrow margins. Was his luck overdue to run out? The one bright spot in it all was that her father wanted her to stay and take over the English language school on the reservation. If Dolf had wanted to return to Alaska she would have gone in a minute, but his current plans meshed with her desire to fulfill her father's wishes.

"On top of the shooting trouble," Dolf said, "we're beginning to have stock rustled." He had been talking to them, to the extent he could manage, in their own language. When he stumbled he reverted to English so Maggie could supply the word or phrase. At the mention of rustling Chief Henry made a rumbling noise.

"I know about that, Morgette," he stated. "My braves see everything that goes on in our country and I hear of it. Many horses"—he made the sign for one thousand—"move in and out. Now the same men are stealing cattle." He laughed suddenly at some thought, then he was silent for awhile, apparently considering the wisdom of telling on himself to a U. S. law officer. (He understood very well what a U. S. marshal was.) He decided it was safe and continued. "We steal from thieves. Indians get blamed anyhow. The thieves try to make their work look like Indians are doing it. My people are not so hungry after we take their cattle. We never take any with the mark on them of our neighbors. We take what comes from somewhere else, probably far away, with marks we have never seen before. That stock would never go back to its owners anyhow even if the white officers got it from the thieves. Maybe it comes from Canada."

Dolf nodded. He wasn't about to squeal on Chief Henry or his tribe. He considered them as much family as his other one in Pinebluff. He remembered his father having said more than once, "A man's first loyalty is to his family. If that isn't worth a damn it doesn't matter what his other loyalties are to—they won't be worth a damn either." That was part of the Morgette creed. It was why it never occurred to him to return to Alaska before the last of the trouble here was completely resolved.

Chief Henry said, "I have fifty of your horses here. We took them and many more from the thieves. I would have sent them back to your brother soon, even if you had not returned."

Matt had previously told Dolf that he had sent Maggie's brother, Buck, and Clem Yoder on the trail of some missing horses. These Dolf thought may be the same horses. Moving fast, on a cold trail Buck could well have missed where the larger herd had been split by Chief Henry's braves. Matt had said he'd given the two pursuers plenty of supplies and money and told them to follow the rustlers to their final destination, no matter how far it was.

When Dolf and Maggie were ready for bed, the Chief ceremonially shook hands with Dolf, then placed his hands on his shoulders and pressed them affectionately. "My son," he said, "my heart is glad that you and my daughter and the little one are home."

Once in their own tepee with young Henry sound asleep, Maggie snuggled close to Dolf, resolved to tell him of her hope to be the local teacher. He kissed her hungrily, telling her, "I'm sure glad to be back with my family." He kissed her again. She decided to put off telling him about her aspirations until morning.

CHAPTER 11

THE local express office of Wells Fargo was in Alby Gould's bank. Doug Hatcher was their express agent. Shipments, however, depended on leased space on the Dawson Stage Line. Charlie Dawson had operated the line *en bonanza* during Pinebluff's first boom, and *en borrasca* when the boom collapsed, almost as a community philanthropy in the latter case, with only himself and one driver, Hen Beeler. In those lean days he was lucky to make horse feed. Now he was rolling in money again, running three stages both ways daily and an occasional extra bullion or mud wagon when treasure or extra passengers warranted. His operation was out of Packard and Underwater's livery stable where he kept his office. Due to space considerations, Dolf located his Wells Fargo headquarters at one end of the stable, putting a desk in Dawson's office. It was a congenial arrangement, since he and Charlie had been friends for almost twenty years. On the other hand, he'd met Wells Fargo's agent, Doug Hatcher, for the first time the day he'd returned from Chief Henry's camp. He eyed him carefully with a poker face, recalling Jim Hume's suspicions of the man.

At the moment, he was arranging his new office as chief of police at the city jail. He planned to function as U. S. deputy marshal from that location too, though he realized he'd probably keep the records of all three official jobs largely under his hat, rather than in pigeonholes in a desk. He wasn't very long on paperwork any more than on talking. He figured the world would do better with a lot less of both. He was, however, sitting at a desk. He was disgustedly reflecting on the fact that, in view of the merely circumstantial evidence, all of the Kelbo boys were out on bail.

He looked up when a tall, angular figure filled the front door and, with Kelbos on his mind, thought at first it might be Old Man Kelbo hunting more trouble. Instead he was happily surprised to see a face from the past.

"Hello, Morgette, I guess you probably weren't expecting to see me again."

Surprised hardly expressed it. "Mike Hanratty. I figured you'd be in Boston makin' a nest with Annie."

"So did I," the tall, red-faced Irishman sighed. "She cleaned me out and took a powder."

Dolf couldn't believe it. Captain Mike Hanratty had had a reputation as one of San Francisco's shrewdest, toughest, and crookedest cops. He had quit after almost forty years on the job. He hadn't asked for a pension. Everyone knew that he was set for life from legal larceny and not so legal blackmail.

"I'm sorry to hear it," Dolf said. He really was. For all the trouble Hanratty had initially caused him in Frisco, he'd ended up liking the big, homely, long-nosed devil.

"Well," Hanratty said, "they say there is no fool like an old fool. I really thought she loved me." He snorted. "Ran off with one of John L. Sullivan's sparin' partners and my last hundred grand."

"Can I do anything for you?" Dolf asked, still nonplussed over the whole thing, especially Hanratty's sudden appearance in Pinebluff. "Do you need some dough?"

"Naw, I got some money. I wrote and told that crooked old bastard, Chris Buckley, I might come back to Frisco. He almost died. I know where all the bodies are that he ever buried. Offered me two C-notes a month to stay away—so I finally got me police pension. Ain't that rich?"

"Have a seat, Hanratty. What brings you here, of all places?"

"Hard to say. I guess I wanted to see a bonanza town again before I die. I got my start in Hangtown in '49, ya know."

Dolf hadn't known. In fact he knew very little about the big Irishman.

"Matter of fact," Hanratty added, "I might be able to do you a favor. I hear yer lookin' for cops."

Dolf began to get the drift and decided to amiably slip in the needle. "You know some tough young bird that needs a job?" he asked. "This place is a hell on wheels."

Hanratty looked pained. "That ain't exactly what I meant."

Dolf feigned surprise. He waited for Hanratty to explain.

"I'm the tough young bird I had in mind. As good as I ever was. Maybe better. I don't take chances any more." He eyed Dolf expectantly.

Dolf grinned. "Sorta had a notion that's what you had in mind. You're hired. It don't pay worth a damn though."

Hanratty grinned now too, his pale blue eyes twinkling like diamonds in his red face. "Who cares? I tried bein' rich. Wasn't cut out fer it. After lettin' that little tart run through me yuh can start an insane asylum with my salary so I'll have some place to retire when I'm ready."

They were interrupted by the arrival of the Wells Fargo agent, Doug Hatcher, in a big hurry. He blurted out to Dolf, "They just tried to knock off another bullion shipment. Shot up Hen Beeler. Hoss Carr thinks he wounded one of 'em. He shot it out with 'em and made a run for it."

"Where is he now?"

"Just wired from the Junction."

Dolf was calculating rapidly. He hadn't had time his first day on the job to organize a quick response to this sort of thing. He had to improvise.

"We'll get on their trail right now. You come along, Doug. I'll need whoever I can scratch up. Wire Hoss to meet me where they hit the stage—and get that information from him." He turned to Hanratty. "How'd you like to go to work for Wells Fargo for awhile too? As of right now?"

"Suits me," Hanratty agreed. "I'll need a hoss."

Dolf nodded. "I'll get you one." To Doug Hatcher he said, "If you know any good men for a posse pick 'em up and get some livery horses. I'll meet you down at Charlie Dawson's office as soon as you can get there."

Hatcher almost bumped into Doc Hennessey at the door. "What's bit him?" Doc asked. Dolf told him very briefly.

"I'll come along," Doc volunteered. "They'll be bringin' Hen Beeler back up here. I'll meet 'em on the road and see what I can do for him. If he ain't hit too bad I'll come with you. Doc Priddy can handle this end. Besides we just inherited a new young sawbones this A.M. Word's gettin' out we're the best gunshot laboratory since the Civil War."

"Suits me," Dolf agreed. "Bring a rifle. We'll meet you at Packard and Underwaters'."

Dolf was thinking they would swing by the ranch on the way and maybe pick up Matt and a couple of his cowboys. He supposed he'd have to tell Morgan Casey about the affair, if Doug Hatcher hadn't done it already. He locked the jail and left a note for Simp Parsons on his desk.

Alby Gould showed up at the livery stable, along with Doug Hatcher, packing a six-shooter and rifle. "I'm going to go along," Alby announced.

"Good," Dolf agreed. He wondered how Victoria Wheat was enjoying her honeymoon. Obviously her life was not going to be dull with Alby Gould, a man of unbounded energy and vast enthusiasms.

Dolf's posse, when he started out, consisted of Hanratty, Doc, Doug Hatcher, Charlie Dawson and Alby Gould. Doug had already told Sheriff Casey about the holdup attempt.

"Is he coming down right away?" Dolf asked.

"I don't think so," Doug said. "He said he'd be along after he rounded up a posse. Said it was most likely a waste of time since they always head up into the Bitterroots."

Dolf hadn't expected much else. He didn't reply. "Let's go," he said. "They can catch up later if they come."

At the Morgette ranch he was able to recruit Matt and Stud Foley, as hard a hand as ever beat it out of Texas a long gunshot ahead of the rangers. Hoss Carr was already waiting for them at the holdup site.

"Where's Hen Beeler?" Doc asked.

"Back at the Junction nursin' a bottle. He jist got grazed in the ribs."

Hoss looked disgusted. "A body'd a thought he was kilt to hear him yell when he got hit. Shit. I got my belly blowed open at Shiloh an' didn't make a sound," he snorted. "Course it hurt so damn' much I couldn't," he admitted with a grin. He dumped out his pipe and turned to the business at hand. "There was seven o' them sonsabitches. They prob'ly never expected me to put up a fight.

Three left like a bat outa hell for town—I followed their tracks a little ways. Four lit out fer the hills. Got a dozen rifle shells where they was a shootin' after us down the road. I hit one of 'em fer sure. Saw him fall, then git up."

Matt exploded, "By damn! So that's what the Kelbos were runnin' like scared rabbits about. I was out after a couple of cayuses that strayed away about nine o'clock and saw the Old Man and two of the boys streakin' it toward town. I figured I was in for some trouble and pulled my Winchester. They didn't even slow down, just looked at me an' kept goin'."

"Where?" Dolf asked.

"About straight west o' our place, where our lane runs into the road."

"That'd be about the right time," Hoss said, "if they got goin' right after they finished pepper'n away after us. I wonder why they hung to the road?"

"Harder to track," Dolf guessed. "Just their tough luck Matt came along an' saw 'em. I'm surprised they didn't try to put you outa the way, Matt."

"What're you aimin' to do now?" Doc asked.

"Go after the other four. We can't prove anything on the Kelbos with only circumstantial evidence. We'll give 'em enough rope an' see if they hang themselves."

The tracks of the four horses headed east toward the high country. They had proceeded perhaps a mile on the trail when they were overtaken by Sheriff Morgan Casey. With him were a half-breed trailer, Chinook Charlie Graves, and to the surprise of almost everyone, Billy Blackenridge, who apparently had been allowed to wear a six-shooter. He was notorious for accidentally shooting either himself or his companions when in a posse.

"Dangerous to follow anybody up there," was almost the first thing Casey said to Dolf. "Besides we always lose the trail when they get up above timberline."

Dolf laughed at him. "If you'd rather go back, go ahead. We're gonna stick to 'em for awhile. Can't be sure they won't double back like the other three."

"What other three?" Casey asked suspiciously.

Dolf decided to get the needle into him good. "Probably Old

Man Kelbo and the two of his boys that ain't in the hospital yet." Both Rafe and Yancey had checked back in with Doc when they got out on bail.

"What makes you so sure o' that?"

Dolf told him what Matt had seen. The others were all gathered around listening.

"Don't prove a damn' thing. They coulda been up there workin' cattle."

"I'll buy that," Matt put in gleefully. "That's Morgette range. If I'm any judge they been workin' our cattle for months—mostly over the divide into Montana."

"Can you prove that?" Casey asked.

"Not yet. I'm workin' on it. Why expect them to turn over a new leaf up here? They've either done time in or been run outa Texas, New Mexico, and Arizona for rustlin' an' stage holdups."

Casey saw he wasn't going to get anywhere with this group, all of whom except his two men were of the Morgette faction. "Well, that's not the point now. I'll go as far as you boys will after this bunch. I brought Chinook Charlie so's we ain't so apt to lose the trail."

"I'll bet," Dolf told himself. He wished that they had Maggie's brother Buck along. He was a pretty good tracker himself. "I'll watch that half-breed," he thought, "to see he's tryin' to follow those dudes rather than lead us on a wild goose chase."

They camped that night just below timberline, then took up the trail again after sun up. Just as it led into the rocky ground beneath the tallest peaks, Chinook Charlie diverged to the south, parallel to the divide. The others started to follow, then Dolf pulled in Wowakan. "Where you goin'?" he yelled after Chinook Charlie.

"They're circlin' back," the trailer said.

Dolf looked disgusted. "You follow that trail if you want to," was all he said. He headed over the divide, followed by his own men. To Doc, who had pulled abreast of him, he said, "He must think we're pretty easy. Those were elk tracks unless I'm goin' blind."

The sheriff and his two men were in a conference back where Dolf had split off from him. "I hope they stay there," Dolf thought. But he wasn't that lucky; after a few minutes they brought up the rear. Chinook Charlie didn't try to lead the tracking again. The trail led over the divide toward the settlements on the Montana side. Once below timberline on the east side it was easier to follow. Dolf led, frequently at a lope. Late in the afternoon he pulled in Wowakan at the edge of the timber above a long meadow. A cabin at the far side had a trail of smoke rising from its chimney. His posse drew up behind him.

"We'll pull back in the timber and circle the place to get closer. Doc, you and Alby stay here in case we flush our birds and they run this way. If they do, shoot their horses. I want them alive so they can sing."

He proceeded cautiously through the timber, never so far back he didn't have the cabin in sight. As they drew closer he was startled by a shot close behind him. Turning he saw Billy Blackenridge with a still smoking pistol in his hand.

"Just checkin' it," Billy explained foolishly. "It went off."

"C'mon," Dolf yelled to whoever would follow him. He touched his spurs to Wowakan and broke from the timber at a run, headed for the cabin where a figure had just streaked out the door at the sound of the shot and around to the rear. In a moment the fugitive reappeared on horseback at a dead run down the meadow. Dolf and Matt, both on superior horses, rapidly closed on him. "Pull up!" Dolf yelled, pointing a pistol directly at him when he came alongside.

The rider eyed him fearfully, yelling, "O.K., I give up." He jerked his mount to a quick halt.

Seeing that Dolf would catch the rider, Mike Hanratty had pulled back, getting Dawson, Stud Foley, and Hoss Carr to follow him. "C'mon," he yelled, "let's shake down that cabin." He rode toward it, rifle pointed toward the door. "Hey, in the cabin," he shouted. "C'mon out and hold 'em high."

One man came outside with his hands up. "Anybody else?" Hanratty asked.

"I'm it," the fellow said.

"Look inside anyhow," Hanratty suggested to the others.

By then Dolf had his prisoner headed back. "Anybody with that guy that ran?" Hanratty asked his man. The other shook his head.

"Nobody in there," Hoss Carr said, coming out of the cabin.

Dolf questioned the two men they'd captured. He was sure from the horse's tracks that the one he'd overtaken was one of the holdup men.

"You ever seen this fellow before?" Dolf asked the cabin owner.

"I reckon. Lot's o' cowboys work this range. He's stopped here before."

Dolf asked, "You know for sure he's a cowboy?" What outfit does he work for?"

The man admitted he didn't know.

"O.K.," Dolf said. "Plenty of time to sweat this guy. We'll stay here for the night."

His posse started to unsaddle, except Stud Foley whom Dolf sent to bring in Doc and Alby.

The local rancher was John Tobin, who said, "If you boys are stayin' you won't mind if I milk my cow, I shouldn't think." He waited for Dolf's approval. "Where is she?" Dolf asked. Tobin indicated around back with his thumb. "In the corral." Dolf walked as far as the cabin's corner with Tobin, who had picked up a bucket from a bench on the porch, then returned when he was satisfied there was actually a cow out there. He had no reason to suspect that Tobin was other than a local rancher until he'd been gone for what seemed a long while. Dolf told Matt, "How about checkin' on the milkmaid. Seems to me he's takin' a long while."

"He's gone," Matt said upon returning.

Dolf got the picture at once. "Goddamit," he cursed. "There goes our other three birds too I bet. That fellow sneaked away to warn 'em. I'll bet they were camped not over a mile from here. An' it's gettin' too dark to track. Well, we'll go after 'em in the A.M."

CHAPTER 12

THE holdup man that Dolf captured said his name was Smith.
That got a general laugh out of everyone. The West probably had
more Smiths of the John Doe variety than any other area on the
globe. This one owned up to being Red Smith. Dolf couldn't push
him on that.

"We got you dead to rights," Dolf confidently assured him. "Your
hoss matches the tracks that were right with the other three all
along. We'll catch them too."

"You'll never make it stick," Smith said. "That's too flimsy for any
court in the West an' you know it."

Dolf eyed him evilly. He had managed to get Red to one side
where Sheriff Casey, if he was still awake, couldn't interfere with his
questioning. Only Dolf, Doc, and Hoss Carr were still up with him,
at one end of the long cabin.

"It won't need to stand up in court," Dolf assured him in a low
voice. "You boys killed a woman an' her kid when the stage made a
run for it. I figure the community'll deal with you long before you
get to court." Dolf's story about a woman and a kid being killed was
only a ploy to scare Red into talking and was working as Dolf had
hoped.

"Aw, naw!" Red moaned. "Aw. I never counted on nuthin' like
that. They said there likely wouldn't be no shootin' at all." He was
thinking desperately now. "Look. I held the hosses. I wasn't even
out there with the crowd that did the shootin'."

Dolf grinned coldly, without humor. "That's what most everyone
would say in yer boots. You don't think we believe that crap do
you?"

"It's the Gawd's truth."

"I might pretend I believe you if you give me the names of the others."

"They'll kill me."

"Maybe. We'll sure keep a heavy guard on yuh to see they don't, I can promise you that," Dolf said.

Red looked desperately uncomfortable.

Dolf said, "We might swing you ourselves if yer so damn tender about yer friends. Or turn you over to the folks in town before you get to jail."

Red didn't believe him and continued to stall. Dolf tried another ploy. "I'll tell you who yore friends were. The three out here with you were Dirty Dick Grant, Dutch Pete, and the Loco Kid. The three that high-tailed it back to town were Old Man Kelbo and two o' his boys. Furthermore I'm gonna have Hal Green put it in the paper that you said so, whether you say so or not. Now, you play our game and I'll put in a good word for you all up the line. You'll get a light sentence, maybe a suspended sentence. In either case you can high-tail long before the rest are outa the pen, assumin' they don't swing, which they probably will." That shook Smith.

"It's a deal," he hastily agreed. "And yer dead right about who the others were. How did you know?" He put his hand out to shake. Dolf pretended not to see it. Nor did he tell him he'd simply been guessing about who the other three were on this end. It hadn't taken a clairvoyant to figure that out in view of Dolf's inside knowledge gained from Wells Fargo.

That's where affairs were when Dolf turned in for the night. He had shackled Red Smith to his bunk, hand and foot. In addition he kept guards on him in two hour shifts.

In the morning they found bacon, coffee, and bread in Tobin's cabin, sufficient to make breakfast.

"Well," Dolf said to Morgan Casey after they'd eaten. "How about you runnin' old Red Smith in to jail. We're outa yer bailiwick anyhow by now. You might as well go home."

"You haven't got enough on him for me to risk my neck draggin' him back outa another state with no papers," Casey protested.

"He confessed last night while you was sawin' wood," Dolf told him. "Named his accomplices too."

Casey looked incredulously at Smith. "That so?" he asked.

Smith hung his head. "Hell, sheriff, I didn't know we killed a woman an' a little kid on that stage."

Casey got the picture and, before Red could say more, hastily told him: "There wasn't anybody killed on that stage, you damn' fool," then bit his tongue over letting the last part slip out. It was plain to all of Dolf's party that the sheriff was trying his clumsy best to get Smith off the hook. Casey knew he'd tipped his own hand but was getting angry enough that he didn't care just yet.

Red Smith blurted to Dolf. "You fellas tricked me. I ain't sayin' another word. And I lied to you about who was with me."

Dolf laughed. "That's O.K. Red. We'll put it in the paper anyhow."

"Who'd he say was with him?" Casey demanded.

"Ask him," Dolf suggested. "I'm sendin' him back to town with Doug as a U. S. prisoner. Alby has to get back so he's goin' too, and just to make damn' sure Smith gets there, Hoss Carr and Dawson are goin' along. If I was you Morg, since you're so touchy about bein' outa your jurisdiction, I'd go too, like I suggested. You and your pal Smith can have a nice long talk."

"Go to . . . ," Casey started to say and remembered who he was talking to. He sullenly joined Dolf's appointed guards, who were taking Red Smith to jail, never looking back, dragging his two deputies along. Dolf yelled after him, "Hey, Morg. Watch out that Blackenridge doesn't check his pistol again. You might get shot."

That left Dolf with his own small posse consisting of himself, Matt, Stud Foley, Doc and Hanratty. "I probably couldn't find a tougher bunch in the West," he thought.

They picked up Tobin's tracks from where he'd crawled out of the corral the night before and legged it for the timber. They never lost a footprint in the loose forest mat, ending up at the other three outlaws' camp. They'd obviously cooked coffee before Tobin had reached them since the grounds had been poured out on the grass. The ashes of their fire were cold. The tracks of men and horses showed they'd hastily saddled up and pulled out.

"One carryin' double, I'd guess," Matt observed. "Tobin musta gone with 'em."

"We oughta go back and burn his damned cabin to the ground," Doc growled.

"I wouldn't bet it was his cabin," Dolf said. "Looked to me like a big line cabin, or somebody's summer camp."

"Mebbe so," Doc allowed.

They hung doggedly to the trail, reaching the small railroad flagstop of Horse Plains just at dark. The little community had a depot, a store with saloon attached, livery stable and about a dozen cabins. Also, railroad section-workers were housed in half-a-dozen converted box cars. The posse had made a reconnaissance of the place on horseback before dismounting at the livery stable. The arrival of five heavily-armed strangers was quickly spread by word of mouth to the entire community. Many drifted out, curious to look them over. Not much ever happened in the little settlement.

At the livery stable Dolf identified himself as a U.S. deputy marshal and asked the hostler, "You by any chance see four men pass through, one pair ridin' double, about four or five hours ago?"

"Yup. Only they didn't go through. Left their cayuses here. They tried to sell 'em to the boss. He figured they was stolen. Said he'd keep 'em 'till they sent fer 'em. The four guys lit out on the train."

"Which way?"

"East. Only train that went through since then. About a half hour after they got here."

"You got a telegraph operator here?"

"Sure. Clem Pearson. About now he's over at the bar in the back of the store." He pointed down the street.

"When's the next east bound due?" Dolf asked.

"About ten A.M. if it ain't late, which it usually is."

"Any place to put up for the night?"

The hostler indicated the hayloft with his thumb. "Cheapest in town. And the onliest—it's free too," he laughed.

From consulting the telegraph operator, who was also the station agent, Dolf realized it was probably a waste of time to wire the sheriffs to the east of there. The outlaws already could have been east of Helena or south of Butte, depending on whether they'd switched trains. Those were the only two towns with enough lawmen to stop four desperate fugitives.

Dolf looked at his companions, who were at the bar with him, listening to his questioning of Clem Pearson, the railroad agent. He shrugged. "They mighta hopped off almost anywhere if the train slowed for a grade. Probably got hideouts all over these mountains. It'll be a needle-in-a-haystack job from here on out. Might's well give it up and go back after we get a night's rest. We can catch a freight back to the Junction tomorrow."

He wired the U. S. marshal at Helena for papers to confiscate the outlaws' horses, then hit the hay at the livery stable. He planned to wire Jim Hume for someone to go down the line later and find out where those four had actually got off the train.

The bankers Angus Kellums and Alex Krieger were at their bank late, along with Sheriff Casey, the first night Casey returned to Pinebluff. They had just concluded a clandestine meeting, the bank's window blinds closely drawn, and had surreptitiously let a fourth party out the rear door into the surrounding darkness.

Kellums asked his partner, "Do you trust that ambitious bastard?" He pointed with his thumb toward the door through which the fourth man had just departed.

"He's bankrolling us," Alex replied, not intending the pun. "He's got big plans. Wants to be governor when we get statehood— probably has his eye on the presidency if I know the type."

"What're his chances, do you think?"

"Who knows? He'll make governor probably. No tellin' about the rest. If some of those generals could make president, why not him? And what've we got to lose stringin' along in any case?"

Sheriff Casey was taking this all in with open mouth. He felt as though the other two had forgotten he was there. Of course he'd known before then who the big money was behind their faction, that money had put him in office as sheriff, but he hadn't known till then the towering ambitions that man harbored. He thought, "I never seen no cabbages growin' on the bastard, but like Krieger says, what the hell have we got to lose?" Then, as his brother Ed had reflected a few days earlier, the case of Sheriff Plummer in a situation like this over in Montana a few decades before came to mind and illustrated what he had to lose. It gave him a queasy feeling in the bowels.

"Well, Casey," Kellums boomed, turning to him.

Casey jumped at the sound of his name. He'd been far away dwelling on his possible fate.

"Were you asleep?" Kellums asked, testily. He didn't wait for a reply. "You got your work cut out for you. Morgette'll be back tomorrow, or the next day at the latest. By then Red Smith has to be gone. And don't fumble it, even if you just let him walk out the door. He's *got to be* gone. He's weak. He could blow the Kelbos out of the water. If they sweat him he'll squeal again. We'll get ahold of Hough over at the *Cryer* and make damn' sure his paper covers it for you so it looks like an outside job."

After Casey left, Kellums turned on Krieger, who had been observing Kellums' agitation during the meeting. Kellums' tic was becoming constant, twitching now at an alarming rate.

"I don't like any of it," Kellums exploded. "Burnings. Stage holdups. Attempted murder. Now we're conniving for a jail break. What the hell's wrong with that greedy bastard?" He rambled on. "We could make it big here all nice and legal. We've got a lock on most of the land. That railroad deal won't make any fortune. Hell, the branch line is only gonna be thirty miles long. How much will a railroad pay for thirty miles of right of way? Not much."

He reached into his desk and pulled out a bottle, taking a big pull directly from it. He even offered it to Krieger, who was beginning to feel like he could use one too and took a big swig. The sight of his partner cracking up right under his nose was unnerving. Kellums is more apt to upset our cart than the boss if he cracks up, he thought. Kellums' next words confirmed that fear.

"I'll tell you something," he said to Krieger. "If that ambitious sonofabitch overreaches himself and ruins my last chance to retire rich I'll kill him, I promise you!" He'd pointed with a trembling finger at the back door where the other had lately departed as he said "that ambitious sonofabitch."

"Get a grip on yourself," Krieger urged. "Maybe you'd better see Doc Hennessey to get something for that case of nerves." He wasn't overly happy himself with the turn events were taking since Dolf Morgette had returned to the Quarter Lien. Well, they'd got the word from the top man, and it was "Get Morgette."

When Dolf returned he was faced with the results of that meeting. As Kellums had promised, Hough's paper, the *Cryer*, had headlined Red Smith's escape:

IMPORTANT WITNESS ESCAPES

*Could have incriminated
prominent local rancher.
Were the robbers chasing
themselves?*

Last evening the accused stage robber, Red Smith, apprehended by the alert work of our Sheriff Morgan Casey, escaped the custody of the undersheriff, with the obvious help of concerned outsiders. Smith had been escorted under guard to the Wells Fargo office of Dolf Morgette to execute papers selling a horse to Morgette's longtime friend, Charlie Dawson. The public may wonder why Dawson needed another horse since he owns over one hundred. The why of that may be evident from the fact that when the undersheriff was witnessing the bill of sale, Smith quietly slipped out and equally quietly mounted a horse conveniently waiting, saddled and with a rifle in the boot, according to witnesses. He was last seen heading for the tall timber at a high run.

It is known that he could have been an important witness against a prominent pioneer rancher who was seen by three reliable witnesses in the vicinity of the robbery attempt shortly after it was carried out. When spotted, this rancher pulled his rifle and the witnesses rapidly fled for their lives. His name is being withheld while authorities investigate further, but it appears that the case against him will be very strong.

Dolf tossed the paper aside. "Bullshit!" he snorted. Nonetheless he gave the other side high marks for cleverly diverting suspicion from the Kelbos and onto Matt. He knew that despite that "name being withheld" business, everyone in the district knew Matt was the pioneer rancher who allegedly had been observed by "three reliable witnesses." The whole piece was a testimonial to Hough's genius as a propagandist, for example, the innuendo that the horse selling deal, during which Red Smith escaped, took place at the "office of Dolf Morgette," without mention that he was far away at the time. Or, the outright lie that Smith had been "apprehended by the alert work of our sheriff." Hough was going to be another thorn in his side, he figured. But he had to laugh over the man's brass. And there'd be a host of fools who would believe his propaganda; there always were.

CHAPTER 13

DOLF was heartily tired of having himself or his family locked up in the Pinebluff jail on trumped up charges. Just in case Morgan Casey planned to arrest Matt he sent him word that any attempt to arrest Matt was going to result in some dire consequences. His chosen messenger, an excellent selection.

"What the hell does he mean?" Casey blustered.

Hanratty fixed him with a very cold eye. Leaning close to Casey, who was seated at his desk, he said slowly and carefully, "He means he'll kill you if you put his brother in the jug you dumb sonofabitch!" With that he turned and marched out on his big flat feet, leaving a thoughtful silence hanging over the office.

Dolf's next worry was moving Junior out of harm's way.

"He's ready," Doc said.

He and Dolf were having a companionable cigar at Doc's office.

"I reckon I'll move him out to the ranch," Dolf decided. "Easier to have someone with him all the time. Also a lot harder for a stranger to sneak up on the place day or night since Matt has a pack of dogs around." He laughed inwardly at the thought of Mum's probable reaction, which he mentioned to Doc. "Mum'll probably give me hell for not bringing the kid up to her house, but she can live out at the ranch awhile herself if she wants to."

"That'll kill two birds with one stone if she does," he thought. "I can put off getting a place of our own for Maggie's and the kid's weekend visits and stay at Mum's." (He'd agreed to Maggie's plan to teach school on the reservation.) He could put off telling Mum he planned to get them their own place. He knew Mum was already ticked off that Henry wasn't going to be around during the week. He sure hated to tell her he wouldn't be around all the time on the weekend either. Dolf's droll suggestion that Mum could always move out to the reservation hadn't improved her humor either.

"Well," Doc was saying, "Might's well move Junior today." They put two mattresses, one on top of another, into a spring wagon and drove him out there. Junior looked a good deal better, getting some color back in his face.

"I'm really feelin' good," he told them. "Be up before you know it."

"If yer up before I know it," Doc told him severely, "I'll fix you so you won't try it again."

Junior grinned. "How?"

"You'll see," Doc told him.

Dolf stayed at the ranch for lunch, then rode back to Pinebluff. He'd told Matt before he left of his recent message to Morgan Casey. "I'd just as soon you shot him as me, little brother. If he comes around with a warrant, bore a hole in him. We'll hide the body where it'll never be found. Even his brother wouldn't miss him if I'm any judge."

"Are you kidding?" Matt asked. All he got in reply was a look that he couldn't read.

Back in town again, Dolf dropped into the telegraph office, hoping for a reply to a coded message to Wells Fargo's chief of detectives, Jim Hume. He got it later that day in an unexpected form. Hume himself showed up, finding Dolf in his office at the jail.

"Long time," he told Dolf. " '80 wasn't it? When we were tryin' to pin that train heist on you?"

They shook hands warmly. "I was scared off a trifle by that old rap," Hume admitted, "but between Will Alexander and Wyatt Earp I had to believe you were my man."

Dolf brought Hume up to date on local events. With respect to finding out where the four fugitives had got off the train in Montana, Hume said, "I've got a better idea. You can bet a five hundred dollar horse that someone right around here knows exactly where you could put the nippers on all four of them right this instant."

Dolf waited for Hume to reveal his plan. The chief of detectives eyed him quizzically. "You know anyone in that crowd that's got a reputation for being gabby?"

Dolf got an instant picture of Billy Blackenridge. He told Hume, "In the old days he was always carryin' news from one side to the other."

"He apt to be in the know enough to know where our men are?"

Dolf shook his head negatively. "But for a price he might lead us to someone who does. How do we get that someone to talk in case Blackenridge turns him up for us?"

"Money," Hume said. "I got the company to offer two grand apiece for those four."

"How about for the three Kelbos too?" Dolf asked.

Hume shook his head. "They're a tougher case. Lots of people will be too dumb to believe they aren't respectable like they're tryin' to appear. So we can't put rewards on them. Besides, they've got political backing. Kellums's and Krieger's bank seems to be behind them with money too. I happen to know. We'll have to get something on them cold to make it stick."

"Won't be easy unless we catch 'em in the act."

Hume was silent. Finally he said, "On the other hand, Tevis—he's president of Wells Fargo—will pay plenty under the table if the Kelbos, or any of that crowd for that matter, have a fatal accident. But that ain't exactly a reward."

Dolf remembered an old story about Hume's providing some notorious Nevada badman a gaudy funeral complete with a headstone with an angel on top and ornately inscribed with the epitaph: "Wells Fargo Never Forgets." In many communities Wells Fargo was the only law. No court ever sat to hear appeals of their verdicts—at least not on the mortal side of the pearly gates.

"I'll hang around a few days and see if you can get this fellow Blackenridge to bring us a canary," Hume stated. "I can run my affairs from any town like Pinebluff that has a telegraph connection."

They had their man before the day was out. Dolf knew that Billy had been a drinking pal of old Mop Finn, who was currently Mum's hired man. Through Mop he had Billy come over to his office just after dark. Hume was present. They explained their need for some information and, without being specific, exposed the color of more money than Billy normally saw in a year.

"Your man for inside dope is Yancey Kelbo," Billy said. "He

needs money and the Old Man doesn't give the boys as much as they think they've got comin', especially Yancey. But maybe I got the information you need myself," he added slyly, fishing after their real purpose.

"We don't want to get you in trouble," Hume stated, paying him off. "Just bring us Yancey if he's getting around yet. I hear he had an accident."

"He's down at the saloon now," Billy cackled, "but yer right about that accident; he'll be ridin' sidesaddle for a month o' Sundays. I wondered who peppered his ass." He snorted again.

Dolf still harbored his suspicion about who'd peppered the two Kelbos but wasn't about to mention it.

"Can you have Yancey come over here the back way tonight?" Hume asked. "I'll try," Billy said. "Should I come with him?"

"Bring him over so he won't be suspicious," Hume suggested. "Then you clear out so he'll talk."

Billy was back with Yancey inside of a half hour. The oldest Kelbo boy looked around the office carefully, both suspicious and fearful. He was obviously scared to death of Dolf, but he knew Hume by reputation and figured he was safe as long as the chief of detectives was there too. After Billy departed, Hume told him what they wanted.

"Naturally," Hume assured him, "we're willing to pay plenty."

Yancey licked his lips. "My crowd'll kill me like a jack rabbit if they ever suspect. How much is plenty?"

"Two thousand dollars apiece, dead or alive."

Yancey whistled. "You must really want 'em bad."

Neither Hume nor Dolf said anything. Finally Hume said, "Well?"

"O.K.," Yancey said. "What do you want me to do? I could tell you where I think they are, but they don't stay in one place for long."

"That ain't necessary," Hume assured him. "I've got a better idea. You tell 'em you got inside information that we're goin' to secretly run out bullion stages from now on without a shotgun guard to throw off the public, but you'll get a tip off on them. Get 'em to come in and gather some place to rob a stage and let us know where. We'll do the rest."

After Yancey left Dolf asked Hume, "You think we can trust him?"

"He wants that money bad. But, of course, I don't trust him. He'll be headed out in the morning though to see those hardcases, whether to sucker 'em into our trap or not. Why not follow him and scoop 'em in that way? Can you get a posse together by sun up?"

"I reckon," Dolf said. He prepared a list of names and showed it to Hume.

Before morning Dolf was able to assemble a posse consisting of his brother Matt, Stud Foley, Charlie Dawson, Mike Hanratty, Hoss Carr, Doc Hennessey and two welcome additions, Buck Henry and Clem Yoder, who had just come back off the stolen horse trail late that afternoon. Hume completed the roster. They assembled at the jail, staying out of sight. Dawson stayed at the livery stable, as he frequently did day or night, in order to tip them off when Yancey Kelbo came for his horse. Dawson hurried to notify the others when Yancey came in to saddle up. Buck Henry had his horse behind the jail and followed Yancey far enough to know where to cut his sign later. Then he returned for the rest of the Wells Fargo posse who were by then saddled and waiting. They left town in the opposite direction from that taken by Yancey and would have run directly into him by accident if Buck hadn't been scouting ahead. He hastily came back and stopped them in time.

"Yancey circled too," Buck informed them.

The trail led up into the high country on the back of the Morgette range. The sun had just set by the time his pursuers felt sure that Yancey had joined his gang. They could hear the distant lowing of a herd of cattle assembled on a bed ground. They retreated well back behind a high ridge while Buck scouted cautiously ahead. Dolf posted a couple of guards, then allowed a small fire to be lit in a depression under a large overhanging ledge where its glow couldn't be seen. The wind was blowing away from the herd of cattle so there was no danger of the smoky smell exposing their presence. They made a meal of coffee, bacon, and bread. A sliver of a moon was riding in the west by the time Buck returned.

"They got about a hundred Morgette cattle," Buck told Dolf. "Plannin' to take 'em over the divide in the morning I'd surmise."

"That's what I thought," Matt snapped. "I can tell a Morgette cow's moo a mile away."

That got a general chuckle.

"Me too," Dolf said. "Especially on your own range." Then he asked Buck, "What's the best way to get 'em?"

Buck considered the question. "Well," he finally said, "they're camped in a little park under some rock cliffs about like these not over fifty yards away from them. Why don't I spot you guys in there one by one? When the sun comes up we can have it in their eyes and yell at 'em to surrender. If they don't—bang! bang!"

That was the plan they decided on. Later when he could talk to Dolf privately Buck told him, "Yancey Kelbo won't be there. He headed right back toward town. I hope it was dark enough he didn't see our back trail. But you'll probably be glad to know his pa is with that outfit."

"How about the rest?"

"I'm only sure of Dirty Dick. Everybody knows his laugh. But where he is you'll likely find Dutch Pete and the Loco Kid. Too dark to tell and too damn' risky for me to try to get closer."

When it began to get light in the east Dolf carefully scanned the sleeping camp below with his field glasses. He was able to make out the cattle in a makeshift corral. That reassured him they weren't apt to be detected by a night herder.

The first one to get out of his blanket roll was Old Man Kelbo, who relieved himself, then started a fire, setting on the coffee pot. He was joined shortly by Dirty Dick. Dolf also recognized their fugitive milkmaid of a few days before, John Tobin, who'd escaped and warned the fleeing highwaymen to skedaddle. There were two others still in their blankets that the odds favored being Dutch Pete and the Loco Kid.

Dolf gave the sun about ten minutes above the horizon so they wouldn't be "skylined." Then he thundered, "Hands up! We've got you covered."

Dirty Dick dived for his rifle. Old Man Kelbo pulled his six-shooter, but before he could shoot, Dolf deliberately cut one of his legs out from under him with his Winchester, then put one dead center into Dirty Dick. The two still in their blankets came thrashing out shooting and were cut down. Old Man Kelbo laboriously drew himself back up, cursing wildly. He raised his pistol and fired one wild shot. Dolf would rather have had the Old Man alive to sweat him but several others were not of the same frame of mind. The Old Man fell back dead, pierced by several shots. Tobin pulled his favorite stunt—running—and disappeared over the opposite ridge among the syringa that grew in an unbroken bed for a mile or more. Several bullets tore up the ground and cut the brush around him but he appeared to be unhit.

"Shall I run him down?" Buck asked Dolf.

"Don't bother. He doesn't know who we are." That had been the only worry Dolf had about letting someone get away, since they'd just had to kill several people—true enough in self defense, but under embarrassing circumstances. They didn't have a warrant for Old Man Kelbo, for example. He discovered they didn't have warrants for the two who'd rolled out of their blankets shooting either. They weren't Dutch Pete or the Loco Kid as he'd hoped. No one recognized them. In any case, Dolf thought, we know what their business was if they were with this crowd.

After Doc assured him the four were indeed dead, Dolf said, "Let's get out of here and back to town as quick as we can. We'd best drift in separately through the day. No sense in givin' Morg Casey another chance to pull us in for self defense."

"And let's not forget, gents," Hume added, "Wells Fargo pays damn' well for folks that are tight lipped. You'll all be hearin' from the company with a little early Christmas present in a week or so."

Riding back to town with Doc, Dolf was a trifle regretful at the thought they'd had to kill Old Man Kelbo. "Sure hated to see him go without a better chance," he told himself. "The old boy had sand, even if he was crooked as a hoop snake."

The newspapers finally picked up the story. Sheriff Casey went out with Doc as coroner. Since they'd scattered the penned Morgette cattle back on the range there was no apparent motive for the shooting. The killings were written off to a falling out among hardcases. Only Yancey Kelbo had the slightest suspicion about what might have occurred. He wisely kept it to himself just then.

Doc grinned inwardly as he wrote his coroner's report. When he turned it over to the sheriff he said, "Probably be an unsolved mystery."

CHAPTER 14

ANGUS Kellums was turning over in his mind many possibilities for getting Dolf Morgette out of the way. Politically it might be possible if Dolf were merely chief of police, though that didn't appear a fair prospect. No sense coming out into the open with no chance of success. Getting him out of the employ of Wells Fargo or fired as a U. S. deputy marshal appeared equally fruitless. But these weren't the big problems. It was the threat of the man himself. The only area where he directly threatened a Kellums' scheme officially was the plan he and Krieger already had well advanced, of exercising their lease rights on Mark Wheat's extensive town lots. There was bound to be an outcry when they jacked up rental prices as much as tenfold. That could lead to mob violence. It would be up to the police force to suppress that. He'd have felt a lot more comfortable about it with a police force in his vest pocket. Morgette might just look the other way if his old friends resisted with force.

"Well," he argued with himself, "we'll just have to risk it. If the big money man wasn't greedy we could do it in little bites with a lot less trouble." A wave of resentment over having to knuckle under swept over him. He managed to calm himself. On the practical side Kellums knew the thing they'd buck was simply the idea of change. Some of the old timers had been getting rent almost at give-away rates, fair enough in the former ghost town, but not in view of current business and they knew it. They'd kick anyhow. But he'd had his orders and knew which side his bread was buttered on. He thought, "If the ambitious bastard actually makes it to the top he may take us the whole ways with him provided we play our cards right." He'd tried to buck the man's orders just once and been treated to an outburst that he didn't care to face again.

For a moment he'd almost forgotten Morgette. The thought of him recurred and caused his stomach to hurt. "Why the hell did Morgette have to come back anyhow?" he asked himself. The answer was obvious—for a wedding. If some maniac hadn't shot his son just then he would probably soon be headed back to Alaska where it was known he had a good paying gold mine.

Kellums, like most locals, figured it was fairly obvious who the only logical candidate was for having shot young Morgette— Yancey Kelbo. That called to mind the recent mysterious death of Old Man Kelbo and those others found with him. Kellums had inside information that the coroner's verdict had been a sham to cover the evidence of drygulching. Doc Hennessey, the coroner, was no friend of Sheriff Casey's, but he had no reason not to go along with the verdict of a shootout among hardcases. The sheriff thought that it would be easier that way to lull whoever had really done the job into a false sense of security so they might be caught later.

Kellums had found Old Man Kelbo useful for doing dirty work such as burning out nesters. He dreaded the necessity of trying to establish a working relationship with his oldest son, now out on bail, who had nonetheless assumed leadership of the clan and their loose-knit band of some hundred or more outlaws. Yancey was due to come see him at any moment. What bothered Kellums was that he realized Yancey wasn't smart. He'd rather have dealt with Dutch Pete who was a lot smarter but a known criminal. "I'm stuck with Yancey for better or worse," he conceded to himself just as he saw Kelbo enter the bank.

Yancey approached with obvious embarrassment. At thirty he lacked any worldly polish, since the Old Man had always kept his boys down. "Jesus!" Kellums exploded inwardly. "What an oaf. I'll have to help raise him." He eyed him narrowly. "Did he really pull a dumb stunt like back-shooting Morgette's boy?" he asked himself. If so, he had perilously bad judgment.

Yancey had always been impressed by rich men. He stood awkwardly, afraid to even offer his hand. Kellums was barely able to stifle a look of disgust. "Come into my office," he invited, relieved at having escaped shaking Yancey's hand. Inside he offered Yancey a chair, which the new outlaw chief sat on nervously. Kellums lit a cigar without offering Yancey one. He took the bull by the horns. "I used to do a lot of business with your pa," he started out. "Did he tell you about that?"

Yancey shook his head in the negative.

"We had a lot of—ah—deals. I'm going to need someone for the same kind of business. It'll pay us both real well."

Prompted by curiosity Yancey got up his nerve to ask, "What kind of deals?"

Kellums debated how much he should let out. He decided to shoot his bolt. "Did you reckon your pa had you boys running out the nesters just because he didn't like hoemen?"

Yancey stared at him stupidly. Actually it had never occurred to him to wonder. He and the rest of the boys just did as they were told; that was how they'd been raised. He'd naturally supposed someone was behind the Old Man just as in the other locales, but he never dared ask who. Now it dawned on him where their orders must have been coming from.

Due to the Kelbos' efforts, the Kellums and Krieger Land Development Company now controlled as much land west of the river as the Morgettes did on this side. The Kelbos had been the sole lever they'd used to persuade the owners of good water rights that homesteading was too risky in the Quarter Lien country. Many of those who'd left, due to innuendos published in Hough's newspaper, had been absolutely sure that Matt Morgette was behind the strong-arm campaign to keep out farmers. The *Cryer* had been a most effective instrument.

Yancey looked now to Kellums for some idea of what the banker might want next. It wasn't long in coming.

"What do you think about Dolf Morgette?" the banker asked.

"Why, I hate the bastard's guts. He damn' near killed my baby brother and knocked hell outa the Old Man," Yancey blurted. "I ain't sure he didn't kill . . . ," then he stopped himself, realizing he might be revealing too much.

Kellums finished the sentence for him. "Your old man?" he asked.

"I dunno," Yancey said, not too convincingly.

"You got any reason to think Morgette did that?"

"Just suspicions," Yancey evaded, not about to reveal his tip off to Wells Fargo, which he suspected may have led them to follow him out to the boys' camp.

Kellums decided to change the subject for a moment. "I know some people who'd pay a good bit to get rid of Morgette and his brother."

"How much?" Yancey asked quickly.

"Five thousand apiece. No questions asked."

"It won't be easy," Yancey said, thinking aloud, but Kellums was happy to see that he showed as few qualms over the idea as his father would have.

"But killing is the only way to get rid of them," Kellums said. He'd thought of all the other possibilities and none offered even a small chance of success. "They can't be run out. And my people—the ones willing to pay—want the Morgettes out." Yancey didn't tumble to the implication of there being higher-ups.

Almost every frontier town was divided against itself. Usually two factions strove for political and economic dominance. Pinebluff was no exception. On one side was Hal Green, backed by the merchants, old timers, and at least ostensibly the mining interests. Ben Page, representing "big mining," sometimes straddled issues, much to the disgust of Mayor Hal Green. Page viewed it as coppering his bet. The other political faction currently controlled only the sheriff's office. But Page fully realized they might completely get the upper hand in any election. If that happened and they had reasons to harbor grudges, they might dominate the county commissioners and try to squeeze the mining interests through confiscatory taxation or regulatory measures.

Page intended to bring Will Alexander to a city council meeting with him so he could see how well the community functioned. Page had been showing Will the mines with a view toward his possible investment in them. "Might as well size us up all around as a community. We've got pretty good government for being a small burg off the beaten path."

"What about the sheriff?" Will asked. "If he isn't crooked he's too dense to pull on his own pants."

Page grimaced. "There'll be an election this fall."

"Well, they'd damn' well better get a good man in his place. The damn' fool mighta let the Morgette boys get killed in his own jail."

They were walking side by side down to the city hall.

"You know, Will, a lot of people wouldn't miss the Morgettes," Page observed. "I don't want to hurt your feelings because I know Dolf Morgette is your friend, but I wouldn't have voted to hire him as chief of police except it's a case of having to fight fire with fire."

Will snorted. "What would you rather have, some copper in a white shirt with a tall hat and night stick? This town'd eat a dozen of that kind alive on any quiet night."

"I know that. And I don't like it. But Morgette's a killer; you can't deny that."

"So am I," Will retorted. "Killed three men in my day because it was kill or be killed. And that's the only way Morgette ever killed if I know him. I'd trust him with my life."

Page didn't reply directly. Instead he said, "Meeting tonight is about Morgette's police force. We voted six men, including him. He's got four now. They want to cancel the other two."

"Probably a big mistake," Will allowed. "Your police force needs to sleep occasionally. This place is hell on wheels day and night from what I've seen. Three or four hundred miners and cowboys, half drunk and lookin' for trouble just for something to do. A half dozen of 'em are always mad because some gambler cleaned 'em. Another half dozen will be gunnin' for each other over a grudge or a woman. Oughta have at least two cops circulatin' night and day and allow for some time off to boot. That don't add up to four men, especially when the chief has to divide his time as a U. S. marshal and Wells Fargo detective to boot."

"I'm not disagreeing," Page said. They arrived just then at the city hall.

Page introduced Will to the council, which consisted of himself, Alex Krieger, Charlie Dawson and Emil Griffenstein, who ran a general store. As mayor, Hal Green presided and was authorized to provide a tie-breaking vote, when necessary.

Hal convened the meeting, then announced, "We have a motion tabled from last meeting as the first order of business. Alex wants us to amend our police ordinance and cut the force to four for the sake of economy. Before we put it to a vote I might point out that this sudden change of heart came about after we got Dolf Morgette as chief of police. You got something against Morgette, Alex?"

"That's got nothing to do with it," Krieger said. "Or maybe in a way it does. With his reputation I think a lot of trouble is going to be scared off. Why not let that fact save us a couple hundred a month? The hospital could use another nurse. The waterworks could use another engineer. We could get both for $75.00 a month each and save $50.00."

Ben Page said, "I was all set to put up a fight for those other two cops, Hal, but what Alex says makes sense to me. Let's put it to a vote."

"O.K.," Hal agreed.

Krieger, Page, and Griffenstein, a thrifty German Jew, voted to reduce the force to four, including the chief.

Hal exploded, "Motion carried. And I think you just made a big mistake." He looked around disapprovingly, especially at his good friend, Ben Page. "I asked Dolf to come around and hear your verdict. I thought you might like to tell him personally why you decided to hamstring his force."

He rose and beckoned Dolf in. Dolf was aware of what was afoot and had decided on his possible response. He'd found his hands more than full with three jobs and had doubts about being able to do any of them well under the circumstances.

Hal said, "Alex, how about tellin' Dolf your argument that convinced Mr. Page and Mr. Griffenstein to join you in cutting his horns off."

Krieger repeated the gist of his reasoning. They waited for Dolf's reply.

Dolf said, "I've worked for the law in this community before, always to my regret. I got my belly full of it in the past because the community never had sense enough to support a good lawman. You can't police this town right with only four men."

He tossed his written resignation, prepared in advance, on the table and walked out without another word.

Hal picked up the resignation and read it to the crowd. "Anybody else got any bright notions?" he asked sarcastically.

Krieger said, "Yah. Why not hire Hanratty for the job? He ran the Barbary Coast for years. His reputation ought to scare 'em off just like Dolf's.

Hal tried Krieger's advice first thing in the morning. Hanratty laughed. "No disrespect to you personally," he said. "I know where you stand. But tell 'em to stick their job. Tell 'em I went to work for Dolf over at Wells Fargo. This town ain't my size."

CHAPTER 15

JIM Hume hadn't left town yet when Dolf resigned as police chief. They were having a beer together later that same evening at the Bonanza.

"Glad you did it," Hume said. "You'll have your hands full without jugging drunks every night. I've got some ideas for you to think over. I'll tell you when we're alone."

Later at Dolf's Wells Fargo office at the livery stable Hume unfolded a simple plan. "I've talked to Dawson already," he said. "He's got some good-sized wagons he'll rent. We'll have Page cast his bullion in two hundred pound ingots. No one's apt to pack one of those off on a horse. We can make a run to the railroad a lot less often. We'll put a bunch of guards on each wagon. We could have hired a half dozen guards for five years with what we've stood in losses so far."

Dolf obtained Hume's permission to hire whatever guards would be needed. "The sky's the limit for now," Hume stated. "The company's reputation is at stake."

Dolf had Hoss Carr already—a good man. He was aware that his police force had decided to quit as a man if he resigned. He didn't want to leave Hal Green in a lurch but they were dead set to do it anyhow. He planned to put them on the Wells Fargo payroll if they did. With himself, Tobe Mulveen, Simp Parsons, Carr and Mike Hanratty, he could take out a bullion shipment with an outrider posted front and rear, and three men on the wagon besides the driver. That, he figured, should discourage anything but an army if casting two hundred pound ingots didn't. The plan to do the latter he intended to widely publicize in the papers.

"We ought to put a stop to losses on this route for good," Dolf surmised. "If we lose anything from now on it'll be over my dead body."

Hume grinned wryly. "And that's exactly the way they'd like to take it. You've got enemies thick as flies up here that'd go after one of those wagons just to get you and never mind the loot."

"How well I know it. The Casey brothers for instance. I could name lots of others still holding grudges from the old days."

"Oh," Hume said, "one last thing. I talked to Ben Page about casting up bars that heavy. He wasn't inclined to be cooperative. Said he'd think about it and made a few reflections on the company's reputation that I didn't like. He's a drivin' man and a penny pincher. He doesn't lose a damn' thing if we get heisted—the company makes good on it. I've seen his kind before. Honest in their own way, but cheap. I told him you'd be up in the morning to talk with him after he thought it over. He also said something about losing interest on the bullion if he only shipped once a week or so. He's close."

"Suppose he doesn't want to draw cards in our game?" Dolf asked.

"Well," Hume said, "we don't serve a few towns for similar reasons. Panamint out in California's one of 'em. You can tell him in that case to haul his own damn' silver."

Dolf laughed. He could imagine how that would sit with a big man used to getting his own way. Although he knew Page and Hal Green were good friends, he'd never cared for Page's type. They didn't know how to take even a few moments of pleasure out of life. After he and Hume had parted, Dolf rode to Mum's. Tomorrow would be Friday and the next day Maggie and the kid would be down for the weekend. He toyed with the idea of chucking all his law jobs and spending the rest of the summer going after cattle and horse thieves his own way. Hanratty would be a good man to replace him. He was sure it would appeal to the big Irishman. Hanratty was looking for a springboard into another job where he could feather his nest again before he got positively too old. He was probably sixty now. He'd mentioned running for sheriff against Casey next fall. If he made a record for Wells Fargo against the local highwaymen that could propel even a newcomer into office.

After having breakfast at the hotel, since Mum was out at the ranch, Dolf walked out to the edge of town where the offices of the Pinebluff Consolidated Mining and Milling Company were located. Hal Green's buggy was parked out front. Dolf could hear Hal's voice raised in heated argument inside. "Thanks to your penny pinchers," he was saying, "we now have no police force at all. Well, you can damn' well find a new mayor too. I'm sick of trying to keep this place peaceful."

"Whoa!" he heard Page say. "Slow down. We made a mistake, so let's fix it."

"No!" Hal stormed. "You fellows fix it. I've got my belly full. I'm callin' a council meeting tonight and turning in my resignation."

Dolf was surprised to hear Hal so hot, especially with a friend. He chuckled inwardly. "Go it, Hal," he said to himself. "Let the careful bastards run it their way and see how they like it."

Hal almost ran into Dolf as he stormed out. "Oh, hi Dolf. I suppose you overheard us."

Dolf said, "I tried to talk those boys outa quittin' on you. I guess I didn't have much room to talk. I left you in the lurch myself."

Hal put his hand on Dolf's shoulder. "I didn't blame you. I'm doin' the same thing tonight. If we need any law around here we can call out the League in an emergency."

Dolf was silent, thinking how ineffectual he'd found miners' meetings in the Yukon. They were a form of vigilantes. Groups were no substitute for one or two good men.

"If you're not going to be here long I'll wait and give you a ride," Hal offered.

"Can't tell how long I'll be. You go ahead. I need the walk anyhow."

Page heard him outside and called, "Come on in Morgette. I been expecting you." As Dolf entered he grinned bleakly. "I suppose you heard me get my dressing down?"

"I guess," Dolf said. "Hal ain't usually that hot."

"I know. Well, I guess I put my foot in it. You wouldn't by any chance take the police force back?"

Dolf shook his head.

"I was afraid of that."

That's your tough luck, Dolf thought. He couldn't really like the man, though he usually avoided snap judgments. He hadn't had a chance to get to know Page, but his bulldog look and snappy eyes somehow aroused in Dolf a distaste for him.

Page eyed him speculatively, "I suspect I'm about to get in dutch with you and Wells Fargo too, but it would cost us a good bit of money to do what Hume wants. Frankly I can't see it. The difference in shipping three times a week and only once amounts to a lot of interest money lost in a year's time. If Wells Fargo can't protect us the word'll get out and it'll hurt their reputation."

Dolf watched him with a poker face. He relished Page's premature look of triumph. He obviously thought he was holding the winning hand.

"In that case," Dolf said, "Hume told me to say that we won't be able to carry your bullion shipments anymore."

"What? He can't do that!"

Dolf silently rose and headed for the door.

"Hey, wait a minute. How the hell are we going to get our bullion out? I'll go to the newspapers and cost Wells Fargo their damn' reputation."

Dolf looked him over coldly. "That's between you and them. Without your business they won't need me here anymore. I aim to wire my resignation and go fishing for the rest of the summer."

He remembered Matt's cattle and horse rustlers and added, strictly to himself, "And maybe catch some real big fish while I'm at it. Might even look into that blind trail Buck and Yoder followed." It had led down to Salt Lake City. They'd returned realizing the Saints weren't about to return gentile horses. It struck him that he didn't need any of his law jobs to tend to Morgette business. The U. S. deputy marshal's badge had come with the Wells Fargo job and, he assumed, would be withdrawn with it. If it wasn't he could resign that too.

He started out the door and was greeted by a bullet splintering the doorframe above his head. A distant rifle report followed. He hastily drew back in, slipping to the window to look for the shooter. He saw a scrambling figure slipping and sliding frantically toward the top of the nearest tailings dump, then over and out of sight. Page joined him at the window.

"You all right?" he asked.

Dolf nodded. "Shot went high. They always do shootin' downhill if a feller don't know enough to aim low. You'll need a new doorframe."

He stepped outside, scanning the pile of tailings some three hundred feet high. When the mines had first opened and Dolf was a newly-wed young man, he had taken a job in them. This tailings pile was from the first mine. He thought, "Maybe I know my way around back there better'n you do, partner." He had an idea where the rifleman had gone and how he might head him off. He wished he'd brought his hound with him.

"I'll come along," Page offered. "Wait'll I get my Winchester." He went back and returned with it.

"Might be risky," Dolf cautioned. "He was after me. Let me have the rifle." He didn't want anyone getting in his way.

Page handed it over reluctantly.

"I'll phone downtown for some reinforcements," he said.

"Don't bother," Dolf advised him.

Dolf rapidly worked his way up the swale between the tailings dump, having an exact idea where he was headed. It took the better part of fifteen minutes to come out on the hillside above where the drygulcher had disappeared. He circled for tracks and soon picked them up.

"That's what I thought," he said under his breath. The shooter had probably left his horse out of sight in the timber behind the hill. "Well," he told himself, "I know a little shortcut." He headed for the tunnel of the old Ajax mine where he'd worked for almost a year. He knew its twists and turns like the back of his hand. High up at the rear was the cave that had led to the discovery in the first place. It had served as an air shaft after they'd poked the tunnel through below. He just might get up there before the drygulcher did.

Dolf found that a heavy plank door had been installed, probably to protect the company from liability if sightseers wandered onto the property. Or maybe they found some new high-grade pockets. The door had a huge hasp on it but the padlock was not latched. He removed it and hung it back on the hasp and entered. He would soon regret not sticking it in his pocket. The light from the tunnel mouth showed him his way back since he had propped the door wide open. He knew that as soon as his eyes became accustomed to the dimness, he would be able to see well enough to get to where the light from the cave on the other end would guide him. It was only some thousand feet through the tunnel. As he slid his feet along, feeling his way, he thought, "I hope nobody punched down any new shafts in here." It was as though his guardian angel had warned him. He felt his exploratory foot move out into empty space and almost lost his balance, pulling back in a wobbly fashion as quickly as he could. He felt around him on the floor, searching for a rock to throw ahead of him. As he did he picked up the sound of water eerily dripping far below, somewhere just ahead of him. Finally he put his hand on a good-sized rock and tossed it into the abyss, counting as he did so. It was a long while before the noise of a splash returned.

"Four hundred feet, at least," he said aloud. "That was a close one." He decided to retrace his footsteps. The entrance now looked very bright to his eyes, which were adjusting to the gloom. Then the light suddenly winked out. Maybe the door blew shut, he thought. But there'd been no wind and he'd put a large heavy rock against it. Someone had to have sneaked up and shut it. "I wonder if the guy I was following knows more about this place than I figured," he speculated. "I sure hope not." He'd have bet he'd find the door securely padlocked this time but had to go back and make sure. If so, he'd have to make his way to the back entrance in pitch darkness, trusting to feel to avoid any more new shafts. He reasoned that he could probably work his way around the edge of them. Crawling would be his safest bet as long as some nice big rattler wasn't using this unused cool tunnel as a retreat from the hot sun during the day. "I'll just have to risk that," he told himself. He was counting his steps so he would have a fair idea when he was back near that shaft, if he had to come back.

He found the heavy door solidly shut. Pushing on it he heard the padlock shift in the hasp. He thought, "If I had a couple boxes of rifle shells I might be able to shoot my way out." Resigned to going the hard, perilous way, he started back in the total darkness. He had a few matches, but decided to save them. If he could find his way back as far as the original stope he expected he might be able to find stubs of candles left stuck in the wall, possibly even one he himself had left.

He proceeded cautiously, counting his steps, but picking up small rocks whenever his feet touched them and filling his jacket pockets. He then tossed them ahead of him as he went. He kept having to remind himself that the yawning shaft that had almost claimed him hadn't moved. He was in solid rock here. If there had been cribbing he could have cut splinters with his jackknife and improvised torches. Long after he felt that he must surely be upon the shaft again he finally reached it. The small rock he tossed did not promptly echo back. He heard its faint splash far below in the water. The thought occurred that but for the grace of God, he might be down there now, dead. "Might yet," he reasoned, "if I don't play my cards just right getting around that thing." He decided to use one of his precious matches. First he searched his pockets for any paper he might have to prolong his matches' light. He remembered his notebook and improvised several twisted paper wicks from its pages, putting them in his pocket. Then he struck a light. The flare revealed that there was a wooden shaft collar that appeared to be in good condition. Dolf banged it exploratorily with the rifle barrel, then quickly lit one of his small paper torches from the match. He examined the overhead and discovered that the shaft continued upward, a stepladder just barely reachable above him. This suggested that there might be a new headwork above somewhere, built since his day. If there were, the probability was that a series of stepladders continued to the surface, nailed into the cribbing that lined the shaft. They would be a risky way of proceeding, however. By now they might be rotten and insecure.

He guessed that he must be at least two hundred feet below the surface of the hilltop. His gamble was either to continue on back in the tunnel, with a chance of running into still another shaft sunk since his time, or to try climbing out this way. The stepladders appeared sound enough at this point, but there was a possibility that one above might not be. A ladder breaking under his weight could plunge him into the shaft, which he knew dropped at least four hundred feet below where he was now. He kept lighting new torches as he debated his position. Another problem with using the upper part of this unknown shaft was that he might run out of light and still be in utter darkness on unfamiliar ground. The thing obviously didn't go straight up all the way or he'd have seen light above.

He decided to work his way across the collar's edge, starting with one foot, putting as much weight on it as he dared. On the far side of it the cribbing started. He figured that if the collar collapsed he might be able to grasp ahold of the first set of timbering and save himself from falling to his death. First he threw Page's rifle across. Then he lit a new slip of paper and tentatively worked his way out on the side of the collar, keeping his back tightly pressed to the tunnel wall. His foot slipped once on a small round stone, almost causing him to sit down and slide off the narrow side beam he was working across. It was only six feet or so to the other side but seemed more like sixty. Once across he wrapped his arm around the first vertical timber and guided himself to safety. This cost him his light and another precious match. He realized that he was now at the edge of the original stope. The ore car tracks were still in place here; they'd no doubt been removed on the side of the shaft from which he'd just crossed and reused elsewhere.

He cautiously proceeded another couple of hundred feet, knowing that by then if he extinguished his light and allowed his eyes to adjust he could see the light from the cave end of the tunnel. He stood in darkness, listening to how loud his own breathing sounded in the utter stillness. He peered around for the expected light spot in the gloom and could discern none. He wondered if there was also a padlocked door at the rear entrance, now? "If there is, I'll have to risk those ladders in the shaft." He was close enough to the cave now that it would be foolish not to check that end of the tunnel.

He proceeded as he had before, throwing pebbles ahead, and running one boot along an ore track to maintain his direction. He risked another match to look around for a candle in the walls, using up several more of his twisted pieces of notepaper and finding nothing. He again proceeded in total darkness, praying there were no more new unknown hazards ahead.

CHAPTER 16

YANCEY Kelbo was not Angus Kellums' notion of a welcome visitor. In the first place he smelled like a goat. In the second, Kellums considered him little smarter than one. He sighed as he saw Yancey come into the bank and look over at him, waiting to be motioned inside the rail. Kellums thought, "If I get rich at this business, I'll sure as hell earn it, having to work with cretins like him." His nerves were more on edge than ever; he'd been sleeping badly, taking large doses of laudanum to get what little he did get, and having serious indigestion. Reluctantly he nodded at Kelbo to come over. He did offer him a chair, largely because he thought he was less obtrusive that way and he hated to have people see him talking to him.

Without preamble Yancey said, "I got Dolf Morgette for you."

Kellums immediately conjectured what he was talking about. "You missed," he contradicted him. "It's all over town that somebody took a shot at Morgette out at the mines—but you missed."

Yancey looked smug. "I know I missed that rifle shot. But that ain't how I got him. You won't be seeing him again."

That interested Kellums. Yancey told him what he'd done to Dolf. "I saw him go into that old mine. He must have been out of his mind. Anyhow I sneaked down and locked him in. He'll never get out of there."

"How can you be sure there's no other way out? That may be why Morgette went in. He may have been trying to take a shortcut after you," he said, making a shrewd surmise. "Don't forget he's a local boy. He may know something you don't."

Yancey's jaw dropped at the unhappy possibility. In his mind, he'd already spent the five thousand dollar reward. He'd planned to go to some big city and see the sights and squire some pretty women around. He blustered, "He's probably stumbled into a shaft and killed himself by now. I want my reward and you ain't gonna weasel outa it. He'll never get outa there and you know it!"

Kellums was taken off guard by how assertive Yancey had become in the few days since his father's death. "Just take it easy," he soothed him. "You're probably right. But I'm not the party that'll pay the money. They've got to be sure. Let's just give it about a week to be sure he doesn't show up. If he doesn't by then, that'll convince our party and you'll get your money."

"I'd better," Yancey rumbled. "I took a damn' long chance sneakin' down and slammin' that door on him."

Kellums admitted that to himself. In fact, Yancey had taken a suicidal chance. If Morgette had stepped out about the time Yancey was nearing the door, the coroner would be working on him at that moment. He made a note to remember that Yancey was capable of desperate, even foolhardy, risks. He wrote it off to his stupidity. Also his avarice. That five thousand dollars obviously was a big incentive to a man of Yancey's stripe.

"One week," Yancey finally said, getting up. "O.K.?"

"One week," Kellums promised. He sincerely hoped that Yancey had got the job done.

Yancey left town at a lope, headed for the ranch. He was using an extra blanket folded across his saddle to pad his healing rear end. He was irritated by that and aggrieved over not receiving his money as soon as he'd expected. He'd had a notion to box Kellums' jaws. At the ranch he found his three brothers with Dutch Pete, the Loco Kid, and several other lesser lights in the gang. He was not surprised to see Billy Blackenridge there as well. Billy often called to peddle gossip and sell inside information if it was worth anything to them. Usually they managed to get him drunk and pry more information out of him than he'd planned to reveal.

Yancey hadn't seen Dutch Pete and the Loco Kid since before his father had been killed. He'd expected to find them with the Old Man and Dirty Dick the day he'd ridden up there with the false news about the bullion shipment designed to toll them into Wells Fargo's net. It happened they had ridden out for supplies and missed the ambush. Yancey hoped that Billy B. hadn't given them a hint of his confab with Dolf Morgette and Jim Hume just before the ambush had taken place. It wouldn't have taken a great mind to put two and two together about that. He wondered if Billy had surmised what had happened. "Maybe it would be best if something happened to Billy," he thought.

Setting Yancey even more on edge with that line of thought, his brother Rafe said, "Listen to what these two found out," indicating Dutch Pete and the Kid with his thumb.

Dutch Pete said, "Yah. Guess who beefed yore old man?"

Yancey turned a little pale, but managed to look innocent and shook his head.

"The Morgettes and a whole bunch of guys with 'em."

"Pete and the Kid saw 'em," Rafe said.

"That's right," Dutch Pete said. "We was comin' back in with supplies and damn' near run into 'em ridin' away. If we'd a been a little sooner we'd a heard the shootin', I reckon."

He told how they'd luckily seen the Morgettes posse first, since they'd pulled off the trail to rest their horses.

"We backtracked the bastards," the Loco Kid said. "Found the boys all laid out with flies already crawlin' in their mouths an' on their eyes by then. A helluva thing to have ta look at."

"Why dint yuh high-tail down an' tell us?" Yancey asked. "Course we found out they was dead anyhow, but that was because Tobin got away."

"Why the hell would we make a fool play like that?" Dutch Pete asked. "We lit out fer the high peaks. Dint know but what the Morgettes might be makin' a sweep of the range. They could just as easy o' hit our back trail and come a foggin' after us. I ain't tetched. It wouldn't a brought the boys an' yer old man back if we pulled some damn' fool stunt like that. We figgered the news'd keep." He added, "Billy B. has some interesting news too." Yancey thought, here it comes and wondered if he could outdraw Dutch Pete, but Pete didn't look the least bit as if he were leading up to a showdown. He said, "The town ain't got no police as of this mornin'. They all quit when Morgette turned in his badge."

After they got rid of Billy B. Yancey gloatingly told them what he'd just managed to do to Dolf, which elicited a general round of applauding remarks.

Dutch Pete drew Yancey to one side. "The situation in town's made to order with no police. I think we oughta hit both banks before they hire a new bunch. We got a whole herd of cayuses corralled up that don't have local brands. We won't be recognized if we wear masks. It's a cinch nobody in town is gonna put up a fight with Morgette outa the way."

Yancey turned that over in his mind. He was still smarting over not getting his five thousand dollars, and he blamed Kellums regardless of his talk about other parties. He'd love to see Kellums' face while his bank was being cleaned out.

Yancey said, "Why the hell not? When should we do it?"

"Today, before they get a new bunch of law hired. We can hit both banks and be more famous than the James boys, even if they won't know for sure who did it."

There were not many people on the streets in Pinebluff at noon, since most were at home eating at that time of day. What few there were took cover in fright at the sight of a dozen horsemen coming out of alleys wearing handkerchief masks. They rushed the two banks by force of numbers, leaving a half-dozen men in the street to suppress any resistance. The only trouble they encountered was Angus Kellums to whom this appeared like the final blow to his aspiration to become rich and independent. He rushed madly at the robbers, shouting and flailing his arms ineffectually. "You can't do this!" he screamed shrilly.

"The hell we cain't," Yancey Kelbo said, and laid a pistol barrel alongside his ear.

It took only a few minutes to clean out the banks and head for the tall timber. Not a shot had been fired. Both banks together lost over one hundred thousand dollars. The robbers paused as soon as they were sure there was no one in close pursuit, divided the loot, then split, leaving a dozen trails behind them. The Kelbo boys were back at their ranch by dark.

They were in a gloating mood, especially Yancey. "Over eight thousand dollars apiece. What a wad of sugar!" It was more than he'd ever had at one time in his whole life. It gave him an idea. To his brothers he proposed, "Why don't we head back to Texas as soon as Billy Joe can travel? It's too damn' cold up here in the winter anyhow—and I don't care about doin' the dirty work of a bunch of bastards too finicky to kill their own beef." He was particularly thinking of Kellums. "How about it, boys? Waddaya say?"

They all looked to him now for leadership just like they had to the Old Man. Yancey was beginning to feel the power that comes from being the accepted leader. He added, "I say, let's do it. We got enough scratch to start a first-rate spread of our own."

"Suits me," Rafe said. "How about you two?" He turned to Lute and Jud.

"Sure," Lute agreed.

"I'm fer it," Jud said. "But ain't we gonna get even first for them Morgettes killin' pappy?"

"Yer damn' right," Yancey blustered. "And I areddy got even with Dolf good and plenty, I reckon."

That set him to thinking about Kellums and the five thousand dollars. He wondered if the banker had recognized him when he hit him over the head. He'd changed his clothes but the old bastard had a sharp eye. He'd see about that when the time came. He wanted the reward too.

The situation in Pinebluff had changed so that Yancey would never get his reward, and it all came with one shocking bolt out of the blue. People had been standing around the streets in little knots talking about the daring bank robbery. There was wild speculation about who had carried it out, none of it touching on the real perpetrators, who had deceived the public into accepting them as honest ranchers. The streetcorner gossips little suspected that a second event would eclipse the first very shortly. It started when Ben Page made his way to the bank to find out the extent of the loss. He was the largest stock holder and largest depositor in the establishment. He found that Kellums had been hurt and taken to the hospital. Doc had put him to bed for a while to observe him for a possible concussion.

Page found Kellums in a hysterical frame of mind. Kellums viewed the robbery, against which the bank was wholly uninsured, as the final ruin of all he'd planned for. Every penny he'd owned had been invested in the now-defunct bank. Moreover, he was almost sure that Yancey Kelbo had been the robber who had hit him over the head. He'd recognized him by the smell, if nothing else. He felt it hadn't been his choice to associate with that sort of person, and he also felt that the bank could have made it without the machinations of the man behind him. That man was Page and he felt a burning hatred for Page's avarice and his sneakiness, letting others do his dirty work, from the Kelbos and their gang to him and Krieger.

Page arrived to offer his sympathy, but more important to work out a strategy to prevent a run on the bank—he thought they could still save it, although it would cost him a big additional investment. He was thunderstruck at the change he found in Kellums, who was in the first stage of a complete nervous breakdown. When Kellums spotted Page, he pointed a finger at him and screamed, "This is your fault, you scheming bastard! You got rid of the police force."

"Take it easy, people will overhear you," Page soothed.

"I don't give a damn who hears me," Kellums shouted. "Your scheming has ruined us and almost got me killed. You bought off the sheriff and hired the Kelbos to burn out the nesters, with me giving your dirty orders. You had your own bullion shipments robbed so you could collect the insurance and sell it again. My bank didn't have insurance, you bastard!"

Page first stood open-mouthed, too stunned to move, then he tried to forcibly restrain Kellums, putting his hand over his mouth. Kellums drew back his legs and kicked him away from the bed. "You know who hit me over the head? You know who robbed the bank? Your goddamned Kelbos and their rotten crew!"

Page rushed back at him and was kicked away again as Kellums was shouting this. Seeing Page trying to rush him again, Kellums reached under his pillow and pulled out a derringer. Page tried to back away but caught the first shot in his arm. The second hit him directly in the heart. He was dead before he hit the floor. Doc and several others had heard it all—the nurse, some visiting townsmen, the other two doctors and young Billy Joe Kelbo down the hall. Billy Joe thought of making a break for it but recognized that he was too weak.

Doc rushed into the room and took the empty derringer from Kellum's now limp hand. "I got the sonofabitch," he gloated. "He won't give me any more of his slimy orders." He laughed hysterically. Doc thought of giving Kellums a heavy sedative, then thought better of it. Better keep him awake and get his statement. Instead he got some whiskey and opium in him to calm him down. They had no trouble getting a statement from him a little later, sworn before Judge Porter who was still relatively sober at that time of the day.

By sundown the news had spread all over town. Hal Green stationed a cordon of vigilantes around the hospital to see that Sheriff Casey didn't try to take Kellums to jail, where he could be permanently silenced. Green knew that this was the final break that the law-and-order forces had been waiting for. This was something the *Cryer* couldn't squelch with its propaganda. They probably couldn't hold Yancey Kelbo for the bank robbery on the uncertain identification of Kellums, but at least they had unmasked him and his brothers. Even if they got a grand jury indictment, it was certain he wouldn't implicate any of the others. But a heavy blow had been struck in the interest of cleaning up the district.

Alby Gould had sent wires to both the governor and the president in Washington, outlining the situation and asking for authority to remove the sheriff and replace him temporarily with the U. S. deputy marshal (whose name he diplomatically left out of the wires). He received his authority in a matter of hours.

"Where is Dolf?" he asked Hal.

"Haven't seen him since morning, come to think of it," Hal said. "He was out seeing Page." That triggered an alarm in Hal's mind. He mentioned what was on his mind to Alby. "Now that we know all about Page, why should we believe his story about someone shooting at Dolf. He might have got him in the back. Dolf wouldn't have had any reason to suspect him. That's the way Dolf's kind finally all get it. From some innocent appearing guy. And you can bet Page was the kind to keep a few men around that would put a body down a mine shaft. We'd better get out there and start investigating."

CHAPTER 17

DOLF, still locked in the old mine, had discovered that the back entrance was as securely locked as the front. There was an air shaft there, but it was heavily grilled and the grill was securely anchored into the rock with cement. By then he'd fashioned himself a handful of torches by cutting long splinters from the mine's timbering. He lit a new one from each previous one, hoarding his precious matches. Back in the familiar stope where he'd worked as a young man, he cut a goodly supply of additional torch material. Some of it he used to look around for a miner's candle or, better still, a carbide light with some fuel remaining in it. They hadn't had these when he had been a miner, but there was always a chance someone had since prospected the old workings and left one there. He had no luck finding a candle or a lamp.

He wondered, hopefully, if Page had seen where he'd gone, or had seen him being locked in, and would sooner or later come to release him. Not very likely, he thought. Knowing Page's kind, he figured he'd probably attacked the pile of paperwork on his desk as soon as Dolf had left. "Pity I didn't let him call town for some help," Dolf muttered aloud. "That ought to teach me something—if I live long enough to use it." He realized that his escape was probably going to be entirely up to him—at least if he got out soon. Even if he were gone for a day or two, it was unlikely that anyone would think to look for him in a mine, even though Hal knew he'd been up at Page's office.

He thought, "I'll be damned if I'm gonna sit over at that front door to this hole, like a dog waitin' for a bone." He wasn't built that way. However, he did plan to go back there and empty Ben's rifle at the bolts on the hasp to try and break them loose. He felt sure the bolts were too sturdy to shatter with a .45 even if he shot up all his cartridges at it, but the rifle might do the job.

He cautiously returned to the entrance and fired his first shot, then tugged at the head of the bolt. He felt a great sense of exaltation when it came away in his fingers. He gloated. "This'll be easier than I thought. Why the hell didn't I try this in the first place?" He had equal success with the second one. Dolf could almost feel himself breathing free air and looking at the sunny landscape. A person didn't really appreciate the outdoors until he got in a pickle like this, or walked behind bars as he had a few years before, knowing it might be for twenty-five years. When he pulled the trigger a third time all he heard was a metallic click. "Bad round," he said to himself. "Probably Page hasn't shot this thing for ten years." He levered another round into the chamber, or tried to, but didn't hear the dud hit the rock floor. The significance of that didn't escape him. He levered the chamber half open and felt inside with his finger. The gun was empty. "Only a goddam' dude would keep only two rounds in a rifle!" he swore, half-aloud. For a moment disappointment overwhelmed him. "Well," he thought, "I didn't think a rifle would bust those big bolts, but it did. Best not give up without giving a .45 a chance." He emptied one of his six-shooters at the third bolt, getting some slivers in his hand in the attempt. It remained as secure as it'd been before his first shot with the .45.

Next he retraced his way to the shaft just as he had before, pitching rocks ahead of him in the dark, hoarding his supply of lights. Once he was able to get up the shaft a ways he figured he'd probably be able to cut some more wood splinters to light him the rest of the way, if his current supply ran low. If the shaft was cribbed all the way, he could probably work his way up with or without ladders, even by feel if need be. Barring a few snakes, he thought. Rattlers had a habit of falling into mine shafts while hunting, then hanging around on beams, getting hungry and testy. He put that thought from his mind. He was in enough trouble without inventing some.

Once back at the edge of the shaft he got his first light going good, using his last match. He hated to think what would happen if he wasn't able to keep a light from then on. He supposed that if he got stuck somewhere above, assuming he even got above, that someone might come into the mine and yell for him, in which case he could yell back. It was a remote possibility, but better than nothing. The first of the step ladders was just above his head. He assumed that they continued all the way to the top. If this first ladder wasn't secure enough to pull himself up on hand over hand it would all be over in short order. He planned to place one light in a crevice in the rock and jam a second into the crack where the first ladder step was, which he could just manage to reach. Once securely on the ladder he could reach down and light another torch, keeping his supply going with a little luck. The main thing that worried him was that he couldn't see daylight up above. He figured, however, from his prior acquaintance with mines, that there might be a floor somewhere above, where the ladders went through a trap door. This would likely be the level where the hoisting engine had been located, in fact, where there still might be one, if it hadn't been removed to use in the new mines.

His luck held at the beginning. The first and second ladders were solid as rock. He scrambled up them, kicking loose some sediment from the uncribbed shaft just below the ladder. He could hear it drop into water far below with a mournful echo. It didn't do a thing for Dolf's peace of mind. Soon he could be making a lot bigger splash himself. He tossed off that gloomy reflection and got his next light going. He held it up, trying to penetrate the gloom. He climbed on up awkwardly, using only three fingers of his left hand, holding the light between the left thumb and forefinger. He made about fifty feet without a hitch and was further encouraged, hoping his problem might soon be behind him. At that point one of the ladder steps unexpectedly broke, pivoting him out into space held up by the three fingers of his left hand. He hastily dropped the loose step and grabbed the ladder siderail and swung himself back again. The broken piece banged its way down the shaft and slapped into the water.

"I hope to hell there won't be any more of that kind," he thought. Dolf paused to fish out another splinter of wood and light it. He resolved to thereafter test each step more carefully before he put much weight on it. He also made sure both hands and both feet were on separate steps all the time. It slowed him down and was rapidly exhausting his supply of lights. He looked above him uncertainly. It appeared that his guess was right. He thought he could just make out a plank floor set on massive beams. If he could crawl out onto the hoist-works floor his escape would probably be assured. It likely wouldn't be more than twenty-five feet below the top of the headworks, and more likely had an unlocked door, or some windows he could get out of.

He lit his next-to-last splinter and moved more rapidly upward, risking another broken step to get close enough to see what the final few feet might be like. He thought of stopping to cut a new supply of lights since the cribbing planks offered large cracks he could work on easily with his jackknife. He set his light into a crevice and hooked his arm over the ladder, fishing out the knife. He fumbled it, almost losing his hold on the ladder before catching it. He knew he had to work fast. Fortunately, the old dry planks split off easily. He carefully lit the first sliver, then cut several more. With these jutting handily from his side pocket and his knife safely returned to the pocket on the other side, he started confidently upward again.

The shaft had been timbered with large planks vertically, with beams set, collar-fashion, about every ten feet to hold them in place. These were in turn supported by beams at the four corners. The vertical planks were rough-hewn two-by-twelves. The ladder's two-by-fours were nailed top and bottom to the beams spaced every ten feet or so. At the bottom of the final section, below the floor of the hoisting room, the ladder played out. The top section was missing. Dolf cursed. Some homesteader had probably swiped it when the mines shut down—they'd carried off everything else, whether nailed down or not.

He kept his lights going and examined the prospect for some hope of a solution. There was no way he intended to retreat. Below he would never be able to manage getting off the bottom of the ladder back into the tunnel. He finally resolved to use the cracks in the vertical timbers to shinny up to the trapdoor that was now visible above. If it was locked he was out of expedients. In that case he planned to use his belt to fasten himself to the ladder and hope someone would find him before he passed out from starvation. It wasn't a happy thought, but he was far from acknowledging he was done. If someone came before he lost consciousness he could yell or fire a six-shooter.

Then he cut a fresh supply of torches. It occurred to him that he could probably light a small fire on one of the huge beams with little danger of it catching fire before he escaped. After doing that he could shinny up and try to open the trap door, using one hand while hanging on with the other. Or, perhaps, if the door hinged in the right direction, he could butt it open with his head. Good thing Morgettes all have hard heads, he thought. He grinned, despite his desperate circumstances. If he could shove one arm through and find something solid to grab ahold of, he had a fighting chance to get out. He realized that swinging out into thin air, feet dangling, while trying to pull himself through the trapdoor, using only his arms, or perhaps only one arm, would be the greatest risk he'd yet taken. Fortunately, on his side, was the fact that he had massive shoulders and arms—like a buffalo as someone had once observed.

He lit his fire, made sure it would go, then, leaving a spare supply of splinters near it in case he had to come back down, he launched himself up the vertical planking. He went like a monkey, hands in the cracks and feet against the boards. He soon discovered that his boots slipped and prevented easy progress. He got back down on the ladder and laboriously pulled the boots off. He placed them on the beam for future retrieval. He was being partially blinded by smoke from his fire while he did this. He ignored that and again started upward. It worked well in his stocking feet. He crowded up as close as he could to the floor, then hanging by the fingers of one hand, he pushed at the trap door. It gave slightly and he could see daylight through the crack he opened. He tried again and, by a tremendous strain, threw the door back on its hinges and heard it fall to the floor above. "At least my light problem is over, thank God," he thought.

Hastily he reassumed his grip with both hands on the cracks between the planks. His hands were tired and cramped. He worked back down to the beam below, standing on it and resting his hands awhile. "It seems like I've been in this hole an awful long time," he thought. He was surprised that it was still light out.

He planned to scramble back to the top just as he had before. The trap door had a four-by-four frame that was now turned upward. That would be his handhold to get out of the shaft with. Once he got both hands over its edge, he could swing one leg up through the hole and hook the heel. After that it would be simple to turn loose an arm and brace both arms across the hole and boost himself out by main force.

"Well, old boy," he grunted, "it's now or never."

The last part of his escape went without a hitch. He found it hard to believe in view of all the other setbacks he'd had. Standing on the hoisting engine floor at last and looking at daylight through the holes that had once held windows, he heaved a great sigh of relief. The missing top section of the ladder was leaning against one wall.

"I've got a notion to shove that down there and get my boots," he thought. "Why not?"

He stepped over to retrieve the ladder and learned why not. All of his pushing and straining to get through the trap door had shaken something loose. Shortly after he'd stepped off the plank floor onto solid concrete, the whole floor around the trap door had let loose and sunk sideways into the shaft, hanging on the cribbing and teetering precariously. Dolf could hardly believe what he was seeing; he thought, my guardian angel was sure with me this time. "Thanks, Lord," he said aloud, and he wasn't kidding.

He was consoled, in looking ahead to his walk back to Mum's without boots, that Pinebluff was located too high to nurture cactus. Just rocks, he thought, as he stepped on the first jagged one. He planned to go to Mum's and stay out of sight. "Someone would like to think I'm down there dead," he reasoned. "Let's let 'em think I am for a few days and see what they do." He chose a roundabout path to his destination.

CHAPTER 18

DOLF waited till well after dark to circle back to Mum's place. He didn't care much about walking around in his socks but had to put up with it. He'd had time after escaping the mine to reflect on his recent series of unhappy experiences. They seemed like a replay of his former role in this community. Why had he been chased by the Kelbos and forced to shoot one of them, jailed by Casey, hired as a lawman and left twisting in the breeze, shot at by some unknown killer and trapped in an old abandoned mine by Lord only knew who? The answer or answers were no longer simple. One inescapable conclusion, of course, was that he was who he was. The community had always expected him to do its dirty work for nothing in return. In fact it had expected him to be persecuted for it. A second reason was that he'd got a reputation as a result of that—a reputation that attracted trouble like a magnet attracted iron fillings. He vowed to break this cycle. Someone wanted him out of the way. Very well, he'd get out of the way for awhile and see what happened. He saddled Wowakan and, taking Jim Too with him, circled by the ranch. He told the folks there what had happened in the mine and that he planned to stay out of sight for awhile and see who did what. "Wells Fargo'll have to survive without me. I'm going to resign anyhow."

"Good," Matt said. "You can pay some attention to your own affairs for awhile."

"Or go fishin'," Dolf said.

"That too."

None of them was yet aware of the shocking events of the day in town, especially the shooting of Ben Page.

As he left, Dolf told Matt, "Be sure to let Will and Alby know I'm

O.K. And Doc and Hal too. But tell 'em, for God's sake, to keep it under their hats. I imagine you can send someone in to the Wheat place so you won't have to see Diana."

"Oh, really?" Matt said. "Well, you got a great imagination. Diana said she might like to be a rancher's wife."

"Do tell?" Dolf laughed. "If she can find one that would have her, I say more power to her. Take care, kid. I'll see you sometime. I'll be out at the reservation—or at least they'll know where to find me if you need me."

He touched spurs to Wowakan and thundered down the lane, Jim Too running behind. He was going home, as Dolf thought of it. Home had become wherever Maggie and the kid were. Although he was an Indian, Dolf liked his father-in-law as though he were of his own blood. Chief Henry, in Dolf's opinion, was a "dead square man."

Maggie was happily surprised to have Dolf arrive at their tepee in the middle of the night.

"How glad I am that you're here. I wasn't really looking forward to coming to town, except to see you. Now you're here. This is a lot more peaceful."

"I know," he said. "I'm plannin' to stay awhile. Let's go fishing tomorrow. And the next day too. And maybe the day after that."

Little Henry woke up and crawled in with them. "Pa is home," he said and contentedly fell asleep in the warm space between their bodies.

"So much for that," Dolf said, chuckling. "I'll see you in the morning, Maggie."

Chief Henry knew that Dolf was back as soon as he arose to greet the sunrise, as he always did, and saw Wowakan grazing with the horse herd in the meadow. He thought, "Ah, we will have much good smoking and talking." The chief was troubled by some things he knew were going on in that country that he knew affected the Morgette ranching interests. He wanted to counsel with Dolf about them.

Maggie knew that her father loved and revered Dolf like a son and would want to be with him as soon as possible. She sent young Henry to bring the chief to breakfast. They came back together, little Henry solemnly leading his beaming grandfather by one finger, which was as much as he could manage to get a grip on.

"Here," the boy announced, as though he'd brought in some firewood and dumped it.

"I'm glad you're back," Chief Henry said. "How is it with your people in the white man village?"

"All fine," Dolf said. "Junior is healing up first rate."

He offered the chief a cigar. He'd got him started on cigars, which the chief had liked from the first. They sat on robes, sociably puffing their cigars and drinking coffee from tin cups while Maggie broiled some venison for them. Dolf had brought a sack of sugar and bread with him, always a welcome treat to Indians, as he well knew.

Dolf told Maggie and her father of his plan to take things easy and stay out of sight.

"Good," Maggie said. "About time we have a life of our own for awhile. I can let school out on my own say so."

Chief Henry said, "We can go far up in the high country where there are lakes that no white man comes to and hunt mountain sheep and catch trout so long." He held his arms to show two feet.

"How long?" Maggie asked.

The Chief grinned and shortened the span a few inches. They all laughed. The Chief invited only a few close friends and their families along on their hunting and fishing sojourn. "Too many disturb the game with their noise," the Chief explained.

Dolf rightly suspected that too many disturbed Chief Henry, who was coming to believe that at his age he was entitled to a little peace and quiet. Like all Indians, the Chief doted on children but was now prone to like them only in small doses. Young Henry was about as big a prescription as he cared to handle at one time.

They transported their equipage on travoises dragged behind several ponies. Two leisurely days' travel brought them to a round emerald lake reposing in a meadow knee-high in thick grass. From the boulder-strewn ridge above, Dolf learned that one could see far into the depths of the lake. A fringe of aspen and willow crowded snugly around the lake, with fingers of dense spruce and lodgepole pine extending above to the timberline. Towering over the landscape was a shimmering grey, granite peak, perpetually covered in snow, from which canyons meandered down. Icy streams of snow-melt ran only a few feet wide and a couple of feet deep downward from each of these, forming the creek that crossed the meadow to the lake right next to their campsite.

Balsam and lupine grew everywhere, as well as blue columbines. Miles of syringa had grown all around them on their route upward. Elk had been so infrequently hunted here that they simply paused and raised their heads curiously, then returned to grazing after watching the cavalcade pass.

Jim Too led a racing pack of dogs to the lake and plunged in, standing up to his neck in the cold water and drinking thirstily. Once camp was set up, with the skirts of the tepee rolled up, Dolf flopped down on a roll of buffalo robes.

"Come sit here awhile, Maggie," Dolf said. He put an arm around her and relaxed that way for a long while, silently savoring the beauty and serenity. "This, as the man said, is the life." He nibbled her ear playfully and kissed her neck.

"Take me now, Lord," he said.

That night, with supper over and little Henry sound asleep, Dolf and Maggie sat together under the bright, winking stars, she close against him with her head on his shoulder. She'd rolled up a buffalo robe for a backrest so he could half-recline in what she knew was his favorite resting position, a second robe beneath them on the soft mat of meadow grass. Their fire had burned down to bright embers from which an occasional flame still darted up. she started to rise and replenish it.

"Stay here," he said, lazily, restraining her. "It's your vacation too."

She smiled. Compared to the squaws of her tribe—or any tribe—almost her whole life with Dolf had been a vacation. She loved to wait on him, but realized he wasn't used to it and that he didn't feel entirely comfortable letting her do it. Just then she recognized that he wanted to be left to his thoughts. She snuggled back next to him and was soon dozing comfortably.

Dolf was completely relaxed, yet he realized that he couldn't really fish the summer away. He hadn't yet submitted his resignation to Wells Fargo or to the U.S. marshal. He knew that he really would be failing his friend, Will Alexander, if he backed out on Wells Fargo, so he was on the fence about that. Loyalty to his friends was a strong article of faith with Dolf. Fealty to his family, even more so. He planned to bring the lawlessness on the range to a stop, first of all. Wholesale rustling could not be tolerated. He would like to go at the gang like Hercules after the Hydra. Since he had no idea who the brains of the gang was, he could hardly do that. He was sure the Kelbos were all deeply involved, as well as Dutch Pete and the Loco Kid, but none of them were of the caliber to run the whole show. He was, as yet, unaware of the startling unmasking of Page as the mastermind of local skulduggery, but even if he had been, he would have felt that a multi-state rustling combine was a little out of Page's line. Under the circumstances, he had an idea that would work as far as freeing his own range from rustlers, regardless of who the overall mastermind was. And that, after all, was what interested him most. The financial well-being of those he loved.

His daughter, Amy, was indirectly dependent on Matt, since he ran the ranch for Theodora, assisted by Junior before he'd volunteered to help Hal out by taking the marshal's job in town. Dolf assumed that Junior intended to go back to ranching to support a wife and family, and expected that he would inherit one half of Theodora's share of the ranch and Amy the other. No matter how he looked at it, the survival of the Morgette ranching enterprise revolved on bringing the rustling to a stop.

"Best I make some medicine with Chief Henry pretty soon," Dolf said to himself. "I'll need his help." His idea was simple and was his father's creed: "The best way to put a stop to the feller that swings a wide loop is with a narrow one."

As a result of the shooting of Page and Kellums' revelations, Alby Gould and Hal Green found themselves the recognized governing force in Pinebluff. Events of the couple of days following Page's death had removed any challenges. Law and order was back in the saddle. Page was already in his grave. Krieger had fled. The Kelbos were underground, or had left the country. Angus Kellums, after a full sworn recital of the evil machinations of Page and his hirelings, was lodged in the county jail. The jail itself was no longer under the control of the Casey brothers, or any of the deputies they'd employed. The Caseys had been given the choice of occupying their own jail awaiting a trial, or banishment. A long wire from Alby Gould to the governor and another to the president had obtained the authority to dismiss the sheriff and replace him. Needless to say, the Caseys had gratefully chosen banishment to prosecution. Morgan Casey knew that Kellums' confession would destroy his reputation with the public, and might even put him in prison for a few years. He and his brother were not entirely certain either that there wasn't some hemp scheduled for their immediate future if they proved balky.

Hal and Alby sent a message to Dolf to see if he was ready to make a public appearance, since they both had him in mind to fill the unexpired term of the sheriff. "It'll be a vindication long overdue," Hal had written in his note to Dolf. The message also filled him in on the sensational happenings in town. Maggie's brother Buck had carried it up to Dolf. The reply that Dolf sent back with him was not what they'd expected, but it was typical of Dolf, and of his current mood. It read:

Dear Hal and Alby,
Send someone else. I've been. Don't expect me back till fall. Tell Matt to bring Junior up when he's able to travel. This is hog heaven. [He was using an old Missouri saying from his youth, referring to Elysium.] I recommend Tobe Mulveen for sheriff and Mike Hanratty for undersheriff. Kopet.
[The close, "Kopet," was an eloquent Indian statement, meaning "That is all."]

Dolf

"Well, what the hell do you know about that?" Doc Hennessey said when Hal showed him the message to see what he thought of it. "The old boy must be slowing down."

Hal nodded. "Maybe he thinks it's time this community learns to wash its own dirty linen. Can't say as I blame him."

"Nor I," Doc agreed. "It's over ten years since they killed his pa and brothers. Same year Chief Henry busted out an' run fer it. The only difference is the Chief gave up that fall. Dolf's been at it, on and off, till just last week. If we really need him, he'd come a runnin' again, you can bet on that."

In addition, Doc suspected that Dolf was hatching plans of his own that didn't require a sheriff's badge. He knew his old sidekick better than anyone. In fact, Doc thought, a badge might cramp his style. "I know him well enough to know he isn't gonna sit up there all summer and see the Morgette ranch rustled out of business. He'll hit 'em good and hard and permanent."

CHAPTER 19

DOLF was seated on a log next to the lake with Jim Too, head on paws, dozing in the nearby grass. Little Henry was awkwardly tossing rocks into the water and squealing at each splash, pleased as only a child can be with such a simple pleasure. They had walked around to the side of the lake opposite the Indian camp. Its noise reached them only faintly.

This is too peaceful, Dolf thought. Warnings from a familiar source he couldn't define, but which were always reliable, were coming to him lately. They told him that the trouble in the Quarter Lien was far from over yet. Chief Henry had told him that the horse and cattle rustling had become a big business. It had to be stamped out. But he sensed some other threat not so specific.

Chief Henry had told him, "My people know where all the hidden corrals are. "There are a hundred or more of them along the old Indian Trail going south, some of them just box canyons fenced in."

"Where do they take the stolen stock?" Dolf asked.

"They usually go through the high passes to the east. Sometimes they go straight south."

"Do you have any idea who is running this business?" Dolf asked.

"Some men from this country"—he described the Kelbos and their gang—"and many strangers as well, who push the stock through that comes from the country of the Grandmother." Dolf knew that by the latter he meant Canada.

"Well," Dolf concluded his rumination on the log by addressing nobody in particular, although Jim Too opened one eye, "it's gonna come to another fight." That was inevitable as long as the

Morgettes intended to stay in the business of large scale cattle and horse raising.

He couldn't help but be attracted by the noisy arrival of some new party at the camp across the lake. He hoped it might be Junior and Matt, and recognized their horses, as well as Doc's. He figured it was about time the kid could move. He walked back over and was delighted to find not only Matt and Doc but Amy, Diana, and Catherine, along supposedly to nurse Junior, though Dolf suspected Diana was going to be more involved in nursing his brother than his son. He was totally displeased to find that Theodora had come along, but this was compensated for by the ostensible reason she'd come—to be with Amy. "Well," Dolf muttered, "she is the girl's mother." But, knowing her, he had reason to wonder what her ulterior motive might be. She wasn't cut out to live in a tent in the mountains.

The newcomers had brought a pack train with their own camping outfits. After the flurry of greetings, Dolf told Doc, "Wait'll you wet a fish line in that lake."

"Can hardly wait," Doc said. "I need some relaxation." Dolf could believe that. Doc, never robust, had lost about ten pounds since Dolf had last seen him in Alaska in '86. Dolf figured that the strain of treating two gunshot cases hadn't helped, especially considering Doc's deep concern for Junior.

Chief Henry knew all of the new contingent of arrivals except Diana. Ever since Doc had been up to his camp back in '85 when Dolf was convalescing there, Doc and the Chief had been close friends, each appreciating the "fighting" nature of the other. Like her father, Maggie had never met Diana either. She greeted her shyly, but not with suspicion or hostility, as well could have been the case. The Chief, who had an eye for beauty, nudged Dolf, and said in his own tongue, "Uh, some looker." Dolf grinned. Then, knowing he was on firm ground among friends, the Chief added, "Ask your brother how many ponies he'll take for her?" This not only belied the Indian reputation for solemnity, but gave away the fact that the Chief understood a lot more English than he let on, and had picked up from the talk between Maggie and Dolf the fact that Matt and Diana were probably "just like that."

Diana, sensing that she was the object of discussion from the eyes of both Dolf and the Chief on her, and the grins on their faces, couldn't contain her curiosity. "What are you two *elders* being secretive about?" she asked.

Dolf said, "I'll tell you later—you might blush in all this company."

"I don't blush," Diana stated.

Dolf shrugged. "O.K. You asked for it. The Chief wants to know how many ponies I figure he'd have to offer Matt for you. He already figured from the way you moon at him that you're Matt's squaw." Dolf threw in the latter sly dig on his own.

Diana giggled, then blushed anyhow, much to her consternation. She got a general horse laugh from everyone, including the Chief. "And I don't moon at Matt," she protested.

"You do too," Matt said. She stuck out her tongue at him.

Diana and Maggie covertly eyed each other from time to time. Diana was surprised at how pretty Maggie was in her dusky, bright-eyed way, with her beautiful long hair and rounded sturdy body, accented by firm, high breasts that obviously would have been the envy of any white woman the way they stood up with no need of artificial support. Diana wondered how much this pretty little wife of Dolf's might suspect about what had transpired between her and Dolf the year before. Or how much she actually knew. After all, the San Francisco papers had announced their possible betrothal at a time when Dolf had believed Maggie dead. Maggie, very practically, suspected the depth of what may have been between Dolf and Diana. She could read it in Diana's eyes when she looked at Dolf. Maggie told herself, "She still loves him. Who can blame her?" She thought, it won't be the first time a woman took another man because she couldn't get the one she wanted. She hoped Matt didn't realize that. Dolf's attitude toward Diana now was very much like that of an affectionate big brother. But Dolf's ex-wife was another matter; Maggie knew that Theodora hated and resented her.

Dolf felt some concern over the possibility of a confrontation between Theodora and Maggie, brought on entirely by his spiteful ex-wife. He had observed on several occasions before Theodora had been in camp long, the ill-concealed looks of contempt that Theodora gave Maggie when she thought no one was watching.

The looks also smugly said, "I could have kept him if I'd wanted him." Dolf acknowledged that that was true—if she had treated him squarely. Even a dog whipped hard enough might bite his master. Dolf now understood that Theodora lacked something that was innate in decent women such as Maggie and Victoria Wheat, and even Diana, for all of her flirty and flighty ways at times. It was character. But he'd known other women only after Theodora had deserted him. Now, unless Dolf was vastly in error, he suspected that he was reading the signs on Theodora of a great regret. He felt a good deal the same, not from a desire to reawaken an old love in himself, but from regret that the past had been the way it was and could not be changed now, no matter how intensely someone might want to make amends. He thought, she will never change. She had tried to patch things up when he returned from prison three years before. He had been as surprised as Theodora to discover that all of the old warmth for her had totally died in him. But, he thought, she'll try again, if only to "show" Maggie that she could have him if she wanted him. "Well, if she makes an unpleasant scene here," he thought, "I'll send her packing right quick."

Their daughter Amy was an entirely different person than her mother. He was finding her a delight to be around. She was a budding adult but she was also still a tomboy, who went fishing and hunting with him and raced ponies with the young Indian boys and girls. She'd been his "little girl" before he'd gone to the pen, when she was eight, and was now very much his "big girl," to the obvious disgust of her mother.

Dolf was considering these things, walking beside the lake under a sickle of a moon, alone except for Jim Too. He was also considering his strange fate: always to be a storm center. Maggie had not accompanied him since she recognized his need to be alone sometimes. She knew that he wandered and pondered strange things, knew this with her Indian wisdom. There was wolf in her man. He was the kind that would fight savagely to the death without fear. His eyes were better attuned to the dark than those of most others. And like an old lobo, he sensed things beyond others' ken, sniffing them out of the air, or from the stars. All of his senses of external things were extra keen, perhaps because he had had to make them that way to survive under the grim necessities of his past. For example, he now knew that someone had followed him from camp, but was sure they intended him no harm. Besides, if they had carried the danger scent, Jim Too would have warned him, or even attacked if the need were urgent. Dolf decided to sit on a dead tree that had fallen beside the lake and wait for whoever was coming behind him.

He sensed that Diana had wanted to talk to him. He could imagine about what. Perhaps she had followed him. "Dolf," a woman's voice called. But it wasn't Diana. He was disappointed to recognize the voice of his ex-wife.

"Over here," he said, but didn't come to assist her across the rough ground as he once would have hurried to do. She made her way closer.

"I can't see you yet. Where are you?" she called plaintively.

He struck a match to a fresh cigar and held the light. She came up and seated herself on the log beside him. She was wearing perfume. How incongruous and unnecessary up here, he thought; and how like her.

"I want to talk to you," she said, slipping her arm under his. He said nothing and sat immobile.

She was silent a long while; he suspected she was having great difficulty forcing herself to say whatever it was she was feeling. Finally she said, "What I did to you was so wrong."

He was glad to hear that she recognized that, and surprised at the same time that she did; even more so that she admitted it. Other than that, he felt nothing, and said nothing. He supposed he should be more elated than he was that she'd grown enough to be developing a little character. He wondered a trifle numbly why she was telling him this now. What could she possibly want from him that he could give? He knew that all her gestures were always designed to gain something for Theodora.

"Don't you know why I had to come here?" she asked. Men to her were all simple to understand, like the lower animals, and she had found most of them as predictable as bulls or stallions where women were concerned. A lovely woman snapped her fingers and they dutifully responded. She had lived with Dolf for years so more than anyone should have recognized that he certainly was the exception to that rule. He had responded to her, many times simply because she had demanded it, though she didn't recognize that. But he had never come to her demandingly at a time when he sensed she would not have welcomed it.

He sat silently, his thoughts wandering to other things. He had no real interest in learning why she had come here, though he suspected why. He wished she would go away. His long silence nettled her.

She jerked at his arm. "I want you back," she said, vehemently. "It can be like it was all over again; like you wanted it to be. I'll make it all up to you. You can't understand what I've been through. I know now it was all my own fault." Panic entered her voice as he remained silent and apparently unmoved. "I never loved anyone but you," she said, desperately. She knew that was actually true now. And even he sensed that. That had been her tragedy. That and the fact that she hadn't had the faintest idea what loving someone had demanded.

"Damn it, Dolf, say something," she snapped.

He had to stifle a laugh. He drew deeply on his cigar, thinking what to say that wouldn't hurt her and could think of nothing, but he had to say something, he realized. Finally he said, "We had some real good times, some good years together, Theo. I'll always respect you as the mother of two real fine kids. But it's all over. You know, though, if you ever *really* need me for anything that I'll always be there as long as I live."

She was silent for a long while. At last she said, "You married her to spite me, didn't you?"

He couldn't believe that she really thought that.

"Maggie?" he asked, wonderingly.

"Who else? That Indian." She gave the word a nasty connotation by the tone of her voice. "The dusky maiden. That damn' squaw."

He disengaged her arm from his, rose and walked away from her, and disappeared into the night. She sat there, feeling numb, mentally and physically, a woman who had destroyed her own life and, at last, recognized it and recognized that there wasn't a damn' thing she could do about it. Finally she cried, her shoulders bowed in misery as she sobbed. She was there a long while with her realization of a great loneliness pouring over her. Junior found her there, recovered from her irrational anger, instead overwhelmed by the dawning realization of a heavy sorrow she suspected she'd carry to the grave.

"Ma?" he called.

"Over here," she said.

"I saw you walk out here. It gets cold up here at night. I brought you a coat." He placed it over her shoulders.

She started to cry again.

"What's the matter?" he asked.

"You're going to be just like your pa."

"Is that so all-fired bad?" he inquired, puzzled.

"No," she finally said in a small voice. "It isn't." Then added after a long pause, "Don't *you* ever leave me."

He hadn't intended to. The thought had never occurred to him to live anywhere but the ranch, even after he married Catherine. He was a cattleman to the core.

"Why the heck should I?" he asked. "You need someone to look after you now that—" He didn't finish the sentence. She knew what he had almost said—"pa is gone."

She felt a little better for the moment anyhow, with him there.

"I know," she said. "Take me back. I think I'll go to bed."

Everyone had retired to their tents except Dolf, Junior, Doc, and Matt. They kept the fire going, smoking and talking quietly to avoid disturbing those in bed. Dolf deliberately contrived to keep Matt chatting, due to his canny sense of humor, since he expected someone might be waiting for him over in her tent. At least for appearance's sake, Matt and Diana had separate tents, but Dolf suspected an experienced tracker might detect some suspiciously heavy signs of nighttime traffic between them.

Dolf allowed, "We're gonna have to fetch this rustling business to a close before fall. I don't aim to miss the last boat up the Yukon."

"How you gonna help us do that if you stay up here fishin' all summer?" Matt asked, slyly.

Dolf grinned. "All part of my plan. I may do some fishin' the rest of the summer, but not necessarily up here. I just plan to stay out of sight for a while. Do us all good to stay up here a few days. In fact I may stay more'n that, but I've got a leetle plan. Don't worry about that."

"How about lettin' us common folks in on it?" Matt suggested.

"Not yet. All in due time. I want you to go on down to the ranch when you're ready and pretend you haven't seen me. Whoever locked me in that mine might just be off guard if they think I'm still in there. That's part of the plan. If you need me before I come down, send for me." Then he turned off the subject by suggesting to Doc, "Why don't you pack up and come back to Alaska with us? The country up there misses Skookum Doc." He used the nickname Doc was known by in Alaska.

"I just might do that thing," Doc said. "Pinebluff's got two new doctors right now and might get more if the boom doesn't bust." Then Doc swung the subject back to the rustlers. "That rustling problem might just have been settled by the time we get back to town. Hal Green sent out four posses of vigilantes to clean up the country."

Dolf thought Doc looked a trifle too innocent and sounded like he was spoofing as well. He decided to go along with him.

"You didn't mention that before," Dolf said.

"Slipped my mind. Besides I hate to think of the fearsome havoc they may visit on them poor defenseless rustlers. At least that last posse might. So far three of 'em walked back in—somebody run off their hosses." He puffed unconcernedly on his cigar.

"No kidding?" Dolf asked.

"A fact," Doc said. "Ask Matt."

"A fact," Matt confirmed.

"So much for vigilantes," Dolf snorted. "Remember those miners' meetin's that Jack Quillen was so proud of up on the Yukon?"

"Sure do," Doc said. "They couldn't find their asses with both hands."

He puffed his cigar contentedly and downed another slug of redeye from his flask. He offered it around and got no takers. "Anyhow," he said, "we can worry about that tomorrow—or the next day. I aim to go fishin' some more tomorrow."

Dolf couldn't have agreed more. He preferred to relax a while longer. Another idea took his fancy. "Hey, little brother," he said to Matt, "why don't you and Junior get some greenhorn to buy you out—book count, of course—and come back to Alaska with us?"

That got a general laugh. "Book count" was a standard Western joke ever since the days when Easterners and Englishmen had flooded the cattle ranges trying to get rich quick. Many of them gullibly accepted the cattle count appearing on a rancher's books just as though they were buying a factory full of equipment, where a phony count could be easily detected in due course. They learned otherwise to their sorrow in the case of cattle. Of course the harsh winter of '86-'87 had acted the part of the foolkiller in their cases and had wiped out up to ninety percent of some ranchers' herds off the over-grazed ranges.

Regarding the book count, Matt said, "It's a pity old Krieger cut and run. He'd have been just the kind of half-smart dude to buy us out that way. Of course he tried to marry half the ranch and do it on the cheap."

"How's that?" Dolf asked.

Matt looked over at Junior to see if maybe he'd put his foot in his mouth. He was relieved to see Junior grinning. "Pa won't mind and I sure as hell don't," Junior assured him. He turned to Dolf and explained what Matt had been driving at. "That dude banker was courtin' Ma. Even she could see through him, I guess. She never batted an eye when she heard he'd cut and run after Kellums spilled the beans on his whole crooked bunch."

"Good," Dolf said.

"Ma's growin' up some," Junior allowed, not realizing exactly how profound he was being.

The idea pleased Dolf. He had sensed a change for the better in Theodora. Amy still needed a mother.

They were able to enjoy a few more days of undisturbed hunting, fishing, and good companionship. Then Matt and the others who had come with him returned to the ranch, or, in Doc's case, to town. Dolf didn't want them around while he put his plan into effect. In the first place he didn't see any sense in risking their hides and in the second they would be staying in that country. He was sure that what he had to do was not entirely legal—by about a country mile, or more.

A few days after the others had left, Dolf got a note from Matt, again delivered by Buck Henry, whom Matt regularly employed at the ranch.

Dolf,

The Kelbos and one or two others shot up the ranch. We killed as many of them as they did of us, I reckon—none in both cases. In fact, nobody got hurt. They left us a note saying they were going to settle our hash sooner or later. The Kelbo kid will soon be out of the hospital, I guess, and I suppose they figure to have a showdown before they drag it out of the country. I figured you might want to come in for the party. I don't reckon they know you're still alive.

Matt

Dolf thought, "If all goes well, they might not be around for a showdown." He planned to move fast now that he knew they'd been seen back in the Quarter Lien.

CHAPTER 20

DOLF was reasonably sure the Kelbos didn't know where he was and might think he was dead. He guessed that Yancey had probably been the rifleman who had fired the near miss at him at Page's office, which was a good guess though he couldn't be sure of it. He figured that either Yancey or Page had then shut the door on him and locked him in. If it had been Kelbo that had done it then he could be reasonably sure that Yancey thought he was dead now and had been for a week or more. "I owe him for that," Dolf thought—if it was him.

Dolf's disappearance had been a subject of much speculation in Pinebluff. The consensus was, "Dolf's a mysterious one. He's up to something, unless somebody finally dry-gulched him and they're hushing it up." There were rumors to that effect also. Dolf wanted to encourage them. What he intended to do would be a lot easier if people figured he might be dead. Therefore, after getting Matt's note, Dolf came to the ranch alone at night, sending Maggie and Henry back with the Chief to the reservation.

Matt told Dolf, "The Kelbos have been out of sight since the shooting at the ranch. May be layin' low or maybe attendin' to some rustling business. Mulveen and Hanratty aimed to put a stop to that by scouring the country with a posse made up from something besides town dudes. I loaned 'em a few good hands. We'll see how they make out."

Dolf didn't comment. He had his own ideas and intended to carry them out regardless.

The good news was that Matt and Diana had decided there were wedding bells in their future. "Maybe me and Junior can make it a double wedding," Matt said.

"Why not?" Dolf agreed. "Sounds like a great idea. The sooner the better—after I do a little chore. I have to be out of town a couple of weeks, maybe. Can it wait that long?"

"The kid ain't ready for a wedding yet," Matt said. "He'll want to be in prime condition, I'd guess, so he won't be a burden on Catherine right off."

"Let's go check with him," Dolf said. "What I got in mind could wait till after a wedding." In fact, he'd just as soon have had Matt and Junior out of the country on a honeymoon trip somewhere. Junior agreed that he wouldn't be ready to get hitched for at least a couple of weeks, though he was coming along great. Dolf knew from bitter experience how long it took to get back on your feet after being shot that hard.

Despite prodding, he refused to tell either of them what he had up his sleeve. "Government business," was all he'd say.

That was loosely the case. He intended to get the government involved through his capacity as U.S. deputy marshal and fervently hoped that he would be the only man in government who ever found out about it, with the exception of the Indian agent out at Chief Henry's reservation. Old Frank Pearson had been a friend of Dolf's father. He was an unlikely sort of Indian agent—honest. He'd come close to being fired for it once or twice, but was still hanging on. When Dolf told him he'd like to borrow about two hundred braves for a federal posse to go after rustlers, Pearson slapped his leg and laughed.

"The Bureau would raise hell if they ever heard about it, but I don't reckon you'd care to have them hear about what you got in mind. Well, if they do, I'd as soon be fired for that as for turning down the Bureau 'big bugs' who wanted me to sell the Injuns' rations to the honest merchants over at town and kickin' back a cut to them. I'll give out a couple of hundred hunting permits in case they get caught off the reservation with you."

Rumors began to circulate in the Quarter Lien that signal smoke had been seen on various peaks. Someone frantically wired the army and Frank Pearson had to send them a reassuring message that all was peace and contentment on the reservation and a roll call showed all present. He acidly added a postscript: "Why not pull a surprise count on the Crows and Sioux. Maybe they're out." He didn't like either of their agents, particularly McLaughlin over at Standing Rock in Dakota.

Dolf was thoroughly briefed by Chief Henry and his braves, who knew very well where the rustlers held their stolen stock and the location of the trails by which they moved them. Their general route was known as the Old Indian Trail and it had probably been in use for hundreds of years before the whites came to that country. The term trail was misleading, however. It could be as much as twenty miles wide or as narrow as a few hundred yards where the terrain dictated. Its route was roughly north and south on the western side of the Bitterroot Range, which divided Idaho and Montana. South of the Morgettes' home range were the only passes through which it was feasible to move livestock with little chance of being observed. The first of these was Lolo Pass, through which Chief Henry and his tribe had fled from the army on their final warpath a decade before. To the east now was the railroad at Missoula. There had been no railroad there then. About seventy miles further south was Nez Percé Pass, between Salmon City and Missoula. Anyone secretly running cattle or horses would use one of these passes. The country was rough, usually heavily timbered and sparsely populated. It was mostly visited by prospectors and trappers among the whites. Chief Henry's tribe hunted freely over all that country and seldom encountered an honest white man.

Dolf didn't intend to interest himself in rustling south of Salmon City. He thought, the folks down there can fry their own eggs. He didn't doubt that some of them were in cahoots with rustlers, if not actually members of the confederation. But he was satisfied that when he slammed the gate shut on the north end of their operation, no one was going to risk his neck up there again, regardless of what went on elsewhere. Dolf's only interest was in the welfare of his own family's ranching activity. He'd learned his lesson regarding the rewards of trying to act in the public good. It had usually ended up with him behind bars, especially when he'd enlisted the law in that pursuit. He aimed to see that no chicken-hearted assistant would someday get the vapors and recite Dolf's sins in some court. Granville Stuart over in Montana had observed the same drawback to legal proceedings on the frontier and had ruthlessly cleaned out the rustlers in the Missouri brakes a few years before. Stuart was still a shining light in his neck of the woods rather than a number up at the territorial pen at Deer Lodge, due to having operated secretly. Dolf aimed to operate the same way. He'd had his fill of pens.

His first need was a reliable organization. He had got that from Pearson, almost legally. The hunting permits given the Indians would cover them if they ran into any army patrols while they were about their business. His most trusted lieutenant was Chief Henry himself. Though most people thought of the Chief as old, he was just over fifty and spry for his age. On a horse he could match any man, young or old, in his tribe.

Chief Henry provided two hundred braves under sub-chiefs Charlie Wolfhead, Black Eagle, Yellow Wolf and Tow-at-way. Dolf explained his strategy to Chief Henry and the four sub-chiefs. He wanted every cattle and horse holding place watched so that they would know when there were gang members at them with stolen stock. The sentinels watching these places would notify one of five dispersed bands, the first under Dolf and Chief Henry and the others under the four sub-chiefs. Whichever one of these was nearest would be called in to capture whoever was at the corral or box canyon involved. They were to be taken away and held in a secret spot until Dolf and the Chief could arrive and pass on their disposition. The rustling ring's operation was so large and far flung that it took fifty braves to cover each of the stock-holding places in that wilderness, which was over one-hundred-miles long and up to fifty wide. This left an average of thirty braves per band. In addition to this small woods-wise army Dolf knew that he had another potent ally—surprise.

After having Chief Henry dispatch the bands and sentinels to their posts, he had a special mission for his own patrol. They quietly surrounded the Kelbo ranch in the dark and waited for early light, when ranch people normally came out to check the weather and see to their horses. Dolf's crafty crew got the drop on Lute, Rafe, and Jud, then waited hopefully for Yancey to come out. It was their bad luck that he wasn't there. Probably in town, Dolf reasoned, knowing Yancey's liking for the joints.

"What the hell is this, Morgette?" Lute blustered. "You can't get away with this. You'll have Uncle Sam's army down on you, monkeying around like this with Injuns, and you'll likely end up back in the pen to boot."

"Yah," his brother Rafe chipped in. Jud just looked scared. All three were obviously plenty scared and it showed in their eyes.

"Tie 'em up," was all Dolf said. He had them placed on their saddled horses with their arms tied behind them, then led the cavalcade up into the timber some distance from the ranch buildings.

"This'll do," Dolf ordered. He took three lariats from a wheat sack he'd had slung from his saddle horn.

"Hey," Lute protested. "We're law abidin' folks. What're you aimin' to do?" There was a terrible fear in his eyes. He knew what they were aimin' to do. His brothers did too. They'd all heard of a grim Dolf Morgette who had become a legend from the old days, but hadn't really believed all they'd heard. Now they were looking into the cold, relentless blue eyes of *that* Morgette. They had never really believed that such a fate as was obviously about to be theirs would ever befall them. Few did.

"No, wait!" Rafe pleaded. "We were just about to pull out back for Texas. We'll get out of here. I promise, won't we boys?"

Dolf ignored them and had the braves place nooses around their necks, swing the ropes over a convenient low and heavy limb on a ponderosa, and tie the ends fast to the trunk. Through Chief Henry, who was interpreting for him and also understood Dolf's Chinook better than the others, he conveyed to the Indians how they would do this. Roughly translated into English, he told them, "We ain't gonna whip the hosses out from under 'em. If we did that the white man's law would say we killed 'em, in case we ever got found out. We're gonna let the hosses walk away whenever they're a mind to. That way anyone can see that it was their own hosses killed 'em."

Chief Henry relayed that information to the group. The reaction would have been a surprising revelation to the whites that always considered Indians stolid and humorless. They laughed fit to kill.

"Besides," Dolf told the Chief, who he knew would understand the added humor of what he said, "them hosses' words don't stand up in a white man's court any better than an Indian's." The Chief caught the irony of that and was quick to appreciate it. Every

Indian knew his word carried no weight at all in a white court. He laughed.

"Morgette," he said, "you're not only a great warrior but a wise man too."

They rode off, leaving the three Kelbos protesting loudly. The last Dolf heard from them they'd obviously recognized the futility of pleading with him and were pleading with the horses to stand still. He heard a prayerful stream of "Whoa, steady boy, stand still." They obviously hoped to stave off the inevitable as long as possible.

It was Dolf's bad luck to be wholly out of earshot when Yancey arrived at the ranch and, expecting his brothers to be around, finally let off a loud holler for them. They answered from up in the trees with, "Yancey! Get the hell up here quick," and as he drew near, "Don't skeer our broncs a comin' in, whatever you do."

He cut the ropes and got their stories from them. "Let's light a shuck," Lute urged. "That was too damn' close. Morgette is crazy."

Yancey was calmer, not having shared their terrible fright.

"Hold on. I'm aimin' to even the score before we pull out."

"I ain't," Lute said. He was joined in that resolve by Jud and Rafe.

"Hold on, hold on. I don't mean right now. We'll head over the line into Canada and let things cool down. Morgette'll think you three are dead. That'll give us a big advantage when we finally hit him. I'll git Billy Joe outa the hospital. You boys lay low for now, then hitch up a wagon when you're sure nobody's comin' back. We'll head out tonight."

"You head out tonight," Lute said. "You can meet me at Smith's place over the line—I'm diggin' out right now just in case Morgette decides to come back and burn us out, or check to see how we're doin'. You boys a comin'?"

They left Yancey sitting on his horse with his mouth open ready to protest. He shook his head disgustedly. "Damn' fools," he said, and reined his horse around, intending to go get a wagon and some supplies for the trail. He trotted slowly toward the buildings below. Then he picked up the distant rumble of many animals running. He hung spurs to his mount and headed at a run toward Pinebluff, with his heart thumping his ribs like fury. He thought, maybe Morgette is comin' back to burn us out, like Lute figured he might.

Dolf had, in fact, thought of torching the place, but decided the smoke could attract some party who might set loose the three brothers. "I can burn them out later," he thought. Buildings keep. Hangin's don't. So it hadn't been Dolf returning that had scared Yancey almost out of his wits. A neighbor's son was driving up a herd of work horses. The kid glanced toward the Kelbo buildings, thinking he might get breakfast there, but noticed no smoke coming from the chimney and hurried on.

Dolf's cleanup took a trifle longer than he'd expected. In a couple of cases they'd met resistance and had to shoot it out with a few hardcases. This posed a problem for Dolf. Chief Henry's braves wanted to scalp their legitimate trophies. He had to explain to them that this would lead directly to serious trouble with the army, should such corpses be found. Another problem had been a couple of rustlers that had only been disabled in a shootout. It went against Dolf's grain to hang someone already seriously injured. Chief Henry recognized the problem Dolf was having with foolish ethics and took it off his hands. He had seen this soft-headedness before when fighting whites and had given thanks for the advantage it gave the Indians; soldiers would hesitate to shoot an armed squaw or a boy and would be killed by them as a result. He considered it damn' foolishness. He craftily decided how to resolve the dilemma for Dolf.

"I will leave some of my braves with them and send for Strong Bull to make them well." He grinned. "Then we'll let their horses hang them." Strong Bull was the medicine man who had, perhaps, saved Dolf's life a few years before. Ground red ants were his favorite potion, which in both Dolf's and Junior's cases had apparently worked—or at least hadn't hindered.

Dolf observed that the braves who had been left as "nurses" were again with them the next day. He pointed this out to the Chief, who leveled a finger at the sky. "The wounded rustlers got a lot worse in the night and the Great Spirit beckoned them."

Dolf could live with that explanation. He hoped the nurses hadn't scalped their patients. He saw no signs of scalps about them—fresh or otherwise. The routine cleanup went well, moving from north to south.

Dolf had decided, after a couple of weeks, to wind up his effort. He was certain that by now most of the rustler gang had stumbled onto the posses' handiwork and read the portents, then made tracks out of the country, carrying a warning with them. He would have bet it would be a few years before any rancher even dared to lay his iron on a maverick and that there would never again be large-scale rustling through that country. He was thinking of heading back north when he got a call to come visit a hidden corral in a box canyon over near Nez Percé Pass. There were five rustlers there as well as a substantial cabin, he was informed. He and the Chief and their band moved that way at a leisurely pace. This one'll do it, Dolf thought. He had a notion to just leave it to the braves, who had really got the hang of their work and liked it. His oracle told him that he had best not do that for some reason—so, as he always did, he followed the urging of his inner voice. If he hadn't and had ever learned what the consequences would have been, he would surely never have forgiven himself.

As Dolf rode up, the first of the outlaws he noticed was John Tobin, the skilled cross-country runner, whom he was especially pleased to catch at last.

"Well, Tobin," he said, "I suppose you've got a milk cow around somewhere, maybe over in the corral? I'll bet you'd like to go over and milk her about now."

Tobin scowled. "Go to hell," he said. He wasn't sure yet what was in store for him or he might have kept his mouth shut. He hoped Dolf might let him off—perhaps for old times' sake. He simply didn't know his man.

"Let's see just what you have got in that corral," Dolf said. Then he noted the kid sitting on a log, trying to avoid being recognized by averting his face. There was no doubt who he was, though he was some three years older than when Dolf had last seen him, and was now almost a man.

The sight carried Dolf back in his memory to Fort Belton, Montana, in '85 when he had been town marshal. There the events unfolded that first took Dolf to Alaska. He'd gone there from Fort Belton on the trail of the murderer of his good friend, Harvey Parrent. The trail had led first to Alaska, then back to San

Francisco's Barbary Coast, where he had finally caught up to his quarry, Forrest Twead. He had intended to shoot him down just as Twead had Harvey shot down, but thought better of it. He figured Harvey's family would feel better revenged by having Twead go home to Montana and the gallows.

Now, here was Harvey Parrent's oldest boy, in bad company and about to be sent to the rope by his late father's good friend. Dolf knew the kid recognized him. He wasn't sure though that the boy knew what was in store for him and the rest. Dolf had made no exceptions to the rule and imposed that upon his red-skin posse. Dolf knew now what he must do. He pretended not to recognize young Harvey Junior.

"Truss 'em all up," he ordered, and turned his back, walking away. He called Chief Henry after him and told him of his foul luck. "It'd be like doin' it to my own son, almost," Dolf admitted.

"This is too bad that this thing happened," the Chief sympathized. "What will you do?"

Dolf proceeded as in all the other cases. He was surprised to see that that great runner, Tobin, was taking it like a man. He gave Dolf a note to send to his family, then faced death stoically.

Dolf covertly watched young Harvey to see how he was taking it. He was white around the gills, but not about to show he was scared by begging. Dolf won his bet that he wouldn't. He was a chip off the old block.

When all the rustlers were on their horses, seated under a stout limb with ropes around their necks, Dolf met young Harvey's eyes for the first time. The kid cleared his throat, and his lower lip quivered as he tried to say something. He managed to croak out, "Mr. Morgette," then seemed to be debating whether to beg. "You know who I am, I reckon?"

Dolf nodded affirmatively.

"Don't tell ma—ever—please."

There were tears in the kid's eyes for the first time. Dolf felt a lump rising in his throat, remembering himself standing at Harvey's grave with the kids and widow, promising them he'd revenge Harvey's murder. His eyes were strangely misty, whether at the recollection or the present bravery of the kid, he wasn't sure.

He noted Chief Henry's eyes on him, inscrutable, but he suspected pleading the kid's case.

"You know what I gotta do, kid?" Dolf said.

Harvey gulped and couldn't say a word. He nodded mutely.

Dolf grabbed the bridle of his horse, saying, "Good. Then you know that I gotta get you down off this fleabag and kick your ass good and hard for yore pa's sake, as soon as we get that rope off you."

He noticed Tobin grin and almost decided to turn him loose too. "Take care of yourself, kid," Tobin said. "Don't get in bad company agin." That did it. "Turn this one loose, too," Dolf told Chief Henry. "He thinks he's quite a runner. If he can outrun a bunch of your boys let him go. I don't want to hear if he does or not."

Later, on the trail back to Pinebluff he got the kid's story.

"The big freeze-out caught everybody back around Fort Belton. Some had as much as a ninety percent kill. We lost what few head we had. Nobody had any money so we couldn't even make our sellin' farm truck off the place, though it did keep us from starvin'. We all helped all we could. Uncle Ben joined the army and gave us most everything he got, so that was the only cash we had. I figured I was just another mouth to feed. I tried to go to cowboyin'—even promised to work for nothin', but even the old hands couldn't get work, so I drifted and ended up where you found me."

Dolf asked, "Didn't you have sense enough to know what a bunch of hardcases those fellers were?"

Harvey laughed. "I was pretty green. They said they'd teach me to cowboy. They made a pretty good flunky and cook of me. I got so I didn't fall off my horse every time it crowhopped." He laughed ruefully. "I didn't even know what a runnin' iron was. I sure do now."

"And how to use it?" Dolf kidded him.

Harvey got red. "That too. But I hardly suspected what they were up to till just lately. We didn't see many other folks while I was with 'em, you can bet, and those we did were in the same business. Tobin was the only decent one. He kept tellin' me to run for it, but the rest of them said if I tried to run off they'd come after me and kill me."

Dolf was silent for awhile. It was an old, familiar story. It was lucky thing he had caught the kid in time. He asked, "You expect you learned yore lesson?"

Harvey looked at him and grinned. "Did I ever," he said. "I damn' near crapped my pants when you put that rope around my neck."

Dolf laughed and clapped him on the shoulder. He said, "I don't blame you. Well, I'll make an honest cowboy of you. And as far as yore Ma and the kids go, I reckon Pinebluff could use a bakery. I'll see that they get out here and I don't want to hear anything about not bein' able to pay me back. When he was killed yore pa was puttin' a roof on my cabin so Maggie would be able to have our first kid in her own home. And first snow was flyin' while he did it, and he should have been workin' on yore place instead of mine. Maybe if he had been he'd still be alive. That feller that shot him may have thought he was gettin' me."

CHAPTER 21

DOLF didn't return directly to Pinebluff following the cleanup of the rustlers, but went instead to Chief Henry's camp. He was surprised to find that he considered this humble place home, rather than the ranch or Mum's. He didn't look forward to returning to town except to attend the double wedding ceremony that was on hold pending his return.

He took Harvey Parrent, Jr., with him. Maggie, who had had her first home with Dolf in Ft. Belton, knew all the Parrents well. They had been taken in by Dolf when, dirt-poor, they had come to Montana to homestead. Harvey's dad had been dry-gulched and killed working on the house Dolf had intended to occupy on a desert homestead there. Seeing young Harvey again was a sort of reunion for Margaret that brought back both happy and sad memories. Dolf didn't tell her the full circumstances of his meeting with Harvey in front of him, but did as soon as they were alone.

He told her, "I aim to leave him out here a few days, till I can line him up a job a the ranch with Matt. Your pa will look out for him, I guess. I think he sorta took a shine to the kid the way he faced the idea of being killed without crying about it. When he may have thought I was gonna go ahead and hang an old friend for a little thing like stealin' some cows, I got the feeling he'd have stopped me before I really did it."

Margaret shook her head. "I doubt it. But he has a soft heart. It wouldn't have done your standing any good with him."

"I got that notion pretty strong. Anyhow I had no idea of doin' more than throw a good scare into the kid."

In the morning Dolf faced with distaste the need to go into town. He also knew Maggie hated towns worse than he did. He wasn't surprised when she said, "You go in first, Dolf. I don't have to come in right away." She dreaded having to attend the wedding at all, but knew it would be considered a snub by all of Dolf's white friends and his relatives if she didn't. Besides, she knew Dolf would brush aside any excuses she might present, short of being next to death's door. She berated herself, as usual, for being such a diffident mouse, but was powerless to overcome it.

Dolf laughed out loud at the next thing she had to offer, which was, "What in the world will I wear?"

"You sound like every woman I ever heard," he said.

"Well," she persisted, "I don't have anything to wear."

"What's the matter with what you got on? It suits me fine."

What suited him was to see her in a loose-fitting, fringed buckskin dress reaching to mid-calf and a pair of knee-high mocassins, the tops intricately beaded in a colorful geometric design. Her hair was braided with red and yellow-cloth into two pigtails, which hung down along each side of her face.

"You're no help," she sighed. She knew he was genty teasing her.

"Come on into town with me then," he said. "We can go shopping for something for you to wear.

Maggie was familiar enough with the styles available in ready-to-wear women's clothes in the stores of the white merchants. She'd look like a homesteader's wife just off the plow. The only way to get something available would be from a seamstress. That would take days, perhaps weeks.

"No," she urged. "You go ahead and let me know when you come in. I'll find something to wear. Don't worry about me." She had an idea about how to prop up her morale and maintain her aplomb around the white women she knew would be at the wedding.

Mum, of course, was no problem. She and Maggie got along fine since Mum was common as an old shoe. But Theodora and Victoria Wheat Gould daunted her; the former because Maggie sensed that she bitterly resented her, the latter because Maggie knew she'd been second choice after Victoria. She knew that Dolf had hoped to marry Victoria and that she would gladly have had him if there hadn't been a disastrous misunderstanding. Besides, the blonde, imperious Victoria was the ideal that Maggie had aspired to ever since she'd first seen her type in the East at the white man's school when she was a girl.

Of them all Catherine Green was the most like Maggie, down-to-earth and practical, not afraid in the least to get dirty or bloody wrestling life. Catherine had been with her in her father's camp in '85 when Dolf had been concealed there from Sheriff Mulveen. At the time, he was lingering close to death from a gunshot wound. While they nursed Dolf, Maggie had recognized that Catherine was in love with him, and she herself had fallen in love with him then.

She smiled now, thinking, "I must be crazy to send Dolf in there alone with that bunch of women. Every one of them wants to marry him in preference to the man they have; even his first wife knows she was a fool and wants him back." In the cases of Diana and Catherine, Maggie recognized that both of them had the attitude that if they couldn't get the Morgette they preferred, they'd settle for another one rather than anyone else. She wondered if those two women consciously recognized what they were doing. She suspected that they must.

Yancey Kelbo and the survivors of his gang were still very much on Dolf's mind as he rode into town. Above all, he'd wanted to catch Yancey, Dutch Pete, and the Loco Kid in his dragnet. He reasoned that they must have left the country, at least temporarily. On the other hand he was fully aware of the Kelbo bent for revenge. He thought that by then Yancey must have found his three brothers hanging from that tree near the ranch. Just to be sure, he had a notion to circle over that way and see if they were still hanging there, but discarded the idea. He didn't particularly care whether they had been found or not, or by whom. He reasoned that certain knowledge of whether they were still there or not would do him no good unless he knew for sure that Yancey had found them. In any case Yancey, who was certainly alive as far as Dolf knew, was always a potential danger. Moreover, he was prone to take desperate chances, assuming it had been Yancey who closed that mine door on Dolf and latched it.

Dolf wondered if any of his posses' other handiwork had yet been discovered hanging around the Quarter Lien country. If it had, he was sure the word would spread fast. People aware of his protracted absence might put two and two together. "Let 'em," he said to himself. "And let 'em try to prove something."

As far as the majority were concerned, he might well be dead. Speculation was certainly still circulating about his disappearance. Inquiries of family and friends had netted nothing for the few nosy enough to openly inquire. The consensus still was, "Dolf's a mysterious one. If he ain't dead, there's no tellin' what he's up to." And that had had to satisfy them.

Therefore, when he rode down Main Street on Wowakan, Jim Too trotting beside, the word spread rapidly in Pinebluff. Figures emerged from buildings along his route, called outside by others who had recognized him coming or passing. Dolf nodded and spoke to those he knew, aware of the excitement his sudden appearance was obviously causing, but outwardly ignoring it. Inwardly he was vastly amused.

In time, as a result of his mysterious absence, there would be over two dozen bodies discovered near the ruins of many old, secluded corrals. Those discovered soon enough would still be hanging. Some were not to be discovered until years later, the rope rotted and skeleton fallen to the ground, the bones scattered by coyotes or wolves. Whenever another one would turn up, then Morgette's name would come to mind again and be on many lips in the community. As the years passed, it would become a bragging point to have known him, or even to have seen him in the flesh. But on this day there were many who viewed Dolf with, at best, mixed emotions. Those who didn't know him personally, and they were a large majority, regarded him with fear—a dangerous man to be avoided if at all possible. Dolf was aware of this, and it too amused him. He considered himself as easy to get along with as any man alive. His friends would have borne out that self-appraisal.

He found Matt and Junior at Mum's where he had hoped he might. He knew that Junior had planned to move back to town as soon as he was able to look out for himself, to be nearer to Catherine. Dolf figured Matt would also play hookey from ranching as much as possible to be near Diana. Before he'd left, they'd both promised to hold up any weddings for his return. Matt had grinned at the time and winked at Dolf, but pointed a thumb at

Junior and said, "The kid ain't in any shape for a honeymoon yet anyhow. I've heard they can get pretty active."

The kitchen was always the social center at Mum's and that was where he found her and the two men now. He stepped in and said, "Well, I'm ready to put on a boiled shirt and be jacked into a monkey suit for them weddings, and be somebody's best man."

"First," Matt insisted, and he was about to say what was on everyone's mind, "I'd like to know what kept you away for a couple of weeks on all that mysterious *business*."

"Me too," Junior said.

Dolf looked at Mum. "I'm sure glad you ain't curious too."

Mum snorted, "I'm sure glad you're dead wrong. Besides I worried. You coulda been dead for all we knew."

Dolf looked innocent. "I coulda been dead all winter too, for all you knew. Anyhow, I been out on a secret project for the U.S. government in my eminent capacity as a U.S. deputy marshal and high muckity muck. Sort of answerin' my country's call. I figured it was the least I could do since I was too dern young for the war."

Mum complained, "That's yore story."

"And," Dolf responded, "you're stuck with it. I will say this much though. I doubt we'll have any more rustler trouble for a spell."

By then a couple of those hanged nearby had been found and the word was out. "Aha," Matt chortled. He tapped his forehead. "I should have guessed. You been out doin' some long overdue stranglin', right? Why didn't you take me along?"

"Do tell? I will admit I was out doin' some reasonin' with a lot of folks that needed it."

"Sure you were," Matt snorted, "with a rope."

Dolf only grinned. "Don't sweat me. I do think though that everybody concerned got the message. It's possible that we won't even be hearin' from the Kelbos any more." And that was exactly all they were able to get out of him.

Dolf had returned to town just in time to join those at Mum's for a dinner to be given that night by Victoria Wheat at her place. Dolf's unexpected arrival with the rest of his family created a ripple. Those present included Victoria and Alby, the Alexanders, Amy, Doc and the three who had come over with Dolf, and a little after they arrived, Hal Green and Catherine. Dolf was naturally asked about Maggie's absence. "She said she's been neglecting her school all summer and would be in the day before the big to-do," Dolf explained. At least Clemmy Alexander suspected what the true reason was; that Maggie was not at ease around Dolf's white friends, especially the socially prominent ones. She made a note to try to put her at ease the first chance she got.

After dinner the men corralled Dolf in the drawing room, cigars lit, and coffee or brandy in hand, with the obvious intention of getting the details of his mysterious absence. They got precisely nothing but an amiable grin. Dolf said, "What you fellows don't know won't hurt me." And all attempts to get him to enlarge on that netted absolutely nothing except Dolf's defensive, "Us ex-jail birds have to be careful. You've heard about giving a dog a bad name."

He finally escaped, he hoped undetected, to the veranda, then stepped into the yard and rapidly circled to the rear grounds to finish his cigar, strolling there under a half moon riding high and dappling the grass, its light filtered by the tall, lacy spruce branches overhead. He was soon aware that someone had followed him and thought it might be one of the men—perhaps Doc—who would have known that Dolf would open up to him privately about where he'd been the past two weeks. Dolf waited and watched, finally discerning the pink gown of Diana.

"Dolf," she called, not able to see him yet. He drew on his cigar, making a beacon for her to see.

"There you are," she said, coming close. He could smell the familiar cologne he'd once known so intimately. He was silent, assuming that she had followed him deliberately and that she had something to say to him.

"I've hardly seen you alone for a minute since I've been here," she complained.

"Not supposed to under the circumstances," he pointed out, unhelpfully, tongue-in-cheek.

"Fooey!" she said. "I see whoever I want to whenever I want to." How well he remembered.

"If Matt's jealous, he'll just have to learn," she added.

Dolf thought, "By George, I believe that." But he didn't say anything, forcing her to come to the point.

"You know why I came out here?" she finally asked.

"Huh uh," he said, again being unhelpful, to say the least.

"The heck you don't," she said. "I came to bid you a tearful goodbye, as the ladies' novels put it."

She stepped close, hugged him fiercely and kissed him hard. He returned the kiss.

"There," she said, stepping back breathlessly.

"Where are the tears?" he asked.

"There aren't any. Maybe if I were doing worse than getting your brother there would be."

She touched his face once, tenderly. "I'll always remember you as the knight that climbed up the wisteria," she said. Then she spun and ran, her head down. He suspected there might be some tears coming then. He watched till she was out of sight, then turned to look at the moon peeping through the tracery of branches overhead. His cigar had gone out. He relit it and puffed to get it going satisfactorily, then strolled idly about. He hoped no one missed him. Social gatherings even among friends were not his idea of a good time.

He noted a light-colored gown coming toward him again and wondered if Diana were coming to say something more. As the figure approached he could see that she was too short for Diana. "Catherine?" he wondered. He was astonished to recognize Victoria's voice.

"Is that you, Dolf?" she asked. He thought, "This crowd of women is a sharp-eyed crew, for sure." He'd thought his departure had been unnoticed. Victoria, of all people, was taking a great risk to come out like this, being a newlywed to boot.

"It's me," he answered, a trifle stupidly.

"I can only be a minute or Alby will wonder where I've gone."

"I shouldn't wonder," he thought.

She stepped close to him, just as Diana had. He knew that she could be as direct as Diana and as audacious. Her queenly appearance was entirely deceiving. She was a hot-blooded woman. He remembered an afternoon she'd spent with him in his apartment in San Francisco, right under Diana's nose.

Victoria didn't hesitate now. She said, "I want you to know it would have been you if it could have been. You're the one I'll always love. I told you that before and I want you to remember it."

Then she kissed him as hard as Diana had and fled.

He mumbled half-aloud, "Don't this beat a hog flyin'?"

His cigar had gone out again and he was just relighting it and thinking that Catherine Green had had a schoolgirl crush on him; the idea went through his mind that all he needed was her to come out too in order to make a perfect circle. He was grinning at the ludicrous notion when she spoke to him close by.

"Dolf?"

"Yup. What're you doin' out here?"

"I wanted to see you alone. This may be my last chance before I'm married."

He thought, "Jeezus, I don't believe this." He had no idea of the effect he had on women. He supposed he should be shocked, since this was the woman who was about to marry his son, but he wasn't. He said nothing.

"I feel a little bit foolish, but I've got to tell you this, Dolf." She paused, collecting her thoughts and searching for the right words. Finally she blurted out, "I wanted you to know that I've been in love with you since I was about twelve years old and stole your horse on a dare. I knew it for sure when I nursed you out at Chief Henry's camp." The words came fast and breathlessly. "I'd have run off with you that night like Maggie did if I'd known you were leaving." She stopped. "How I wish I had."

She kissed him breathlessly, then fled.

His cigar was out again. He threw it away and turned toward the house. He thought, "I sure as hell hope none of their men saw any of that. Or suspected." He decided it would be better if he didn't come back in too soon. He couldn't think of anyone else who might come out and embarrass him, so he risked lighting another cigar. He smoked it down before he went inside. No one else had come out. He had expected that maybe Doc would, but Doc knew he was given to spells of wanting to be alone.

When he returned, he stepped into the middle of the final wedding plans. It was Monday. The wedding was scheduled for Friday morning so the honeymooners could catch the afternoon

Northern Bullet at the Junction, even if it happened to be on time. They were planning a double honeymoon in California, starting in San Francisco. Diana simply had to show them her town, Dolf thought. Wait'll they see that thirty room "shanty" of Will's, as the latter had described it to Dolf before he'd ever seen it. Three stories too, Dolf thought. That ought to impress the country kids, like it did me.

Later Dolf's mind dwelt on other things besides a wedding as he lay on one of Mum's big beds trying to get to sleep. His mind was still focused on the possibility of danger. His sixth sense had been sending him the kind of signals he never ignored. Then too, he was still employed by Wells Fargo, though he figured their problem was solved and he could resign. The same went for his job as U.S. deputy marshal. He intended to resign as soon as the wedding was over and he had the young ones safely on the train. After that it would be back to Alaska for him and Maggie and the kid. He hoped to make it before freeze-up in the Yukon, but if he couldn't get up there he and the family could stay in their cabin at Dyea where Henry had been born. They could then go north as soon as the ice broke up in the spring. At least there would be the vast solitude and stillness he'd come to love so. True, it was cold up there, but if one didn't *have to* go out in stormy weather, the cold was welcome when one dressed for it. Besides he'd learned to like sleeping late. That was easy to do where the sun stayed below the horizon until mid-morning.

Closer to home, the whereabouts of the remnants of the Kelbo gang still worried him. He intended to be on guard every moment. Naturally he assumed the Kelbo clan proper had been cut down to only two boys, Yancey and Billy Joe, but there was still the hardcore dregs of the old gang, Dutch Pete and the Loco Kid. Four desperate and unscrupulous men could pose a grave danger, to Matt and Junior particularly. They weren't as wary as he was, nor as ready to shoot first and argue the morals later. "They never will be either, if I have my way," Dolf thought. Getting that way left too many inner scars that a man could best do without.

CHAPTER 22

DUTCH Pete and the Loco Kid evaded Dolf's cleanup purely by chance. They were running a herd of stolen horses over into eastern Montana. They returned with a couple of tough recruits to fill the local gang's somewhat depleted ranks—Dusty Rhodes and Phil Cranston. Both had cut their teeth on violence along the Mexican border and had judiciously headed north just a jump ahead of the Texas Rangers. Dutch Pete was, as yet, unaware of just how badly depleted the ranks of the local gang had become. Since he and his men returned by the quickest route, the railroad, they didn't stumble across the ample evidence, hanging from trees in their usual haunts, that would have warned them. From the Junction, where they unloaded their horses, they took a circuitous route to the Kelbo ranch and, of course, found no one there. Dutch Pete was immediately on edge over that unusual circumstance. He thought of heading for the timber and camping out till he could be sure what was behind the Kelbos' mysterious absence.

"I don't like the looks of this," he said to the Loco Kid.

"Aw, they're probably all in town. Yancey's a lot looser than the Old Man. You know what a boozer he is too, and the rest ain't far behind."

The Loco Kid's guess made sense, but Dutch Pete still had the "spooks." He said, "All the same, I'll head into town as soon as it's dark and find out, 'less someone shows up afore then."

After checking over the ranch's grub supply, Dutch Pete was again on the alert. "Ain't been anyone here for at least a week, I'd guess. Bread's dry and hard. Bacon's rancid. I'm draggin' it for the high country till we know what the hell's been goin' on here. But I aim to slip in and see Billy Blackenridge afore we pull out too far."

They moved to within a few miles of town and camped in heavy timber, waiting for night. When full dark came Dutch Pete rode to town alone, tethered his mount in a gulch well back from the outskirts and slipped into Blackenridge's shack. He found Billy at home reading a penny dreadful about the exploits of the James' gang.

"You got any grub?" Pete asked. "Ain't et since this A.M."

"Got some spuds and beans on the stove," Billy offered. "Heat 'em up."

"Got any meat?"

"Nope. Cain't afford it."

Dutch Pete wondered why the hell he didn't rustle out and shoot a deer or elk, or steal a cow. He hated shiftless and improvident people. He could understand people too lazy to work, but didn't see how anyone could be too lazy to take something free or to steal.

Dutch Pete slipped Billy some cash. Go in and get us a bottle and bring back some steaks—big ones." While Billy was gone he got the stove going to heat up the spuds and beans, gnawed a crust of bread while he did, and refilled the coffee pot.

Billy was soon back, anxious to crack the bottle. He poured them both a big shot in two of the jelly jars he used for glasses. Billy tossed his down quickly and poured another. The fact was that Dutch Pete and his kind made him extremely nervous, though he tried to mask that fact. He knew they were unpredictable. A man could never tell when they might decide to plug him over some fancied offense. Or just to see him kick, if they were drunk enough. He'd heard that Pete had offered to buy a fellow a drink in a saloon somewhere over in Montana, and shot him when he ordered wine, while Pete had ordered whiskey. The Loco Kid was even more of a crazy. In a cow camp where he'd worked, he'd killed a Mexican cook with a shovel for serving him tea when he wanted coffee.

However, Dutch Pete was not about to shoot the likes of Billy. He found him too useful as an informer. But, he knew Billy could be cagey. He was sometimes evasive if a fellow seemed too anxious, and prone to expect to be paid more for his information. You couldn't blame him for that, though. In any event, Pete knew it was best to get him oiled before putting the first question to him. If he'd blurted out what was on his mind to Billy as soon as he'd come in, he'd likely have got no more out of him than a blank stare, even if Billy had known where the Kelbos were. So Pete cooked a couple of steaks for them, kept Billy's glass full, and had a leisurely meal, followed by coffee and a cigarette, before he mentioned what was on his mind.

"You got any idea where I might find Yancey about now, Billy?" he asked. He could have said, "I was out to the Kelbo ranch and nobody was there," but that would have been the wrong way to get anything out of Billy.

Billy had as good an idea as anyone where Yancey was and why. For that reason he suspected that Dutch Pete had been out to the ranch, found no one there, and was damned anxious to find out why. Billy had been in the Bonanza Saloon the morning Yancey had cut loose his brothers from that tree up above the ranch, then been spooked by the kid driving a bunch of horses. Billy had seen Yancey's hasty arrival out front and his beeline for the door as though he could use a bracer. Yancey had busted through the batwings and headed for the bar without waiting for his eyes to adjust to the gloom, ordered a whole bottle and a glass, and hastily tossed a couple of big slugs down. Only then had he bothered to look around. He'd spotted Billy and motioned him over. He hadn't beat around the bush. He had signaled the bartender for another glass and had poured Billy a big hooker.

"Billy, I'm gonna hafta wait for a fella here in town," Yancey had lied. "I'm gonna need a wagon and team from the ranch right quick too, but I cant afford to go out myself right now." He'd put five silver dollars on the bar. "How about you goin' out and havin' one of the boys hitch up and come on in." Of course he knew that Billy would find no one there, and had added, "If the boys are all out somewheres, you know where stuff is. You fix me up a rig. Throw in some bedrolls and a cookin' outfit—or be sure to tell the boys to do that if they're there. If you have to do it your own self there's an extra five in it."

Naturally Billy had been curious about the all-fired hurry and what Yancey was het up about, but not curious enough to make Yancey mad and maybe blow that five, or even a ten. He'd gone out to the ranch, found it deserted, and done what Yancey had asked. He hadn't missed the signs of many horses' hoofs, most of them unshod. Only Injuns, as a rule, rode unshod horses. The question naturally occurred to him whether some of Chief Henry's young bucks were on the rampage. Regardless of what the explanation for them was, Billy would have bet whatever caused all those tracks was the reason Yancey was in a sweat. At the thought of Indians, a definite feeling of uneasiness gripped him. He could feel the hair standing up on the back of his neck, and looked around carefully all the way into town for signs of an ambush. If there were Indians out, why hadn't Yancey given the alarm? Even he wasn't that depraved. The mystery was one too many for Billy, but he resolved to carefully watch Yancey's movements after getting the wagon to him.

Billy had collected his extra five, then watched Yancey from a distance after he'd left. By then the rustler was pretty full and staggering noticeably as he walked. Nonetheless, he'd managed to get his young brother, Billy Joe, out of the hospital, then go over to Price's Mercantile. He was jawing all the way, and Billy would have given a lot to know what Yancey was saying. Apparently Billy Joe was in pretty good shape since he was able to help Yancey load a lot of supplies onto the wagon. On their last trip they both carried Winchesters. That had really set Billy wondering. He mumbled to himself, "They bought new Winchesters. Sure sign Yancey wasn't about to go back to the ranch, fer some reason." They hadn't let any grass grow under their feet about heading out of town either. They had gone north on the road toward the Junction. Pullin' their freight fer sure, Billy had thought. And that bastard Yancey sent me out there to the ranch to rake his chestnuts, knowin' I might run into whatever scared hell out of him. He had vowed to get even with the son of a bitch the first chance he got. Dutch Pete's question was to give him his chance, though Billy didn't suspect that.

Billy told Dutch Pete everything that had happened the day Yancey had dusted out in a hurry—except about the unshod horse tracks.

"Where d'ya suppose he was headed?" Dutch Pete asked, but he was thinking aloud to himself as much as talking to Billy.

Billy said, "My guess is he's probably in Canada for awhile. Something scared hell out of him." He wasn't sure why he didn't mention all those unshod tracks, but he'd found out that secrets usually had a way of being saleable eventually.

Dutch Pete had been pouring steadily for Billy and was amazed at his capacity, though his words were getting a trifle slurred. Pete was gambling on that bonus tidbit he often got when Billy was really full. He wasn't to be disappointed this time, either. Billy looked at Dutch Pete, conspiratorially, and said, "I reckon I might know something else about Yancey that you'd be interested in."

"What's that?" Dutch Pete asked, casually.

Billy held back for a half a minute, the whiskey having made him less afraid of the outlaw. Sometimes he was able to manage a bigger bribe without antagonizing Pete. The latter fished in his vest pocket and pulled out a five dollar gold piece, placing it near his empty plate. Billy still hesitated. "Worth mor'n that," he allowed. "Yancey'd kill me if he found out I told."

Dutch Pete now eyed Billy with intense interest. His eyes turned both mean and threatening. He had a notion to scare whatever it was out of Billy by shoving a six-shooter under his nose. He was feeling the whiskey himself and would have done it for the laugh as much as to find out what he wanted to know. Instead, he said, "Spill it. If it's worth more, I'll pay more."

Billy was scared now, but couldn't back out. "I seen Yancey, one night, a havin' a confab with Dolf Morgette and old Jim Hume." He carefully neglected to mention that he had arranged the meeting for money.

"How'd you see that?" Dutch Pete growled, suspecting the truth.

Billy's eyes became fearful. He realized he'd said too much and not been smart enough about how he'd said it.

"How come you didn't tell me that sooner? How come, Billy?"

"I dint have a chance!" Billy quavered.

"Bullshit!" Dutch Pete dismissed his alibi. "You was prob'ly at that meetin' yerself."

"They wouldn't let me," Billy blurted out, then caught himself too late.

Dutch Pete eyed Billy steadily, sweeping out his pistol and aiming it between Billy's terrified eyes.

"No!" Billy pleaded. "Please!"

Pete grinned evilly and slowly eared back the hammer so the two distinct clicks were clearly audible. "Bang!" he yelled, then guffawed. Billy almost collapsed from relief. He'd dirtied his pants both ways out of fear.

"You sure you don't have any idea what Hume and Morgette got out of Yancey?"

Billy said, "I don't know, but I can guess."

His guess was the same as Dutch Pete's, whose nimble mind had immediately put two and two together when Billy spilled the beans. Pete thought, "No wonder those bastards knew right where our camp was. Serves old Yancey right that his big mouth got his pa killed by accident. Well, I owe Yancey for that one."

Dutch Pete nodded. He figured to get the drop on Yancey the first chance he got and even up the score by cutting him down. Then an idea occurred to him that appealed even more and caused him to almost laugh aloud. Billy wondered what was going through the hawk-nosed outlaw's evil mind. Pete stopped grinning and fixed Billy with a harsh stare as he stepped to the door. He pointed his finger, threateningly. "You ever hold out on me again and I'll pull that trigger the next time."

"I won't," Billy assured him in a shaky voice. "I sure won't."

With that Dutch Pete slipped out and was gone. Billy gingerly took down his pants and removed his drawers, carefully transporting them to the outhouse, hoping no one saw him in only his pelt. Returning a trifle unsteadily, he hung his drawers on a nail outside the door. "I'll wash 'em tomorra," he thought. He was thankful Dutch Pete had left the remains of the whiskey. He took a long pull then set the bottle down, mumbling to himself, "Damn' lucky to be alive. I've got to get out of this country." But he had no idea how he'd manage that.

He was beginning to get back a little courage now that he was sure he wouldn't need it. Anger at Dutch Pete and the whole damn' bunch of them swept over him. He was glad he'd saved a tidbit of information that might have been of use to Dutch Pete. He knew that rumors were sweeping the country of people having stumbled across some of Dolf's and Chief Henry's work with ropes. Let him find out for himself, Billy thought. He didn't know that the stranglers had completed their sweep. He surmised that somehow Yancey had been warned and that had been the reason he'd left suddenly. "I hope they get 'em all," Billy mumbled as he tumbled into bed and passed out.

CHAPTER 23

DOLF was mindful of the need to remain on guard against any last-ditch retaliation by the Kelbos or other surviving elements of the rustler gang. For that reason he remained in town and kept an eye on things and, at the same time, especially tried to stay away from women. He was gratified to manage, in the process, to spend some time with Will Alexander. He had Will over to Mum's rather than go over to the Wheat mansion, so that he didn't have to rub elbows with Diana and Victoria. Will and Dolf smoked and reminisced about the exciting time they had had on the Barbary Coast the year before. Will revealed some of his plans for the railroad he was assembling in California to break the Southern Pacific's monopoly. He also told Dolf that he had bought the Wheat mansion from Victoria, to be given to Diana and Matt as a wedding present. Dolf grinned inwardly at the probable reaction of Matt, whom he knew would have been satisfied with a bottle of bourbon, or a box of cigars, and would have considered a gift of both luxurious.

Will casually explained his motive. "They'll need some sort of shebang when they come to town from the ranch." Shebang brought to mind Will's thirty room "shanty" in San Francisco.

"Naturally," Dolf agreed. His own taste ran more to the big one-room cabin he owned up on Spruce Creek. He had frequently thought of semi-retirement up there, with Margaret and Henry. He could raise quality horses and cattle on a small scale and make out. The income from his Alaskan gold claim had made him moderately well-off anyhow, so that he really wouldn't have to work unless he wanted to. However, the call of Alaska was strong on him and he would undoubtedly go back for at least a few years.

True to her promise, Maggie had managed to find something suitable to wear to the wedding. She arrived Thursday, escorted by her father and some forty braves. Chief Henry was a prudent man and had considered the possibility that some shrewd, evil mind among the outlaw confederation may have divined who had decimated their ranks. What a revenge it would be to retaliate on both Dolf and the Chief by killing Maggie and young Henry. He intended to forestall such a possibility. His contingent of fighting men pitched their dog tents on Mum's ample grounds and turned their horses into her large corral.

This would not be the first meeting between the redoubtable Mum and her red-skinned relative by marriage. She and the Chief bore one another a certain wary respect, recognizing in the other a kindred soul. He was able to overlook the fact that she was *only* a woman, and a paleface at that, and she was able to overlook the fact that he was a pesky, thieving Injun.

Maggie stole the show at the Indian pageant, which had attracted a lot of townspeople, especially kids. She came on a large, black Apaloosa that had the classic white dappled rump known as a "leopard" pattern. She rode a saddle with pommel and cantle a full foot-and-a-half high, both decorated with a huge silver saucer on top. The saddle was covered with doeskin, bleached white. Under the saddle was draped a white and red, fringed blanket woven with geometric designs in black, green, and gold. Behind the saddle a waterfall of white buckskin thongs were pendant in two clusters on each side of the horse's rump, reaching almost to the ground. A breast band of coarse woven blanket material with a Maltese cross design bore a hemline fringe of red porcupine quills. The bridle and reins had been traded for in the south, perhaps from the Navajos or even in Mexico, and were of black glossy leather, carved and heavily ornamented with conchos whose silver was engraved in intricate designs. Maggie was dressed in all the finery of an Indian princess, which she was—the foremost of her tribe, daughter of the hereditary "old man" chief.

Maggie wore a pair of white doeskin pants under an ermine skirt that reached to just below her knees. This permitted her to ride astraddle. Her blouse was plain cotton of a faun hue, trimmed with sea shells in long strands across the front and along all the seams.

The back of her ermine dress had a sleek beaver hide attached to the belt, ornamented with beads and porcupine quills, both dyed in red, blue, green and yellow. Her raven hair was a glossy, unrestrained cataract flowing down to the small of her back, and had a single eagle feather attached on the left side. (This represented the lone coup she'd scored with her father's coup stick while saving Dolf's life in Alaska.) She wore sky-blue mocassins, reaching to her knees, ornamented with a beaded strip from ankle to knee and tied at the top with thongs that had tinkling bells on their ends.

She remained on her horse hoping that Dolf would be at Mum's and come out and see her in all her tribal finery, which he'd never seen her in before. She was not disappointed. He looked astounded.

"Holey Moley!" he exclaimed. "Is that you, Maggie?" He came up beside her and pretended to squint.

"It's me, all right," she said. Then she leaned over and added in a voice only he could hear, "Come help me get off this damn' saddle."

He laughed. As she leaned over, he took her under the arms and hefted her lightly to the ground.

"How'd you get up there in the first place?" he asked.

"Had to be helped," she admitted. She looked drolly at him. "How do you like what I found to wear?"

"Great," he assured her. "You'll steal the show."

She almost did. The young white women at the wedding reminded Dolf of carefully cultivated roses. His Maggie was an exotic mountain wild flower—unique among them. The women had all examined and exclaimed over her native finery—except Theodora, who avoided her.

The double wedding was a civil affair. Neither the Greens, Alexanders, nor Morgettes were church-goers. Doc Hennessey and Hal Green constituted the committee to keep Judge Porter sober till after he performed the ceremony. Doc was Junior's best man; Dolf Matt's. All the men had been stuffed into black suits with frock coats, insisted on by the ladies as proper. (Doc had leaned over to Dolf and snidely whispered, "Do you feel all frocked up?") These suits had been special ordered by Clemmy Alexander from Marshall Field's in Chicago, by telegraph. She had even insisted that all the men come in and get measured—she'd done this even before Dolf and the Chief had gone on their hunting trip after rustlers.

Chief Henry arrived in the formal costume of a war chief. Dolf recognized this and wondered if any of the other whites did. Might be kinda appropriate for matrimonial affairs, Dolf thought, remembering his own first marriage. The chief wore a headdress of eagle feathers that reached to his heels. Dolf eyed him to see if he had any scalps hanging from his belt. It wouldn't have surprised him. Chief Henry's breeches had been donated by the cavalry, in this case a legitimate present from General Howard. They had a gaudy yellow stripe down the leg. Over these the chief wore a multicolored breech cloth, heavily beaded. His shirt was an ornamented white buckskin, over which he wore several chains of wampum suspended from his neck. He hadn't forgotten the possible threat to all of them, however. Under his loose shirt he had concealed two six-shooters and a bowie knife. He had found such appurtenances appropriate for white man's ceremonies of other kinds in the past.

The Morgettes had made the necessary compromise with appearances by wearing their six-shooters in shoulder holsters. Dolf looked himself over in the mirror and thought to himself that the shootin' irons hardly showed. He wryly reflected that having a civil ceremony under the circumstances had a hidden advantage—an unworldly sky pilot might have objected to the artillery. Judge Porter would merely see the good sense in their preparations.

Diana and Catherine looked like brides should, at least according to the customary newspaper description—"lovely and radiant." Both best men managed to find the rings at the right time and everything went off, as Doc later commented, "slick as axle grease." When the "I do's" were over, Judge Porter kissed the brides right after their new husbands had and the rest of the men lined up to do the same. Chief Henry had the good sense to stand back, sensing that his contribution might not be appreciated. Diana noticed and stepped over to him and pulled his head down, smacking him on the lips. "You too," she said. "You're family now. Probably a second something-or-other, maybe once removed." Not to be outdone, Catherine followed suit. The Chief loved it.

"Uh," he said. "First time kiss white squaw. Not bad."

Everyone laughed. They moved into the dining room for refreshments, where the Chief assured everyone that his tribe wouldn't be shamed by a lack of performance, even at the punch bowl. Dolf had a trifle more than his customary one. Feeling expansive, he banged a glass with a fork and got everyone's attention. He looked quite solemn, or at least hoped he did.

"You're Morgettes now," he told the new brides. "You know what that means."

Matt interrupted. "What does that mean, Dolf? Tell us all."

Dolf was unruffled. "Damfino," he admitted. "I thought it sounded pretty good, though. Probably means they'll be in a lot of trouble from now on, along with the rest of us."

"Till death do us part," Diana added. "I, for one, will love it."

Dolf said, "I got a big rig down at Packard and Underwaters to carry you all down to the Junction in style. Even got fringe on top. I think Packard won it off a circus in a poker game. Anyhow, we'd best get down there if you don't plan to miss the Northern Bullet and have to camp out the first night of your honeymoon."

"Why not bring it up here?" Will asked.

Dolf winked and humorously explained. "Cain't. Got a surprise down thataway. We can take our own buggies down from here."

"I love surprises," Diana said.

The newlyweds were showered by confetti as they went out the door to their buggy with the old shoes and tin cans tied on behind. Amy caught Catherine's bouquet when she threw it to the crowd and wished she hadn't. She thought, "I don't want to get married young—if ever." Diana deliberately aimed her bouquet at Chief Henry, who caught it deftly, smelled it, then quickly passed it to Theodora Morgette Pardeau, who happened to be standing next to him. Theodora held it as though it might explode, but had the grace not to throw it down.

On the way down to the livery stable Dolf and Maggie rode in Will Alexander's buggy with him and Clemmy. "Now that us girls are alone," Will said, "what's that all-fired big surprise down at the stables?"

"Got the fire department band down there hid in the barn. We aim to play 'em down the road in style."

"Ah," Will said. Clemmy added, "You old sentimental softie, Dolf. People always misjudge you."

"And a lot of 'em that did are in graves due to that 'sentimental softie's' personal attentions," Will thought.

Dutch Pete had found the Kelbos at Smith's ranch in Canada. From them he heard how Dolf's posse had left the three Kelbo boys with ropes around their necks, sitting on untethered horses. By then, other fleeing rank-and-file members of the gang had filtered through with strange tales of finding hanging corpses around their familiar haunts.

Dutch Pete had no trouble conjuring a picture of himself on a ship to some banana republic. Before he left, however, he was willing to run a considerable risk to get revenge, on Morgette for ruining his soft racket, and on Yancey Kelbo for almost getting him killed in the ambush that had accidentally netted Yancey's father. He'd played on Yancey's vanity and vengefulness equally, to nerve him up to go after the Morgettes. Yancey had boastfully assured him on previous occasions that he and his brothers would gladly meet the Morgettes face to face if Dutch Pete and the Loco Kid would side them. The now possible addition of two other formidable bad men, Dusty Rhodes and Phil Cranston, made such an uneven match look even more to Yancey's liking—especially when he had some liquor under his belt. The manner in which Dutch Pete proposed to add his reinforcements appealed to Yancey particularly. His pappy had raised him to "allus git 'em fa'r 'n squar, Texas style, right whar the suspenders cross." That's how Dutch Pete planned to do it. Dutch Pete described what he had in mind to Yancey and his brothers. "The best place in town to git the Morgettes whipsawed like I got in mind is down at the livery. You call 'em out in that corral and be lined up facin' 'em. Me and the boy's 'll be up in the loft with scatterguns. They won't git to bust a cap afore they're dead."

That appealed to Yancey. He looked to his brothers for their reactions. The look on their faces was plain to read, especially on Billy Joe's. He gloated, "I damn' near beefed young Morgette at that ball park. This time we'll get him."

"You did that?" Yancey almost gasped. The rest of the brothers were equally taken aback.

Billy Joe nodded. "Why the hell not? You shoulda been glad. He kicked hell out of you the night before." His eyes had a sort of crazy glow when he said it. They'd all seen the look before. As Yancey had observed before, at least he hadn't cracked his marbles on a wagon tongue, like Billy Joe. His remark didn't leave much to say unless Yancey wanted to cry over spilled milk. "Sure I was glad, except that the finger pointed straight to me. Well, it's done now and no sense arguing about it." He forbore to mention that Billy Joe had probably got their pappy killed as an indirect result. What was done was done. Then a final reservation occurred to him. To Dutch Pete he said, "How we gonna explain buckshot holes in the Morgettes' backs?"

Pete regarded him with disgust. "Was you aimin' to stay around and stand for office or somethin' after the shootin'? We're gonna haul our freight to hell outa there, yuh dang fool!"

Dutch Pete had more than one option to accomplish his end. He thought, "If I didn't show up at all it'd get even plenty with old Yancey. On the other hand," he told himself, "if we just wait awhile before we cut loose, the Morgettes'll git Yancey an' probably his brothers. Then I can get them too. Depends on how much risk I want to run." He calculated the odds of beating it out of the country ahead of Morgette's friends. Chief Henry's possible revenge was what worried him most.

Dutch Pete came in close to Pinebluff and set up a secluded camp. "We're gonna go in before daylight and get stashed in that loft. Lots of saddle bums sleep it off up there. We'll be under hoss blankets sawing wood so far as anyone guesses, till we hear you out back. Leave the rest to us."

"When should we come in?" Yancey wanted to know.

"Happens I found that out from the local paper," Pete said. He'd sent Phil Cranston in for a paper, since he was not known in town. "The Morgettes are havin' a double weddin' in the morning. Too bad they'll be havin' a triple funeral in a couple of days. Figure to git in right after the reception. They plan to go down to the Junction afterward. I'd say high noon would just about catch 'em right."

That had been the way preparations had been laid out for the second reception of the day. The Kelbos had just reached their posts in the corral when the wedding party got to Packard and Underwaters'. The Morgette men and Doc were gathered out front with friends who were saying goodbyes. Dolf and Doc, along with a tough crew, intended to see the newlyweds safely to the Junction in their big surrey. They hadn't anticipated Chief Henry's contribution of a *really* tough crew to the escort, but were happy to accept the offer.

During this final flurry of farewells and best wishes, the hostler approached Dolf, looking frightened and agitated. He motioned Dolf closer and whispered to him, "The five Kelbo boys're out in the corral. They said I should tell you to come get 'em if you ain't too yellow." He hastily added his explanation of the latter remark, "Yuh understand that Yancey said that about if you ain't too yellow." Like a lot of people, he had no intention of ever laying himself open to being misunderstood by a Morgette. Dolf nodded, grimly.

He called Matt, Doc, and Junior over and told them what the hostler had said to him. "Halleluiah!" Doc said. "Leave the young one to me. I didn't have the heart to castrate him with a scalpel, but a .41 Colt will do as well."

Will came over just then to see what the confab was all about; Chief Henry, who had an infallible nose for brewing trouble, came too. Dolf told them what was shaping up. "Keep the rest away," he cautioned Will. "This is a family affair."

The four marched resolutely down the side of the long barn, dressed in funereal black, coattails flapping in a rising wind. Chief Henry joined them as they passed under the big overhead livery stable sign, which was swinging in the wind and creaking from a rusty hinge. As though sensing carrion, a flock of ravens drifted overhead with the wind and disappeared behind the big barn. Dolf glanced at Chief Henry as though to caution him to stay away. The Chief pointed a finger at his chest and uttered one word: "Family." Dolf grinned for just a second.

This determined group turned the corner and were out of sight of the apprehensive watchers being held in check by Will's stern admonition: "Dolf said it's man for man. It's the code-of-the-West."

They all understood and accepted what that meant. It was inviolable to proud men who valued honor above life.

As the five in Dolf's party rounded the corner they could see the five Kelbo boys spread out, roughly abreast in the corral some fifty feet away.

"Spread out a little, boys," Dolf ordered.

Little puffs of dust rose from their marching feet and hurried away on the stiff breeze. The only sounds were from their measured tread and the squeaky hinge on the livery stable sign around the corner. Dolf halted his party some twenty feet from the Kelbos; who neither moved nor spoke.

"I'll take the three on the left," Dolf intoned, laconically. "You boys divide up the others." He was careful to see that Doc got Billy Joe, as he'd requested.

Yancey was hopefully eyeing the big hay mow door for signs of his murderous reinforcements.

Dolf growled, "You sonsabitches have been lookin' for a fight, so fill yore hands!"

None of the Kelbos made a move. They all knew what was supposed to happen next, only it didn't.

Dolf was growing exasperated. "Goddammit!" he yelled. "Fill yore hands!"

Frantic, Yancey finally blurted, "No! No!" Then forgetting himself, "Somethin's wrong! It wasn't supposed to happen this way!" He desperately eyed the hay mow door for signs of the shotgun brigade. Surely they could have heard the yelling. He suddenly got a sickening picture of Dutch Pete far away, riding out of the country—laughing.

"Fight, or throw down yore guns," Dolf ordered. "Toss 'em down slow and easy one at a time." For the first time he snaked out his own pistol and covered them.

Just then the fire department band, getting their signals mixed due to the many voices out back, assumed they were supposed to come out that door. They burst into the corral, horns blaring and drums banging. The Kelbos were just shucking their pistols into the dust, and finished accompanied by the lively strains of *Oh! Dem Golden Slippers*.

When it came Billy Joe's turn, he yelled, "No, by damn! I almost beefed yore son, Morgette. I'm gonna get you or die a tryin'!" He jerked his pistol with surprising speed and fanned it rapidly, with the predictable result of that sort of folly. The first shot plowed into the ground not four feet in front of him. Dolf could easily have killed him even before his pistol cleared leather, but gave him his chance. He could see the kid wasn't apt to hit anything and merely covered him. The Morgettes and Doc, all dead shots, had all heard of green shootists who were so scared or angry they emptied their guns blindly, at almost point blank range, and never hit a thing. Dolf realized he was watching such an exhibition now.

Doc watched the first three shots, then snorted. Billy Joe noticed that and screamed, "You sonsabitches," blasting his last three shots into the side of the plank horse trough, the bell lip of a tuba in the band, and a horse in the barn, which he just grazed. It kicked a board loose in the side of the barn in startled resentment.

Billy Joe eyed his pistol disgustedly and threw it down. He had flabbergasted his brothers, who all stood with open mouths, afraid to move either to restrain or abet him. Billy Joe charged at Dolf, awkwardly flailing his arms like a girl with fists doubled. He obviously didn't know any more about fist fighting than he did about gun fighting. He screamed, "You killed pappy, you big pisspot!" Dolf grabbed him by the front of his shirt and swung him around, transferring his hold to the back of his belt.

"Cover his brothers," Dolf ordered the others, who then drew their weapons for the first time. He jerked Billy Joe over to the horse trough, seated himself and turned the kid over his knee, whaling him with a loose board that had been leaning against the trough, used for skimming off moss. As Dolf whaled away he felt something running down his leg and wondered if he'd been grazed by one of the bullets and failed to notice. He glanced down and saw the small stream of water flowing from the trough where Billy Joe's .45 had punctured it. He disgustedly got up and pitched the kid into the trough head first.

Doc noticed Dolf examining his leg and pulling off his boot and came right over, thinking he might have stopped a bullet. Before he could ask, Dolf had the boot off and was pouring the water out of it.

"Hell, Dolf," Doc said, snidely, "I didn't know you scared that easy."

Dolf eyed him amiably without answering, meanwhile pulling the boot back on and getting up. And that was the substance of the famous showdown at Packard and Underwaters' Corral, destined to be fabled in Western lore in a later century. At that point acting Sheriff Mulveen and undersheriff Hanratty rounded the corner and took the Kelbos in charge, Billy Joe still sputtering and coughing up water.

Later, at the Junction, Dolf and Maggie stood arm in arm, watching the famous Northern Bullet, which had been only a half hour late, chug away to the west, growing smaller and smaller, finally winding out of sight up a canyon with just a thread of smoke visible above the timbered ridge, high on the mountainside.

Dolf squeezed Maggie companionably and sighed. "Now maybe we can have a little peace," he said.

Back at Mum's house, where she'd been baby-sitting young Henry while the others went to the Junction, Dolf and Maggie slipped quietly in by the kitchen door. There didn't seem to be anyone around. They peeked into the parlor. Mum was in her big chair, snoring lightly, while Henry was securely cuddled asleep on her huge bosom, right under her chin.

Dolf felt like he could sleep for about a week himself. All the tension of the past weeks was draining out of him, yet he coiled inwardly when he heard someone slipping in the back door. He was poised to jerk his pistol when Chief Henry's head poked into the parlor; he took in the scene and grinned; motioning them to the kitchen. He gestured with his thumb back toward the parlor and whispered in his own tongue, "The old, fat one promised me some huckleberry pie and coffee."

Glenn G. Boyer was born in a log cabin in Wood County, Wisconsin. He spent twenty-two years in the U. S. Air Force and retired as a command pilot with the rank of lieutenant colonel. While an Aviation Cadet in Santa Ana, California, Boyer met members of the Earp family and went on to become the doyen of historians of Wyatt Earp and his brothers, amassing a vast research collection that became the basis for numerous publications. Among the most notable of these have been *The Suppressed Murder Of Wyatt Earp* (1967), concerned with the development of the Wyatt Earp mythology, publication of the memoirs of Josephine Earp as *I Married Wyatt Earp* (1976) that also served as the basis for a motion picture for television, and more recently *Wyatt Earp's Tombstone Vendetta* (1993). He is currently at work on a definitive book collecting his numerous articles and essays about the Earps, Doc Holliday, and other historical personalities involved in the Earps years in Arizona. With *The Guns Of Morgette* (1982) Boyer launched a second career as a novelist of the American West. In his series about the adventures of Dolf Morgette and together with the novel, *Dorn* (1986), he readily established himself as one of the finest authors of the Western story, with fiction as notable for its sharp and penetrating characters and grippingly suspenseful plots as for the authenticity and accuracy of the historical backgrounds and settings.